THE PORTABLE NINE

Pete Mesling

Other Kingdoms Publishing, Seattle

ISBN-13: 978-0-578-73256-5

Cover design by: James T. Egan of Bookfly Design
Copy editor: Kate Jonez
Library of Congress Control Number: 2020913545
Printed in the United States of America

ADVANCE PRAISE FOR THE PORTABLE NINE

"A compelling tale of vigilante hit men that'll keep readers on the edge of their seats."—**Roy Lee**, producer of *IT*, *IT Chapter Two*, *Doctor Sleep*, and *The Stand*

"A dark blend of *Ocean's Eleven* and *Mission Impossible*, Mesling's *The Portable Nine* pits a team of mismatched miscreants against a nefarious villain in an age-old tale of intrigue, betrayal, and revenge. With whip-sharp characterisation and a network of plot-lines, Mesling proves his mettle in this cinematic thrillride."—**Lee Murray**, three-time Bram Stoker Award nominee and author of *Into the Mist*

"Pete Mesling has gifted us with an intriguing cast of characters and a complex, fast-moving plot in *The Portable Nine*. This one gets off to a fast start, and never stops to catch its breath. (Borderlands Press Writers Boot Camp lightning strikes again!)"—**Tom Monteleone**, five-time winner of the Bram Stoker Award

PRAISE FOR JAGGED EDGES & MOVING PARTS

"Pete Mesling leads the reader through many a harrowing tale in this collection of short fiction. The wide variety of stories, long and short, grabs the reader and holds on. Be prepared—the going will get tough. You are not getting through this book unchanged."—**Alan M. Clark**, author of *The Prostitute's Price* and *Mudlarks and the Silent Highwayman*

"The writing was as beautiful as the stories were uncomfortable. Pretty pictures of ugly things."—**Well Read Beard (a.k.a., Kevin Whitten)**, reviewer and BookTuber

"Each short story is a new and exciting world … A brief glimpse into a horrific painting before being ripped away at the conclusion … Pete Mesling can write. Wow."—**Steve Stred**, author of *Invisible* and *Wagon Buddy*

MISCELLANEOUS PRAISE FOR PETE MESLING'S WORK

"Claustrophobic and terrifying; you'll be holding your breath."—*Rue Morgue*

"Pete Mesling's None So Deaf gave me a serious dose of the creeps. Herein lies an assemblage of horrors that, when it isn't reminding you of Bradbury at his grimmest, will have you double-checking the locks and turning on all the lights. Wonderful stuff indeed."—**Kealan Patrick Burke**, Bram Stoker Award-winning author of *The Turtle Boy*, *Kin*, and *Sour Candy*

"Reminiscent of the best and darkest work of David Morrell and Dan Simmons, the new collection by Pete Mesling, None So Deaf, crackles with malignant life and death. You can smell and taste these stories, which are written with a surgeon's eye for detail and a mortician's sense of drama. Highly recommended!"—**Jay Bonansinga**, New York Times best-selling author of *The Walking Dead: Invasion* and *Self-Storage*

"We've got the genealogical report in on Pete Mesling. There's some Fredric Brown. Some Kafka. And even some Brautigan. But mostly there's Mesling. And that's 100% unique and original. As is *None So Deaf*, this memorable collection."—**Mort Castle**, author of *Moon on the Water*, *New Moon on the Water*, and *Knowing When to Die*

"With his debut collection of mad scientists and classic monsters, childhood wonders twisted into nightmares, and *Twilight Zone*-style morality plays, Pete Mesling reminds us what's fun about horror—and adds serious chills along the way."—**Norman Prentiss**, Bram Stoker Award-winner, author of *Invisible Fences*

"Flashes of darkness ... moments of the macabre captured like the snapshots of a scream ... or an impaling. Short, fast, and deadly moments of discovery!"—**John Everson**, Bram Stoker Award-winning author of *Covenant* and *Sacrificing Virgins*

"Pete Mesling's *None So Deaf* explores the darkest regions of the human soul in readable tales that take no prisoners."—**Nancy Kilpatrick**, *Nevermore!: Tales of Murder, Mystery & The Macabre*

"A terrific new author. His work is fresh and different."—**John R. Little**, author of *Miranda*, *The Memory Tree*, and *Soul Mates*

"Lean and masterful prose. Buy this book."—**Wayne Allen Sallee**, author of *The Holy Terror* and *Proactive Contrition*

"Pete Mesling's fiction is definitely the kind of old school horror I grew up with. Short, sharp shocks that touch on the fears we all have—stuff like claustrophobia, the anger of strangers, carnivals, spooky houses. Definitely give them a whirl!"—**Paul Kane**, Bestselling and award-winning author of *Pain Cages*, *The Hellraiser Films & Their Legacy*, and *Lunar*

"Pete Mesling is a brawler of a writer. Whether his touch is light as a feather, like Bradbury, or a hard left hook, like Lansdale, he has you exactly where he wants you."—**John Bruni**, author of *Tales of Questionable Taste*

"Pete Mesling's *None So Deaf* takes the reader on a whistle-stop tour of American gothic, traditional and modern, with unsettling carnivals, kids breaking into decrepit houses on a dare, and corrupt preachers in the Wild West. Nasty new stings in the tail alternate with tilted perspectives on horror tropes for this box of entertainingly poisoned chocolates."—**Narrelle M Harris**, *The Opposite of Life*

"Just when you think you know what's going to happen, Mesling pulls the rug out and down the trapdoor you fall, spiraling into expertly crafted nightmares. I'm already looking forward to Pete's next offering!"—**Robert Essig**, author of *In Black*, *People of the Ethereal Realm*, and *Stronger than Hate*

"*None So Deaf* spans the horror spectrum from fearsome to fun in the spirit of *Skeleton Crew* and *Strange Highways*, making it a great read for any fan of the genre!"—**Matt Hults**, Author of *Husk*

For Christine.

CONTENTS

PREFACE

The book you hold in your hands has been banging around for a while. I suppose that's often the case with first novels. They take some time to come alive. Well, it's alive, as Victor Frankenstein and Larry Cohen would say. But what is it, exactly? Maybe the question is worth spending a little time on, since I'm mostly known for my short stories in the horror and crime genres. The Portable Nine is not a horror novel, but it's not exactly a crime novel, either. It's a suspense thriller set all over the world. It's a novel of intrigue and subterfuge, but it also has a sense of humor and exaggeration. I like to think of it as a work of literary pulp. The A-Team meets Quentin Tarantino in the back alley of a Dean Koontz novel.

I wanted to examine morality in an age when the concept has been almost completely untethered from its religious associations. I wanted to see how strongly I believe in the concepts of good and evil as played out in the earthly realm. What I didn't want was to sacrifice a rollicking good time for the sake of thematic concerns. What kept the story fun—and alive—for me over the course of its gestation was allowing myself to play a little fast and loose with reality. There are realistic elements here, I think, in both psychological and societal terms, but the emphasis is on the deployment of action.

There would probably be no *Portable Nine* to talk about, however, if not for three key moments of raw inspiration. Chapter 2 was the first chapter written (a version of it, anyway), and the idea for it came from whatever strange sea all ideas come from. This was inspirational moment *numero uno*. I knew I had something bigger than a short story or novella on my hands, but I really had no idea where it was headed. All I knew at that point was that there was a story belonging to this character called Davenport that I desperately wanted to tell.

The next lightning strike of inspiration came from the most unexpected of quarters: a short-form documentary by German filmmaker Werner Herzog. *La Soufrière* is a wonderful piece of work about a small Carribean island with a volcano that was in imminent danger of erupting in the mid-1970s as Herzog and his skeleton crew climbed the caldera to interview an old man who refused to leave, even though everyone else on the island had long since evacuated. Herzog seems convinced in the film, almost hopeful, that the volcano will blow, much as Mount Pelée outside of Saint-Pierre, Martinique, had done—with cataclysmic effect—near the turn of the 20th century. Immediately upon viewing the film, I knew its subject matter had a role to play in Davenport's story. Unable to decide for the longest time whether I wanted to use the actual eruption of Mount Pelée or the would-be eruption of La Grande Soufrière as a backdrop for *The Portable Nine*, I eventually decided to combine elements of both stories and fictionalize them accordingly. Hence Chapter 1 of the finished novel.

Still, the largest gear wheel had yet to snap into the machinery. Now, I strongly recommend that any aspiring writers know more about their basic plot than I did when I started tunneling through a first draft of *The Portable Nine*. Writing blind is a slow boat to completion, but progress is progress, and here we are. The puzzle piece I was waiting for without realizing it came when I was between jobs and had taken a part-time gig driving a school bus. One morning I drove past a set of portables on the grounds of a high school on my new route. The wall of one of these structures was labeled in large black script, as you might guess, *Portable 9*. I think that almost before the true meaning of the phrase registered with me, I had the notion in my head of a band of misfits traveling the world to fight crime in their own twisted way.

If you like, maybe we have the underfunded nature of public education in America to blame for the existence of *The Portable Nine*, then—maybe in more ways than one, it will likely be pointed out by some. Such notions might be fun to consider, but at the end of the day, what matters most to me is that I've written a novel of joyful sarcasm and playful rebuke. That its tone is dark should be expected from a writer who will always be a horror enthusiast at heart. If it has moments of illumination, maybe they aren't so easily explained away or accounted for. If any of this is true, I can lay down my pen content. May you turn the final page in a similar spirit.

—Pete Mesling
Seattle, Washington

PART I: THE GATHERING

I can look back now and say that in many ways this was the absolute apogee of my life, the point to which everything before led upward, and from which everything after fell away.
—Scott Smith, *A Simple Plan*

Fire is the devil, hiding like a coward in the smoke.
—The Log Lady, *Twin Peaks*

CHAPTER 1

The Island of Basse-Terre, the Lesser Antilles

1976

J acques LeGrand's first clue that he had left reality behind was that the sun still hung in the sky. Mollymawks cackled and swooped overhead and a warm Caribbean breeze brought with it the countless scents of island life, some salty and fresh, others hinting of decay. He couldn't remember the last time he'd seen or felt the sun, and he knew he wasn't really seeing it now, but knowing didn't diminish the illusion of warmth on his dark skin, or the phantom beads of sweat that popped on his arms, neck, shoulders, and back. He stood at the edge of a small courtyard, wearing only a pair of muslin pants tied at the waist with a leather cord. Behind him was the prison, before him a domed concrete chamber built into a hill, where only the worst of the worst ended up. In his dream, he longed to be its sole inhabitant, and the force of his longing drew him across the yard to its arched doorway, as though he were a wraith. He pounded on the heavy iron door, alternating with both fists, but no one answered, let alone admitted him. "Laisse moi entrer!" he shouted. "Let me in!"

✱ ✱ ✱

A chill shook his body and he awoke with a start. The dream sweated out of his pores and pooled between his naked back and the slab of spring-work that passed for his mattress.

It was obscene to dream such a thing, when in truth he was trapped inside the very structure his dream-self wanted so desperately to gain entrance to.

His eyes focused, as they did every morning, on the half dozen bars of sunlight near the top of the cell's tall door: an architect's kindness, perhaps, allowed to seep into the dungeon's design. Though it wasn't the same as actually seeing and feeling the sun, the crude window of iron bars was his only connection to the reality outside his cell. Not only did it let in a squint of tropical sunlight, but he was sometimes able to hear the conversations of guards and other inmates during yard time. He stopped breathing and listened. No chatter among guards on their morning rounds, which meant he'd awoken earlier than usual. That was bad. His wait for breakfast would feel like forever.

He rose from the mattress and laid his hands on the door, which was his way of gauging the weather outside, or at least the temperature. The iron door was cool to the touch, as he knew it would be so early in the day, but now he'd have a reading to compare his next one to. Not that it mattered much, but it gave him something to do. That was no small thing in solitary confinement.

The events that had landed him in Basse-Terre's only prison began their slow circulation through his brain as he pressed his hands against the door. This was a daily routine. It wasn't as powerful an escape as dreaming, but any kind of mental engagement was a welcome diversion. Who knew when the next dream—or nightmare—would come? The archipelago of Guadeloupe enjoyed a civilized climate—often the *only* civilized thing about the place—thanks to the Caribbean trade winds, but it was on a wet, chill night in spring, three-and-a-half years ago, that he had committed his crime. The charges against him weren't any more severe than those of other inmates, were in fact considerably less serious than those of some. They certainly weren't equal to his sentence. Yet everyone, from the prosecutors to the warden, had given special consideration to the fact that Jacques's transgression had involved his own brother, while ignoring the fact that he'd acted in self-defense. That he had buried a machete deep enough into his brother's arm to necessitate amputation was sufficient. They didn't want to hear how his brother had come after him, wild with rage, to accuse him of stealing a sock stuffed with money from a drawer in his apartment. They had no patience for Jacques's insistence that he hadn't taken the money. They didn't even care that his brother had attacked him with a knife behind their mother's home when Jacques returned late from a party, cut him several times and tried to stab him. The machete blow had cast a shadow over all other facts and suppositions in the case.

Still, it wasn't the prosecutors who had damned him to solitary. The guards had taken a dislike to him because he was smarter than they were. He'd get them hooked on one of his schemes for running cigarettes or setting up conjugal visits with the town's professional girls, but the screws never got what they'd expected or thought they'd been promised, which made them bitter. Unfortunately, he'd needed their cooperation to pull off his deals, so he'd been forced to live with the reality that intellectual inferiority was a breeding ground for ill tempers and petty revenge.

Revenge of a not-so-petty variety had come eventually in the form of Jacques's being called to the warden's sweaty office and told through a fog of cigarette smoke that he was to serve the rest of his sentence in solitary. Something about his being a bad influence on the prison population, which would have made him laugh if applied to anyone other than himself. Maybe the simple truth of the matter was that his past had caught up to him at last and he was paying not only for disfiguring his brother, but for all the other crimes he thought he'd gotten away with. God knew, it was a long list.

His thoughts returned to the present as he pulled his hands away from the door. On his way back to the mattress, he sensed that something outside had changed as his fingers were peeling away from the iron. A far-off rumbling grew in intensity until the ground beneath him shook. He dropped to his haunches and planted both hands on the dirt floor, as if he were waiting for a gun to fire so he could begin running laps around his tiny cell. Instead, gritty plumes of dust blew in through the bars at the top of the door.

What the hell's going on?

The rumbling turned ferocious, deafening. And the dust modulated to a darker shade of gray. Black flecks drifted throughout the ugly cloud, their added weight seeming to draw it down into the cell. Grayness enveloped him and he was beset with coughing. Then came the burning. It felt as though his skin was being torn from his back in sheets. He collapsed face first in the dirt and lost consciousness.

* * *

When he came to, he had no way of knowing how much time had passed. The floor was covered with several inches of ash, tiny swirls of smoke rising from it in places. His back felt raw, ached from numerous burns. Only a dull haze hung at the door's vent now. His cell had never felt more tomb-like. He rose and crossed the room, ash stinging his feet as he went.

"Help me!" he called out in French, his cheek pressed against the door, which was very warm now, but the words came out hoarse and dry, and uttering them made him cough hard. He might have given himself up to the cloying terror of his situation, to the lure of inevitable death, but he noticed that something had changed about the door. The lower half was hidden in a drift of ash, but at the top it had come free of its jamb. Not by much. Maybe two inches. But suddenly there was hope in his breast. The dream was still fresh enough to add luster to the sensation. He almost let a tear fall to think that he might once again enjoy the sun and air on his skin, even though every inch of him felt alive with the pain of his burns, which screamed for ointment and gauze. Could he slide his fingers into the slender gap and hope to dislodge the door? *Hope will only drive you mad.* That was rule number one among the prison population. But if the state of the door farther down was ...

He dropped to his knees and began scooping away hot ash. It burned like hell, but he welcomed the distraction from the more serious burns that throbbed along his back.

Hope broke free of its reins when he discovered that the bottom half of the door was indeed pushed slightly outward. That meant that the door sat twisted on its hinges, which meant, in turn, that with a wink of divine magic he might just have a shot. It would sure as hell be easier to push out the bottom than pry at the top. He knelt down and battered his shoulder into the door, grunting with each strike against the hot metal. His entire arm was soon another source of agony. He couldn't endure the pain forever and was about to take a break when he saw that his work had wrenched the door several inches farther on its hinges. His hopes renewed, he quickly stood up to have a go at the upper half. For what might have been thirty minutes, he alternated between pulling at the top and pushing at the bottom, until at last the top hinge screamed free of its housing and Jacques was able to bring down the door completely, which sent a fresh cloud of ash billowing throughout his chamber.

Unfortunately, what met his gaze as he looked out through the open doorway was no better. The world beyond his cell was not the sun-dappled tropical paradise of his dream, but a dense blizzard of ash.

CHAPTER 2

Present

Davenport stepped out onto the balcony and let the cool late afternoon air flow into his open jacket, fluttering his indigo silk shirt against his chest and stomach. The jacket was stylish but comfortable, a light brown canvas affair with a collar like a suit jacket and dark wooden buttons down the front. With a crippled hand, he drew a cigarette from a silver case, lit it, and leaned against the parapet. The crowd below thickened with pedestrians. The central region of Florence was closed off to most vehicle traffic at this hour. It would be all the cover he needed. He adjusted his signature black leather fedora—as rumpled and creased as he sometimes felt, though not today. He knew that some found the hat pretentious, but he couldn't have cared less. It was an ironic thing with him. The jacket, on the other hand, was pure style. These were the sweet times, the hours before a hit. For all other occasions in his life—weddings, funerals, high-speed pursuits, sex—Davenport's blood pressure remained even, his demeanor flat and hard. But in anticipation of a kill, he was always a changed man, an enhanced man, if only briefly. And the brevity didn't really bother him. What joys in life ever lasted very long?

He smiled at the rising September moon, a fat crescent, and took a long, delicious drag from his cigarette. It made him hungry for more pleasure, and he stepped inside to refresh his drink, knowing the rest of his cigarette would taste even better chasing fumes of bourbon down his throat.

* * *

An hour later, he had his man in sight. Forty-six-year-old Max Brindle: bald on top, wide in the middle, short on the bottom. He wore a brightly colored sport coat—a patchwork of tweed—with beige slacks, and he wove through the crowded streets with a swiftness and agility that belied his awkward looks. On his head sat a tan porkpie with a brown satin band, all pretense. The man's haste amused Davenport. As if anyone could outpace the Mad Marksman of Malta—a nickname he'd earned almost a dozen years ago. As if anyone could outpace Death.

Davenport's weapon of choice was a Colt King Cobra with a four-inch barrel and a wooden grip. No one used them anymore. Not sexy enough for the modern gangster. But to Davenport the Colt meant business, from hammer to sight, and it felt good and heavy in his grip. It was a loud sonofabitch, and its recoil could kick your ass if you weren't paying attention, but these were traits he had come to respect. He held the weapon now, inside his pocket, as he shadowed Max Brindle. The way the cold steel warmed from his touch made him feel strong, almost invincible. The gun was his to control, a snake that would strike only at his command.

He was closing in on him now. Slowly the noises around them disappeared in concentric circles. First to go was the distant blare of car horns and the occasional squeal of tires. The next ring to disperse contained the ambient chatter of pedestrians and the clinking of dishware at alfresco cafés. Soon the only sound to claim Davenport's attention was the click of his and Max Brindle's footsteps on the cobblestones, which took on an exaggerated quality resembling the work of an overzealous fledgling soundman in the glory days of cinema. One second Davenport's footsteps were the louder of the two. The next they were background to Brindle's. He could imagine the close-up camerawork that would be used for the scene. Meanwhile, dear old Max had no idea that his executioner was staring at the exact location between his shoulder blades where a bullet would enter to do the most damage. But it wasn't quite time.

Too many onlookers. Besides, Davenport grew distracted by the rich aroma of various sauces and baked goods that filled the avenue. He wished he'd taken a moment to have a bite before setting out on this errand.

"Excuse me, sir?" Davenport said as he came up alongside Max and touched him lightly on the shoulder. "Please, come with me for a moment."

"Beg pardon?" Max's response was indignant, accompanied by an arching of his wiry eyebrows, but when his eyes met Davenport's, his temper cooled visibly. Davenport had that effect on people.

"Don't look back," Davenport whispered, "but I think someone's tailing you." It was amazing how often this simple ruse worked, but the men Davenport was hired to kill usually had more than one reason to keep an eye over their shoulder.

The two men ducked into a narrow alley with boutiques and more cafés lining its curved length. It wasn't nearly as thronged with tourists. The odd restaurant patio sported a gathering of clientele, but most of the day's light had drained from the sky and people were in search of postprandial entertainments. It was a fine spot for the deed. The moon caught Davenport's eye again, and he gave it a wink as he slid the Colt from his pocket and aimed it discreetly at Max Brindle's back. He applied pressure to the trigger as the sound of a woman's tipsy laughter rose up into the deepening purple night from somewhere nearby. A little more pressure to the trigger and ...

Jammed. The gun's hammer wouldn't budge.

He stopped suddenly and held the firearm in the palm of his hand to eye it like a turd someone had handed him before he could refuse it. His temples pulsed with a mixture of disbelief and disgust as he thrust it back into his pocket, quickly realizing he had to worry about his cover again. He'd never botched a job before. Never.

Max, noticing Davenport was no longer protecting him, stopped and turned.

"Anything the matter?" he asked, his eyes a little wide and

nervous.

"No," said Davenport, gritting his teeth against anger that wanted to rise within him like some dark and heavy drift of timber riding an incoming tide. "I think we've given him the slip. I'll be on my way."

"You mind if I ask why you took such an interest in my welfare? Don't get me wrong; I'm appreciative, but ..."

Max's double chin trembled as he spoke, and he swallowed excessively when silent. Davenport stared at his throat as it tensed and released, tensed and released. He wanted to tear it open with his bare hands, keep digging through the red, wet tissue of the neck until his fingers poked through the other side. He had to get away from this little man before he was forced to do something regrettable. His anger might cause him to lose control, and he couldn't afford to let that happen.

"I used to do a bit of government work for the U.S.," he said, doing his best to make his gritted teeth come across as part of his normal inflection. "Guess I developed an eye for trouble."

"Well thank you," said Max. "I do a bit of government work myself, and it hasn't earned me a lot of admirers. You may have saved me the inconvenience of a mugging." He rocked on his heels and smiled.

Davenport pulled at the brim of his hat and continued down the alley. It was automatic with him never to retrace his steps if he could avoid it.

The air had grown more brisk in the last twenty minutes, but the temperature had yet to get uncomfortable since his arrival. It was almost as if the weather knew the city to be a kind of paradise on earth and kept itself from going too far in any direction. A mild gust enlivened him, almost against his will. He wanted to hang on to his fury for reasons he couldn't explain to himself, but the September evening worked its charms, and by the time he'd crossed the Arno and trailed back through the Piazza del Duomo to his hotel, he was in a much more agreeable state. He almost wished it were the off season so he could enjoy the city without its crush of tourists.

* * *

Back in his room, he poured himself a drink and retired with it to the balcony.

His temper was quelled, but he still had the shakes. He felt robbed of his prize, and yet it was almost as if he'd followed through on the hit. Mentally he'd been as prepared as ever to take a life. He'd gone after his man and confronted him, even pulled the trigger, or tried to. Had the firearm not malfunctioned, he'd have murdered again. Surely it would count against him on the cosmic scorecard, which was why it seemed unfair that he shouldn't have anything to show for it. Worse than that, his client, one Mr. Samuel Gutterson, wouldn't be pleased with the outcome. Some days he really thought this solo shit was for the birds, and he longed for the old days ... the old *team*.

His head pounded, and the bourbon only made it worse, but he kept drinking. Davenport had never harbored a moment's guilt for any of his past jobs. If he was hired to take a man out, that man was taken out. If he couldn't justify the act to his own moral satisfaction, he didn't take the job. It was as simple as that. He was well respected for his sense of duty and eye for detail, as well as his impeccable completion rate. Now, a mechanical failure in the cylinder mechanism of his pride and joy threatened to change all that. Davenport, the Mad Marksman of Malta, had failed.

The question now was, Would he pick up the spare? He knew he could find Brindle again before the man would have an opportunity to leave the city. That would have been the professional attitude. Davenport should have dusted himself off and counted on going after his target again the next day. But he couldn't get excited about the idea. He was more intrigued by Max Brindle the person than Max Brindle the hit. What was Brindle doing right now? Why was he in Tuscany? What joys and sorrows would he now be exposed to, all because Davenport's

Colt King Cobra had refused to open a hole in his back?

This of course led to the question of how many sorrows and joys Davenport had stolen from past victims. He held his glass up to the moon in his good hand. A couple of ice cubes banged around inside. He remembered a line from Dickens, of all things, and he recited it in full voice: "Or would you know the weight and length of the strong coil you bear yourself? It was full as heavy and as long as this, seven Christmas Eves ago. You have laboured on it since. It is a ponderous chain!"

As with his love of Bach, and so many other things, he owed his familiarity with Dickens to his Aunt Meredith. She had tried to put him on a better path. If only he could make her understand that the one he was on had its own merits. Maybe the next time he visited her he could make some headway on that score.

He staggered drunkenly, smashing the glass of bourbon on the brightly colored tiles that made up the floor of the broad balcony. Eventually he found his way to bed.

* * *

Gutterson didn't expect to hear from him for two more days, so he devoted the next day—once he finally woke up—to seeking out Brindle again. The man had a curious hold on him, and Davenport felt that he must see him again, if only to prove to himself that he still drew breath. Maybe then he'd seem less like a ghost.

He first caught sight of the unmistakable patch of gaudy tweed winding along near the Piazza della Signoria, a kind of Trafalgar Square for the Tuscan adventurer. Neptune, along with one of many copies of Michelangelo's David that Davenport had observed throughout Florence, kept a watchful eye on the square from a prominent location near the Palazzo Vecchio, which served as town hall to Florence. Or maybe it was the adjacent Loggia dei Lanzi they watched over, making sure none of the statues in that covered gallery were molested by vandals. Somewhere a plaintive harmonium turned air into music, most likely for coins tossed into a cup. Not knowing exactly what he hoped to gain by catching up with Brindle, Davenport followed at a safe distance until at last his quarry took a table at a bustling street café with the alarming name Fine del Viaggio. Journey's end. Finding an unobtrusive table of his own, Davenport sat down and kept watch.

Brindle appeared to be waiting for someone. He kept checking his watch, twisting it back and forth on his puffy wrist. Soon there was a tall, slender glass of something icy and intoxicating on the table in front of him, as though he'd ordered up his exact physical opposite. He poked the paper umbrella up and down in the drink a few times. Davenport ordered a coffee and settled in for a long stakeout.

Nothing could have surprised him more than the arrival, two umbrella cocktails later, of a tall woman who seemed to move within a constant shadow. Her hair was straight and black and melted into a slinky dress of equal darkness. Between the hem of the dress and her jet-black shoes was some reprieve, for her black stockings did allow a bit of flesh color to show through. Her face also offered some paleness, but not much, with large, dark sunglasses covering most of it. She sat down next to Max and smiled icily. He leaned over and kissed her cheek, which pleased her. Then he became extremely animated, gesturing wildly and talking at a great clip. He appeared to be delighted by the woman's attention, and Davenport couldn't say he blamed him. She looked like trouble, all right, but she was beautiful.

It had never occurred to Davenport that men like Max Brindle enjoyed the company of women like this. Or any women at all, for that matter. He always thought the Max Brindles of the world just sort of fell into marriages somewhere along the way and spent the rest of their unhappy lives working one angle or another. Maybe it was easier to kill a man if you told yourself he half wanted to die anyway.

The woman kissed Max, a lingering press of her lips on his, before leaving him to his drink. Her smile had said there was plenty more where that came from. That made at least two kisses that Brindle never would have known if Davenport's Colt had done its job the night before. It was almost enough to make a hired gun cry.

He stopped at the restroom on his way out. He'd had enough of Max Brindle and the guilt he inspired. It was time for a new line of work. Maybe even something legit. Something that didn't involve adding too many more links to that ponderous chain of his. He splashed water in his face and stared down his mirror image. It was older than it had been the last time he bothered to check, but still a good face. Hard and more mean than otherwise, but appealing.

But was it a face that could belong to anything other than a killer? And was he qualified to do anything else?

Before he could dry his hands, much less answer his own questions, the bathroom door swung open and in walked Max Brindle. At first he just nodded politely at Davenport and headed for the urinal, but he stopped halfway, knew he was being watched.

"Well, I'll be," he said, facing Davenport. "You're the man from last night. Saved my neck."

Davenport rolled his shoulders, uncomfortable with the encounter. "Just on my way out."

"Oh, now wait a minute. This is the second time life has put you in my path. I'm not sure I can ignore that kind of coincidence. Why don't you join me outside for a drink? Maybe it turns out we have something in common, you and me."

"I don't think—"

"I insist."

The last thing Davenport needed was to make friends with this man, for Christ's sake. There was danger in obsessing over how much he could learn about him, knowing that every tidbit, every observation, would have been impossible had he fulfilled Gutteron's wishes. Where would it lead, and when would it end? Max's invitation proved too tempting to refuse, however. The spigot would have to be cranked off at a later time.

"Okay." He wiped his hands and face. "We'll have a drink."

"Splendid." Max held the door for Davenport and led him back to his patio table.

Apparently nature's call could wait a little longer.

"What'll you have?" a sharply dressed waiter asked Davenport in Italian.

"Bourbon with a skim of water, two ice cubes." His response was an admixture of Italian and English, a trick he'd used to charm waitstaff the world over. It was tied to his broader policy of always treating the collateral players with enough respect to keep him in their good graces but not so much as to draw unwanted attention.

"Certainly, sir. And another for you?" Heavily accented English this time.

"Oh, I suppose you could talk me into one more," Max said with a smile. Then, to Davenport, "You know you're a regular when the waiter's willing to speak English at you." This ended in airy laughter.

For a moment, Davenport feared that Max might slap him on the shoulder, or something equally horrible, but he was spared.

The drinks arrived and both men toyed with their glasses before getting down to any real drinking. Max let his eyes linger on Davenport's deformed left hand for a moment but wisely kept any comments to himself.

"It's a funny thing, running into you again," Max said. "Something's been on my mind since last night and I didn't think I'd ever have an answer to it."

Davenport eyed him cautiously, said nothing.

"When you approached me, you addressed me in English. Now, I know this is Florence. English isn't uncommon to hear, but ..."

"How can I put this delicately?" Davenport said. "Americans tend to make an impression."

"You sonofabitch. Well I'll be damned. If that isn't something." Max paused to sip his drink, fumbling with the umbrella before finally adding it to the pile he had going. "Say, where are you from, anyway? Your accent isn't Italian."

"English born. Greek raised."

"Well, it's damn good to know you. The name's Max Brindle. What do they call you?"

"Davenport." He brought the bourbon to his lips to avoid shaking hands.

"Davenport what?" Again he let out a laugh.

Davenport wondered if Max would make a similar sound if his throat were being squeezed shut. Would there be any discernible difference between this irritating, put-on laughter and the sound of his final, choking gasps?

"Just Davenport."

"Say, how does a fellow like you earn a living, you don't mind my asking?"

"This and that. Things come my way, you know?" He paused to light a cigarette. "I'm in the lucky position of being able to turn down what doesn't appeal to me."

"But it's kind of a hardscrabble existence, isn't it? Living according to the whims of chance and all that?"

"Chance favors the prepared mind, Mr. Brindle."

"Chance fav …What's that, Shakespeare?"

"Pasteur."

Max nodded his way back to his drink. "Didn't he invent the cotton gin?"

"No." He could tell Max wanted him to ask about *his* line of work, but he wasn't about to. Max would volunteer the information any minute now, especially with all the alcohol in him.

"Tell me, Mr. Davenport, have you ever done much in the way of quality control?"

"I like to think that every job I do has a measure of quality control to it. Perhaps you could be more specific." He blew a cloud of smoke over Max's head, where it haloed for a moment before thinning to blend with the Tuscan sky.

"Cargo's my business. I'm in charge of moving things around this planet. By boat, train, airplane, truck. You name it, I make the deals that get merchandise moving. Of course, I can't personally keep an eye on what gets put on the boats and planes. I need help with that kind of work."

"Quality control."

Max pointed at him as if his thumb and forefinger were a gun. He winked and flicked his thumb to shoot. "Blam-o," he said and followed it with a broad grin. Then came the forced laugh.

Davenport gave a politic smile. "This work you have in mind, does it pay well?"

"Ah, a man who gets down to business. Good, good." He clapped his hands and rubbed them together. "The compensation should be suitable for someone in your position."

"What position is that?"

"Why, the lucky position of being able to turn down what doesn't appeal to you."

Max Brindle had some depth to him after all. Davenport would have to watch his step with this one. "Fair enough. We can talk money another time."

"You're interested, then?"

"Curious, for now. It may develop into interest."

"You'd have certain demands, I imagine."

"I won't kill anyone."

Max's features twisted a degree, as though he thought Davenport was joking. Something must have changed his mind, though, because his features soon hung slack once again.

"I hope not. I won't either."

Davenport considered asking about Max's lady friend but decided to keep that card in his hand for now. Max didn't know that Davenport had seen them together. Why change that?

"In that case, I think we'll be able to talk further. But not here. Not today." Davenport pressed the butt of his cigarette into an ashtray. "I'll be in touch, Mr. Brindle."

"Please, call me Max."

Davenport swigged the remnants of his bourbon and once again avoided a handshake. He touched the brim of his hat as he rose and merged into the foot traffic that pressed through the busy square. He heard Brindle ask how they'd get in touch, but he chose to ignore the question and keep moving.

Max's cryptic offer wasn't without appeal. It was unlikely to be an above-board proposal, but at least Max seemed averse to bloodshed. Just the kind of boss Davenport was hoping for since murdering the man the previous evening. *Almost* murdering, he reminded himself. The guilt was really lingering. He'd never felt this way after an *actual* hit. Why now?

He was pleased to discover that he could walk off the nagging sensation more easily today. Strolling along the Arno calmed him, and the always startling Ponte Vecchio claimed him entirely. Crossing the ancient bridge, he passed by clots of competing jewelry shops, strings of garland and lights crossing overhead. The constant aroma of espresso followed him the entire way, as if the coffee-thickened air hung trapped among the shops and dwellings that lined the bridge. The crowds were dense but navigable, and eventually his feet carried him back to the Hotel Aggregio. Perhaps he would be able to rest peacefully, clear his conscience now that his future held hope for a better way of living. Maybe he'd even get in a cat nap.

"Signor Davenport?" the young woman at the desk called as he crossed the lobby, headed for the staircase.

He turned and stepped briskly to the counter, giving a sharp nod.

"There is delivery for you," the desk clerk said, her English labored. She retrieved a large brown envelope and slid it to Davenport.

"*Grazie.*" Davenport touched his hat. "Who dropped it off?"

"Was here when I came on."

He turned the padded envelope in his hands as he wandered back toward the stairs, searching for some indication of who it might have been from. There was none. When he reached his floor, he tucked the parcel under his left arm so he could fish out his key with the other hand. Once inside, he switched on a table lamp and examined the envelope anew. It was rectangular, about the thickness of a legal pad, but heavier. When he tore it open and tipped it upside down over the small table, a tablet computer slid out.

A sticky note was affixed to the screen. On it were scrawled two words, upside down to him, and in French, but he was able to read them: *Quelle honte.* Shame on you.

He could think of only two things that anyone could possibly try to hold over his head. There was, of course, his long history of violence, his ponderous chain of sin and guilt. And now there was the more recent incident, his failure to live up to that past. It seemed impossible that his client could have learned that Max Brindle was still alive already. It was less than twenty-four hours since his gun had malfunctioned and changed his life course. Gutterson didn't have the brains or the staff to get a status report on Brindle that fast.

But that meant the message on the sticky note was in reference to a past job, which was a little disquieting. If that was the case, the package could be from one of a dozen potential enemies, even after selecting for those with brains and resources. It also stood in defiance of the three ideals Davenport prided himself on his adherence to. 1) Always finish a job at the first opportunity. 2) Never leave a mess for someone you don't trust to clean up. 3) Cover your tracks like a wolf in a blizzard. It was unthinkable that his past was catching up with him at last. He'd been at this game for almost twenty damn years.

The only thing he could be sure of was that if he speculated much longer on the origins of the tablet, he'd end up painting a picture that was likely to be far worse than reality. Facing this would be better than fearing it, as was almost always the case, in his experience. He took the tablet to the bed and, sitting on the mattress's very edge, powered it on.

A customized home screen came to life and the tablet

quickly found the Wi-Fi connection. From the center of the screen, a single application stared at him like a threat, or a dare. There was no title or caption, only the image of a match head aflame. He tapped open the app and leaned closer to the screen as it went black. A moment later, a shrouded figure appeared in a video that took up the whole screen. Davenport tried to make out the face of the figure but saw that not only did the person have a monastic cowl draped about him, but his head was bowed to the floor.

"You have made a grave error in judgment by killing Brindle, Mr. Davenport." It was a man's voice, rich and deep, tinged with French. "I understand that it may ruffle the feathers of an employer or two, but do stay out of my affairs. As things stand, you have a far worse thing at your back than a disgruntled boss. You've got the Black Phantom nipping at your heels."

As the man in the video spoke these last words, he lifted his head and threw back the hood of his cowl, revealing the leering face of a bald man whose skin was as dark as Davenport had ever seen. The eyes had an aspect of fire in the midst of all that black. At an utter loss for words, all Davenport could manage was to drag back the video's progress bar to ascertain whether it was live or prerecorded, paranoid as the question seemed in retrospect. Of course, the video repeated itself.

Following the portion he had already watched, the footage cut to a tripod shot of a steep, crooked street that wound up a hill cluttered with narrow houses, all of them painted in various pastel shades of yellow, blue, and green. Balconies adorned most of the homes. Davenport's pulse quickened. Recognition was dawning but he was caught off guard. Everything was out of context. His aunt's house? Yes, two in on the right. It was her house on Crete, in the city of Chania. He hadn't been there for years, but it was as familiar as his own name, now that he'd made sense of what he was seeing. His heart began to gallop in his chest. What the fuck *was* this? Aunt Meredith. One of the few people in the world he gave a damn about anymore.

An explosion blew a corner balcony out of his aunt's

house and rocked the camera. Davenport jerked back as though present at the scene. Debris rained down onto the roughly paved street as fire blazed in every direction from the source of the blast, spreading with terrifying swiftness amid the tightly packed buildings. Smoke rolled into the crisp blue sky.

"*No!*" He bolted to his feet.

By the time the video went black, the house was beyond rescue. As was his aunt, if she had been inside at the time. As was the baby grand piano she had taught him on when he was a boy, convinced he had the makings of a concert pianist—until he lost the use of his left hand. The Steinway had been her prize possession, and therefore his. Even if she hadn't been home when the bomb exploded, the piano was surely gone, and that was crime enough.

The application shrank back down to a thumbnail on the home screen. After a moment, the app disappeared altogether, leaving the screen utterly blank. He tried to reset the tablet, to no effect. It wouldn't even turn off. Playing the video had crippled the device.

With a trembling hand he set the tablet computer flat on the floor and stepped on one end of it. Leaning over, he pried the other end up until it began to bend and finally cracked apart. He dropped the remains into a wastebasket and leaned on a dresser with both hands, staring at his reflection in the mirror and breathing like an incensed beast. He could hear his pulse as blood rushed through his head. His face burned red with anger. His blood pressure must have been through the attic.

Now the need to turn his life around after failing to dispatch Max Brindle seemed a rash resolution. Maybe all he required was a shifting of focus. The anger and murderous detachment that was part and parcel of a hit man's life ... Why couldn't it all be concentrated on seeking revenge against the Black Phantom? The man's video threats would prove mild by comparison to what Davenport would visit upon him.

Yes, why not make the Black Phantom's extermination his sole ambition? He would have to discover why the bastard had singled out Davenport and his aunt anyway. Why stop at fact-finding? What was he going to do with the information he gathered? Provide it to the police? No, the Black Phantom had picked the wrong parade to rain on.

No one laid a threat on Davenport's doorstep without there being repercussions.

No one dug into his past and used it against him.

No one told him what to do unless he was in their employ.

No blue ghost.

No purple wraith.

No black phantom.

No one.

CHAPTER 3

T he lobby of the Hotel Aggregio was quiet but not empty. Davenport sat in a plush burgundy armchair, intent upon his evening bourbon and paper. It was the best way he could think of to regain a facade of equanimity. If he had stayed in his room to brood, who knew what manner of untenable plots might have begun to hatch. His gnarled hand angered him, though. Some days he was almost able to forget about it, but he used it now to drink his bourbon, making it difficult to bring the glass to his mouth without spilling on his tan jacket. Each splash of liquor was a cruel reminder of what he might have been with two good hands.

After a long time spent staring blankly at the paper, a story about security flaws at a large shipping port in eastern China caught his interest and reminded him of Max Brindle's offer. But when the woman in black emerged through the main door of the hotel with a man on her arm, Davenport forgot all about the newspaper and his job options, if not about the likely fate of his aunt. He had seen the way this slinking black mamba had kissed Max the day before, and now he saw how she pressed her slithering form against the tall young stranger on her arm. It surprised him how much he enjoyed having a secret to keep from Brindle. It might prove useful. The woman could be a lady of the evening, Davenport thought. Max Brindle seemed the type to enjoy a call girl's company. Then again, the twenty-something on her arm now didn't look like he'd have any trouble hooking a date. No, Davenport had a feeling she was playing these men for something more than pocket change. And his feelings about such things were reliable—had, in fact, positioned him as the de facto leader of the Nine. When an FBI agent had tried to ingratiate himself to the Portable Nine in 2008, Davenport had been the one to see through the man's compliments and tales of derring-do, eventually convincing him to forget he'd ever so much as learned their names. From that point forward, Davenport had been the one the Portable Nine all turned to for matters requiring a judgment call of any significance.

He set the newspaper aside and uncrossed his legs. The woman working the desk had gone on break, leaving the lobby to the care of a man about her age wearing a tight-cut hipster suit. The main door swung open again and in walked two men. He watched them out of boredom at first, but the taller of the two looked more familiar with each step they took across the red lobby rug. They were in conversation and didn't look in Davenport's direction, which was fine with him, for now he knew where he recognized the man from. He had been present when Sam Gutterson relayed the details of the hit he wanted Davenport to make on Brindle. Even then Davenport had pegged the man—Jaggert—as a climber. The way he'd stood off to the side without uttering a single word had left Davenport with the feeling that the man had asked to be present rather than wait for an invitation. Something about how he'd taken everything in but commented on nothing had conveyed more of the ambitious hood than the browbeaten henchman.

Jaggert was the same man today, though not so still and quiet: his posture and stride full of bravado, his instructions to the man at his side emphasized by gestures, the face behind the long, flowing hair a mass of sharp angles and scars. The smaller fellow had on a wide-brimmed hat, which kept Davenport from getting much of a read on him as the duo drifted out of profile. Soon all he saw was their backs as they waited for the elevator, then stepped inside. They appeared to have the car to themselves, and Davenport watched a brass dial above the elevator entrance light up each number as it passed the corresponding floor.

Two … three … four.

It went all the way to five, the top floor.

Taking a moment to down the remnants of his drink, he donned his hat and made a move for the staircase. His rooms were on the third floor, but he passed by a couple arguing on that landing, a cloud of their cigarette smoke following him up the stairs. He hadn't had a chance to troubleshoot the problem with the King Cobra, but it was reassuring to have it on him. A gun, even one that wouldn't fire, could be brandished, and it was remarkable how quickly a person's mood changed at the sight of a firearm. The pugnacious look of the King Cobra was especially helpful in this regard.

There was only one problem: At the door to the fifth-floor hallway, he remembered he hadn't put the Colt in his jacket pocket. It still sat in the drawer of his bureau, tucked between two of his favorite shirts. Time was precious, but instinct told him to retrieve the impotent weapon.

The couple was no longer on the landing when he retraced his steps to the third floor, but the stale smell of tobacco smoke lingered, and he could make out their squabbling voices somewhere down the hall when he opened the door to the corridor. His rooms were in the opposite direction, occupying a corner of the hotel. As he turned the door handle and stepped into the entryway, he realized his error. He had locked the door when he left, but it was not locked now. Odd that he hadn't even thought to get his keys out, as if his subconscious had wanted him to play into the hands of whatever fates conspired against him.

The bastards had gone to the fifth floor as a ruse, then doubled back. It could have been torn from his own playbook.

He tried to catch the door before it could swing closed, but it was no use. Glimpsing a dark and slender blur of motion at the corner of his eye, he had no time to avoid the cudgel's blow.

* * *

"There's life in him after all."

These were the first words Davenport heard upon waking. His vision was blurred and he detected a faint taste of copper at the back of his throat. His wrists throbbed. He tried and failed to bring words to his lips.

"Not for long." This was a different man's voice, meaner and tight.

Davenport's senses normalized by degrees, triggered by a dark, oily smell. The low light of wherever he was didn't provide much visual stimulation, even as his consciousness returned, bringing with it a rounded ache that pounded at both temples. And of course there was the sharper pain of the blow to his right parietal, a pain that felt as if it had frozen in time and would constantly renew itself. Maybe he saw a large opening in a wall across the way, but if so it was nighttime and all he was seeing was the glow of exterior lights. Through all of these discoveries he remained silent. Until he had an idea of where he might be, he intended to keep his cards close to his chest. He was tied to a metal pole with his hands behind him and appeared to be sitting on a floor of creosote-laden timbers. There was interior lighting, he saw now, but only a row of low-wattage fixtures hanging from the high ceiling. He figured he was in a warehouse, or maybe a covered marina.

"Mr. Davenport," the second man said from somewhere off to Davenport's left, "I trust I don't have the distinction of being the first to tell you there's a certain pecking order in this life. There's always someone above you, and, if you're lucky, someone below you. Of course, it's your subordinates you want to look out for. They're the ones who can't wait to see you slip. Dying to fill your shoes, the vultures."

The American accent had sounded familiar right away. East Texas. Now Davenport's weary mind placed it. "Jaggert."

"The very same."

The first man laughed in darkness.

"Does Gutterson know you're off leash, or is this a bit of freelance work?" Davenport asked.

"Hit him, Ned."

Jaggert's lackey shuffled into view, no hat to cover his pate now, his face a mass of incongruities and healed traumas, as if he'd been beaten as an infant and traipsed through life expecting nothing more. He delivered a stinging blow to Davenport's left cheek, then retreated out of sight. Before Davenport could utter a word, Jaggert was squatting and leering before him. His features lay mostly in shadow, but memory filled in the rest. *No sir, you haven't changed a bit, Jaggert, old chap.*

"See what I mean about that pecking order?" Jaggert's hair hung in sweaty strands. "My days of taking shit from people like you are over, Mr. Davenport."

"Perhaps. And perhaps your boy ... Ned, is it? Perhaps Ned will surprise *you* one day."

Jaggert gripped Davenport's jaw with one hand. "Don't you worry about that. You have plenty to worry about without being philanthropic." He let go and stood up. "To answer your question, Mr. Gutterson does not know that I'm in Italy, or that you've fucked up a job. A very important job. But he'll find out soon, just not from you."

"Yeah? From who, then?"

"Look at it as a blessing. Would you really want to be the one to break the news to him? I'm not looking forward to it myself, but at least his mood will lighten when I tell him about your unfortunate demise."

"And how did you get wind of the news, as you call it?"

"Eyes and ears, my friend. Eyes and ears everywhere."

Davenport wondered if they'd taken his gun from the hotel room. He assumed so. But which one of them had it? Or was it in a vehicle somewhere nearby? Or—and Jesus, here was a thought—dumped at the side of the road?

"Jaggert," he said at last, "I don't have the energy to argue with you or trade insults. It was the end of the line for me whether you got to me or not. Why don't you do what you're going to do and save us all a lot of time."

Was it water he heard nearby, lapping at a pier, perhaps?

Very likely a marina, then. They'd done some traveling while he was unconscious if this was the coast.

"What a splendid idea, Mr. Davenport. Stand up."

For a moment, he thought Jaggert was kidding. How could he possibly hope to stand with his hands tied to a pole behind his back? But the man's face was a shadow–mask of earnestness. Davenport pressed his back against the pole and drew his knees up before him. This gave him enough leverage to push himself—slowly and painfully—up the pole. The phantom bludgeon continued to press into his skull. He labored as much to keep the difficulty of the task from showing on his face as to bring himself to an upright posture. The latter he eventually accomplished. He couldn't be sure about the former, not that it mattered much in the bad light of the place.

"Good," muttered Jaggert. "Ned, take him outside and shoot him in the neck, from behind. No need to make it look like an execution. I plan to tell Gutterson we tried to bring him in alive but he made a run for it." He turned his attention to Davenport. "You understand."

Ned undid Davenport's bonds as he responded. "What should I do with the body?"

"Fish food, you idiot. Why do you think we came to the water to do this? I fucking hate Livorno."

Livorno? It was only an hour or so from Florence, but still … Ned must have delivered him quite a blow (it was always the Neds of the world who carried out the violence). No wonder his head still throbbed like a heart kept beating under glass in a mad scientist's laboratory.

There was no sense making a scene when he was so obviously out-muscled. And there was a certain code to dealing with goons like Jaggert. They were small men with large ambitions, and they thrived on signs of weakness in their adversaries. Part of Davenport's code involved denying such men every possible satisfaction.

With his eyes more or less adjusted to the level of light in the place, he could discern the shapes of pleasure craft suspended by cranes in the darker recesses of the space. Ned led him across the uneven floor of what he now assumed to be a marina's covered repair facility to the large doorway he'd noticed earlier. The soupy smell of seawater blended with the rich scent of creosote into a swampy stench that called to mind the jungle settings of comic books Davenport used to read as a kid.

"Outside," Ned said in a voice that suggested crooked teeth. He'd been walking behind Davenport with a gun at the ready.

It was dark, except for a handful of hanging bulbs along the pier, and the city lights of Livorno beyond. Davenport felt a sense of unease at how the days were slipping away from him, as if he were losing control of his life.

"All right," said Ned, "Let's get this over with."

They stood facing each other on the pier. Away from Jaggert, Ned seemed a different person. Not quite nervous, but not nearly as cocky as he'd been inside. He let his gun dangle at his side, uninterested in further theatrics. Davenport noticed that he had close-cropped hair the color of fire, where he wasn't completely bald.

"What would you like me to do, Ned?"

"Um, start walking down the pier, I guess, away from me." Ned's accent was also American. Midwest corn fed. With marbles.

Davenport nodded. "I don't know which one of you has my gun..."

Ned patted a jacket pocket, a proud, stupid smile on his face. Davenport had to suppress one of his own. No matter how much talent you had, you could always do with a spot of luck. Then again, as he'd pointed out to Max Brindle, chance favored the prepared mind.

"I see," Davenport continued. "I don't want to waste your time, son, but I think you could use some friendly advice. And seeing how it's my last chance to—"

"Spit it out." The gun at Ned's side waggled a little.

"It's just that I know these guys you're humping for, better than you do. They're petty. They like tokens and symbolism."

"You've got ten seconds to tell me what you're getting at." He brought the gun up, aimed it at Davenport's face."

"Remember, Jaggert wanted a neck shot from behind. I wouldn't give it to me in the mug if I were you. But getting to the point, it might be seen as a clever gesture on your part if you were to shoot me with my own weapon."

"What? Why?"

"Insult to injury. That kind of thing. Just something for you to consider."

"Why do you care?"

"I don't, really. But I like you a hell of a lot better than Jaggert. One of you is bound to move up through the ranks. I don't see why it has to be him, do you? Offing me with my own damn gun … Well, it's the kind of thing that will get you talked about. For years."

Ned stared at him without moving, but wheels were turning behind those eyes. Yes, they were.

Finally Ned holstered his gun between his belt and the paunch it held in, then reached into the jacket pocket he'd patted earlier. "It's all the same to me. One gun's the same as another."

Davenport gritted his teeth at the thought of such an ignorant whelp handling his precious King Cobra, but he let it go. Timing was everything. Ned drew the beauty out and wagged it to indicate that it was time for Davenport to get moving.

It was thrilling to think he might be dead in mere seconds. He didn't expect the Colt to work, but it might have fixed itself. Or maybe the difference in Ned's grip would give the trigger the leverage it needed to fire. Most likely not, though. He was counting on most likely not … Had it all riding on most likely not.

He charged Ned, half expecting a round to explode from the barrel of the Colt and tear into his flesh. But the report never came. Nor did the pain. They wrestled upright for a moment, but Ned was no physical match for Davenport, who quickly wrested his pride and joy from the younger man's hand and kicked him into the sea.

Without so much as a glance back in the direction of the marina, Davenport fled for cover.

CHAPTER 4

"Yeah," the Butcher said into the phone as he surveyed the cracks in the wall of his shithole apartment, and several waves in the carpet where the glue had failed. "I need to talk to someone about a stolen vehicle."

"One moment," came the apathetic response from the man who'd answered at the police station.

"Can I help you?" A new voice. Still male, but deeper.

"Someone stole my Bronco. I watched them drive out of the lot where I live about ten minutes ago. Seemed to be heading west."

"Can I get your name?"

He gave his name, at least the name he'd purchased the Bronco under. Not the name he'd rented the apartment under, or the name he'd soon be purchasing an airline ticket under. Earl Saunders, Mitch Williamson, Clay Fundt. They were only the most recent in a string of identities the Butcher had concocted. He could afford to answer their silly questions. Name, address, make, model, year. It didn't take long. The conversation was soon over, the report filed. They wouldn't touch him in a million years, because he knew where to go and how to get there.

The Butcher always knew exactly where to go because life was a matter of planning and waiting. Oceans of waiting in between thrills. Gulfs of hypothetical reasoning. The ecstasies were islands in that vast sea—necessarily few and sparsely arranged, but they *were* oases. They gave him fuel and balm, and they provided him with purpose.

Purpose loomed large on the Butcher's horizon this particular afternoon as he slipped into his suede-collared denim jacket, sweeping his locks from between the jacket and his back, and pocketed the cream-colored envelope that someone had slid under the door of his apartment while he dozed. He retrieved a hatchet from the hall closet and dropped it into the loop he'd fashioned on the inside of his jacket.

Los Angeles seemed to comprise the entire world as he stepped out onto the sunbaked aggregate the walkway of his balcony was paved with. Neighborhoods like city–states under his command called to him. Smog-ringed skyscrapers gleamed in chemical refraction, and wild hills stood guard over it all from a voyeuristic distance. Everything the human animal was capable of accomplishing was happening right now within his range of sight. Even what he was about to undertake was surely being visited upon someone, if on a smaller scale.

A much smaller scale.

This outing was more for himself than anything. The card inside the envelope had only requested his presence several days hence in Seattle. No signature. Just three capital letters, typewritten like the rest of the note. *MMM*. The stiff paper. The lack of indentation. The triple-M sign-off. There was almost no chance it was a forgery. It had all the earmarks of an authentic message from the Mad Marksman of Malta, and that meant there was land ahead for the water-logged Butcher.

It had been a long time since his last official assignment. He was rusty, but today's festivities would slough away the rust. Would crack the knuckles of his idleness, clear the throat of his watchful patience. He would travel to Davenport a shiny, sharpened blade. It was the surest he'd felt about anything in ages.

He quickly descended the steps to the parking lot, slipped behind the wheel of his black Ford Bronco, and gunned it for the trailer park where Bradley Madder lived in East L.A., ever since his release from state prison.

* * *

The Butcher knocked on the door of the mobile home. After a moment it opened, just wide enough for him to recognize the face within.

"Yo, Bradley!" he said, like they were buddies.

"Who the fuck are you?"

"Who the fuck am *I*? Who the fuck are *you*?" He pushed his way in using both arms like battering rams.

The man who'd answered the door fell back into a tattered arm chair upholstered with a yellow-and-orange-dappled fabric that bore a striking resemblance to vomit.

"I'd stay right where you are for a minute if I were you." The Butcher closed the flimsy door behind him and dropped his jacket to the floor, hatchet and all. "Wouldn't wiggle a goddamn toe."

The man tried to look angry, but he didn't budge. He remained in the awkward sprawl that the Butcher's forced entry had landed him in.

"Let's talk about who the fuck you are. See, I read the papers. Did you know you can still get an actual newspaper delivered to your doorstep in this big old town? Well, you can. And I do. I've done my share of reading about you, yes I have."

The listener seemed to shrink into himself.

"You've been out, what now, six months? Less than a year, I know that. It wasn't the crime itself so much that bothered me. A lot of convenience stores get hit these days, and there's often some violence attached."

"Look, I don't know—"

"You will keep that fucking clam-hole shut until I ask you to speak. Is that plain?"

Two slow, shaky nods convinced the Butcher that it was.

"Good. you were just kind of on the edge of my awareness right after the story broke. Another small-time cockroach who'd found the end of his line. But the way you started whining to anyone who would listen about how unfair the whole thing was … The clerk should have known better than to jump the counter and come at you with that yard stick or whatever the hell they said it was. What, did he think it was a cap gun in your hand? Of course it went off! What did he expect, huh?"

The Butcher could read real fear in Bradley's eyes. Not too surprising. He was a little startled himself by the foamy saliva that ran from both corners of his mouth as he delivered this diatribe.

"Now ask me, Bradley Madder: Why did that get my goat? Go on, ask me."

"Wh-why did that get your goat?"

The Butcher moved in close and smiled.

"Because I learned how to read *between* the lines before I knew how to read what's on 'em. And suddenly I saw who you were. You weren't Bradley Madder, the dangerous hoodlum. You were Bradley Madder, the arrogant little fool who had never taken the blame for a goddamn thing in his miserable fucking life."

Bradley looked like he wanted to speak. Probably wanted to defend himself against the truth. But he only trembled, no doubt remembering very clearly what the Butcher had said about keeping his clam-hole shut.

"I don't suppose guys like you keep up with the stories you set in motion, but details continue to emerge, if a fellow keeps his eyes peeled. You maybe knew that the clerk you killed had a teenage boy, but did you know that the boy killed himself a little over two years after his father was shot to death in the store where he'd worked for twelve years? Now, suicide's a tricky thing. Difficult to trace back to its dominant causes, especially when there's no note, which there wasn't. But you file these things away and start piecing the facts together. Maybe the boy's mother would have disappeared anyway, but it wasn't more than a month after she found him curled up on the floor of their garage—some weird, lifeless nautilus—that she vanished like a wisp of smoke. You can call that what you like. I call it one hell of a coincidence."

"What are you ... going to—"

The Butcher bent down, reached inside his denim jacket

and gripped the smooth wooden handle of the hatchet. It was free in a flash, and as he rose, he held it at chest height, tight and motionless. Ready to strike. Bradley Madder curled himself up as tight as possible on the vomit-colored chair. The Butcher wouldn't have been surprised to see him pop a thumb into his mouth and start nursing it like a babe.

It was time.

In the Butcher's line of work, he had to believe in the greater good. It wasn't enough to count himself lucky for having such release at his disposal. The license to end lives only took him so far, only *extended* so far. If he didn't feel there was lasting value for humanity in the work, insanity became a very real concern, as absurd as that seemed on the surface. As with God, the Butcher's work was mysterious and inscrutable. He alone understood his motivations, needs, and limits fully. Others were left to judge him by his results. Some of them got it right. Most did not. It was all the same to him.

"What did I tell you about uninvited back-sass, cowboy?"

Bradley Madder probably didn't care what kind of engine revved behind the wide eyes of his attacker, or what it burned for fuel. All he could have known was that the small axe was coming at him fast and hard, and that there would be pain, maybe even death. Nothing else was worth knowing.

The first blow went to the side of his neck. A splitting whack to the chest followed quickly. Then a deep cut to his upper arm. Finally, the finishing strike to the top of his head.

The Butcher watched him wriggle and bleed for a moment before stalking off to the bathroom, letting the hatchet hang from Bradley Madder's head. Breathing hard, he scrubbed his hands and face clean and unbuttoned his blood-spattered shirt to reveal a fresh one underneath. After stepping out of his cowboy boots he did the same with his jeans. He'd purchased the outer set of clothes a size larger than his usual. The oversized shirt and pants had sat folded on a shelf in his closet for over a month. He'd had a feeling he would need them before long.

Retrieving his jacket from the floor, he donned it and removed a balled-up garbage bag from an inner pocket. He snapped the bag open and stuffed the soiled articles inside before stepping out to toss them into the back of the Bronco. His eyes darted from side to side. He was as aware of his immediate surroundings as a trained dancer, knew that a shade had gone up in a nearby trailer, but that the sun would obscure him from the prying eyes of a nosy neighbor. He also had an instinct that wasn't much less reliable than his keen observational talents. It told him that if the curious neighbor was stymied in his or her efforts to snoop from the window, the matter was likely to end there. In Los Angeles it was impossible not to wonder about the affairs of others, but it was dangerous to show too much interest. Personal safety almost always won out. It was an axiom he counted on for the next several minutes.

Back in the trailer, he did his best to avoid the largest puddles surrounding Bradley Madder's gruesome throne. Gore dripped into one of them from an elbow. Gripping the hatchet firmly with his claw-like right hand, the Butcher wrenched it free of the man's skull, sending one last posthumous shudder through the lifeless body. He exited the trailer purposefully with the bloodied weapon and deposited it next to the garbage bag in the Bronco before returning for a last look at the scene he'd created. He'd lived up to his name again. The work had been messy, but exhilarating and simple. He was ready.

Pulling the trailer door shut behind him, he stepped across a small rock garden to the driver's side door of the Bronco and slid behind the wheel. The day was heating up, but he left his jacket on as he drove calmly out of the trailer park, heading for South Central L.A. A novice would have done all of this at night, thinking it's easier to stay out of sight in the dark. *Maybe*, the Butcher thought. But he knew that people tended to remember things they saw at night. What they witnessed in daylight they were less likely to perceive as out of the ordinary.

He pulled up the music library on his phone, which he then tossed on the seat beside him. The Bronco was soon filled with the nasty ferocity of Motörhead. Lemmy screamed about the Ace of Spades over and over again as the Butcher grinned, one hand at the top of the wheel.

"Land ho," he muttered, but it was lost in the din of grinding guitar, big drums, rumbling bass, and Lemmy's unmistakable vocals, like the cries of something that yearned to be as free as it felt.

Halfway between East L.A. and South Central lay an empty lot. It was hemmed in on two sides by rows of date palms. The other two edges of the property were more or less open to view, but it was an obscure part of town. The perfect place for what needed to be done before he could consider his day's work complete.

A small brick building sat at one corner of the lot. Some kind of unused utility shack, the Butcher figured. He didn't remember it from previous drive-bys, but he was pleased to discover it. The Bronco all but disappeared into shadow as he pulled alongside the structure and paused his music. Without wasting a moment, he jumped out, swung open the rear gate of the vehicle, and yanked out the bag of bloody clothes, along with a small can of lighter fluid. Skulking around to the back of the structure, he dropped the bag of clothes and peeled it back like a giant foreskin. The can of lighter fluid squirted its contents onto the exposed clothes, and a single match set the heap on fire. It went up quick, bag and all, and the Butcher was on his way again.

The drive to South Los Angeles was quick. Traffic was uncharacteristically light the whole way. All that remained was to drop off the Bronco in the seediest area he could find and hoof it to LAX.

It was good to be back on dry land.

CHAPTER 5

The world unraveled itself on the television news as Twitch Markham sat cross-legged in his favorite armchair, chewing his nails and counting his regrets. He'd settled on Wichita after his last job, thinking the pace might bring him some long overdue peace of mind. So far it hadn't panned out that way. He was as nervous as ever, but now it was worse, because if sleepy Midwestern Wichita couldn't calm his nerves, what hope did he have that he would ever be released from the constant grip of anxiety?

He stopped chewing his nails, but only so he could light a cigarette, which he took a deep drag from with closed eyes before letting the anxiety back in.

This business in Los Angeles had him particularly worried. A small-time hood found murdered by hatchet, of all things, in his mobile home. No one in custody. No solid leads. No whiff of a motive. Even for the US of A this was remarkably novel. How could such a thing have been done by anyone other than the Butcher?

He heard the flower pot on the front porch totter before he heard the whisper of something being slid underneath his door. He didn't turn away from CNN or put out his cigarette, but all sounds not coming from the direction of that door receded into a gray place in his mind. There was time to get a description of whoever was on his property, maybe even catch the bastard. But for now he sat, and listened.

There was only one man he'd ever known who was capable of the raw ferocity required to pull off a thing like what had been done in L.A., and the fact that he knew one such man made it pretty clear what had just been slipped under his door. It was either a warning, a farewell, or a job offer. No one cared enough about him to issue a warning about anything. He didn't care enough about anyone else to expect a farewell. That left option number three. And that meant Davenport.

He shot to his feet, stabbed his butt into an ashtray, and switched off the television before whirling into the kitchen. There he stood, chewing his nails again as he stared out the window. There was nothing to see through it but the blackness of a late summer night in Kansas, and his own reflection. God, he was gaunt. He used to be strong and full of energy. Not half bad with the ladies, either. Shit, he'd be lucky to score with a hooker the way he'd let himself go. Stringy hair, mostly bald at the top. A wife-beater tank top stained with who-knew-what. Pinstriped sweats better suited for a twelve-year-old than an adult. Pathetic. That's how he looked and that's how he felt. Sometimes you *could* judge a book by its cover.

"Fuck it," he muttered and ran back through the house to the front door. Throwing it open he flung himself down the broad flagstone steps and across the winding driveway to the street. He threw a glance to his right. Nothing but pools of light from a row of streetlamps. To his left, also nothing.

Wait, a figure taking a corner two blocks down.

Twitch gave chase. Action was the only antidote to the unease in his belly. It had always been that way. It was in his blood.

As Twitch reached a hedgerow lining a driveway, he saw the bastard's leg shoot out in front of him, but not soon enough to do anything about it. His legs went out from under him and he landed in a sprawl at the opposite edge of the drive. The stranger was on him at once. He was a little guy, difficult to get a hold of. Little hands clutched and squeezed at Twitch's throat. He punched the little man in the neck, but the grip remained strong. Another pop to the throat, followed by a weakening of the fingers. Twitch pulled back for another punch but didn't have to follow through. The man released his hold, breathing heavily and rubbing his neck. He was a young guy with long hair and a bad complexion.

And then there it was: the old, familiar conundrum. As Twitch lay there planning his next move, he wondered if it was too late for him. He walked through life chewing his fingernails down to uneven shards and assuming that he was a doomed man with a damned soul. But what if he wasn't … yet? What if God was so far willing to turn the other cheek and give him one more chance for the big prize: life everlasting in the Kingdom of Heaven? What if all he had to do was let this little punk go and all would be forgiven? But kill him and it was flames and pitchforks, friend.

"What did you slip under my door?" he asked his prey.

"Why didn't you just pick it up and read it? Jesus."

"Ask questions before shooting? Not my style. You had the nerve to sneak onto my property to deliver something. That makes you potentially as interesting as whatever you delivered. Who are you?"

"I'm nobody, man. Just a messenger. I have no idea what's even in the fucking envelope."

It was the truth. Twitch was surprised how sure he was, but the kid wasn't lying. It reminded him of some of the snap decisions he'd had to make in Mexico on one of the Portable Nine's precarious missions. He'd feared that many of his old skills were lost from disuse, but maybe they were only dormant. Besides, what had he expected, that Davenport himself would have delivered the note? No, he wouldn't even use an acquaintance for something like this. Money would change hands and trickle down to a qualified stranger who would get the job done and disappear into the night. Chasing this punk had been a foolish misstep on Twitch's part. He was indeed rusty. If Davenport had in mind what he suspected, Twitch would need to sharpen his wits—and his skills.

First he needed to make sure things were as they appeared, and that meant releasing his hostage and trotting back home with his tail between his legs so he could read the goddamn note. He stood up and brushed pebbles and dirt from his shirt and sweatpants.

"You're free to go. I don't ever want to see you in Wichita again."

"How do you know I don't live here?" the kid said, also standing.

Twitch laughed a little. "Been around the block a few times, son. You don't smell like Wichita. Now start increasing the miles between us. Oh, and you were never here. Got it?"

"Drove through Kansas once, I think. Don't remember passing through Wichita, though."

"That's the spirit. There's hope for your generation yet."

He was out of breath the whole way back to his porch. How times had changed. His high-strung nature used to propel him to work his body and maintain it like a machine. With more than a little worry about his ability to meet whatever challenges lay ahead, he opened the door, stooped over, and retrieved a cream-colored envelope from the olive-green shag carpet. No writing on either side. He tore it open and pulled out a stiff, unfolded card, slightly darker in color than the envelope.

Twitch,

Your presence is required at Shallot in Seattle on September 24, 7:00 p.m. There is no need to R.S.V.P. I trust you will be there. This is as important as it gets.

MMM

Though the Mad Marxman of Malta surely knew that Twitch was likely to be out of shape and out of practice, he had assumed he could rely on the Kansan's deep-rooted commitment to professionalism. That, as much as anything, separated the Portable Nine from the workaday thug and cookie-cutter hit man. They lived by a code—a rare thing in this day and age. They were outcasts, criminals, egotists, and lunatics, but they had their code, and it was shared only among the nine of them. They were a country unto themselves. A portable country. A lengthy period of inactivity and separation had kept the group out of the covetous arms of the law and the groping claws of the depraved. But now it was time for a gathering. Twitch's body went still, a solid core of anticipation. Already he felt the strength of numbers coursing through his veins, for that was in his blood, too.

CHAPTER 6

A slightly nervous man, but also a very dangerous one, Gar sat in the booth adjacent to the women, rotating back and forth a little inside his leather jacket. The one he was interested in—a raven-haired Japanese beauty with ghost-pale skin—had good taste in bars. More queers than he would have liked, but it was like that all over New York City anymore. You couldn't swing an aluminum bat these days without connecting with a cocksucker. So be it. He would adapt. He always did. There was no good sense in making yourself stand out from the crowd over the little shit. "Pick your fights!" his dad had been fond of yelling at him whenever he complained about anything. Then he'd knock him upside the head so hard it throbbed for a while and patches of black-and-white traveled across his vision. That's one reason it was more of a blessing than a curse when the old man finally pulled up stakes and moved out of St. Louis. Gar and his mom had a rough go of it after that, but it was a better kind of rough.

The plan had been to ditch the envelope in the bitch's coat pocket or something. Easiest job of his life. But now he was getting caught up in the conversation she was having with her bitch friends, all of them lookers, in a hot-off-the-superslut-assembly-line way. Maybe he could get a little more out of this night than he'd signed on for if he played his cards just so. *Joker's wild, motherfuckers!*

Her phone rang. "Hello," she said. "Yeah? Oh, hi. Sure, okay. I'll let you in. No problem. Later." Her phone beeped.

"What was that all about?" one of her friends asked.

The high back of the bar booth separated him from them, but his ears were trained on their chatter.

"My building manager. He locked himself out."

"And you can let him in with your phone? That's pretty cool."

"Yeah, if the call comes from the buzzer outside the main door. I take the call, and if it's legit I press and hold the star sign for a few seconds. Voilà."

It was enough to make a small-time hood believe in God. He couldn't have prayed for a better opportunity. It added risk to his undertaking, but the apple at the end of this bough was going to be well worth the trouble.

"Be back in a minute, girls," he heard her say. "Gotta pee."

That was the cue he was waiting for. Once she disappeared around a corner he picked up his glass of beer and moved to their table.

"Hello, ladies. Mind if I join you?" He was already sliding into the empty booth across from the two of them.

"By all means," the brunette on the left said. "Feel free to make us into one great big woman." She laughed a little, but she was the only one.

"Huh?" the other one responded.

She turned to her blond-haired friend. "It's something my dad used to say. He got it from some British show."

Gar had no idea what she was talking about, and he could tell the blonde was equally in the dark. But his hand was already in one of the pockets of the jacket his mark had left behind, searching for her phone.

If she took it with her to the bathroom I'll fucking kill her.

Ah, there it was. He transferred it to his own jacket pocket in an instant.

"I don't suppose there's any chance of us—"

"There's a chance," said the brunette, "but it's so remote you'd be better off buying a lottery ticket and throwing it away without even looking at it."

This one had a certain intelligence that he didn't care for. She was cocky. If he was freelancing she might have paid for her brashness, but he had a job to do and the pay was good. He was already going off the rails because of his dick. He couldn't afford to let his temper enter into the thing as well.

"Well, I'm not going to beg." He trained his gaze on the blonde, but there was even less interest in her expression. She was showing signs of too much drink, honestly: a droop of the features that conveyed apathy and sickness. It made for easy pickings, but there was no challenge. Any cock in the county could slither into something as messed up as her, and he wasn't just any cock. "And I don't want to be a bother. You're both very pretty, and I gave it a shot. Can't hold that against me, I guess." He smiled and pulled a cigarette out of an inner pocket as he stood up again. "Have a good night." He lit the cigarette with a Zippo and disappeared into a dark recess of the bar to watch and wait.

It didn't take long. He must have been right in his assessment of the blonde's condition. The other two practically had to carry her out of the place. His girl of the remote apartment access had arrived separately from the other two. He hoped that was the planned arrangement for their departure as well. Things would get tricky fast if she decided to stick with them. He'd been so careful in setting this up. Now he was getting careless. But he'd get the job done. He always did. That's why he was never without work, unless by choice.

Absolutes. Black and white. Good versus evil. What was true yesterday remained true today. It was the mindset of the common criminal, the only language he knew. In some barely pulsing lobe of his brain he knew that the whole shebang was held together by a fragile web of belief, from the effectiveness of monetary systems to the faith required to step onto an airplane. But it was damn sure above his pay grade to separate fact from fiction. Hell, he wasn't even sure he had a choice in the matter. Maybe choice was nothing but an illusion as well. He was on his path, and so far he'd made out okay by it. Tomorrow would be his reward or penalty. Tonight was now, and it was filled with promise.

Raven Hair tried in vain to hail a cab about three blocks

from the bar, her friends in tow. Foiled, the trio continued up Church Street. Gar watched from the dark entryway of a tobacco shop that was either closed for the night or closed forever. An old man, devilishly drunk, staggered in among the group of females, turning clumsy circles and making threats he couldn't have made good on sober, let alone in his current condition. They easily left him in the dust, and Gar waited for him to pass, too, before continuing his pursuit.

Car horns blared and laughter cut the night, coming either from the next block over or the far side of the moon. It was nighttime in the city, the way it should always be in New York. No goddamn business suits clogging the streets, or limousines dropping them off for a day of fleecing the masses. No safe, bright bustle of humanity. At night, New York became the edge of the world. Some folks had to go over that edge. Some folks did the pushing. Gar knew goddamn well which one he was.

His beauty led her mice around a corner onto Walker, where she finally managed to get a cab's attention. He grew nervous that they'd all three board when it pulled to the curb. Only the brunette and the blonde got in, however. Raven Hair stepped back and waved them off. She was on foot, then. Good.

At the end of the block, she descended into the subway and he followed at a cautious distance. A rat the size of a house pet crossed between them on the platform, but he barely registered its presence. His eyes had more interesting meat to take in. Each rise of her ass cheeks as she moved seemed to slide her tight red skirt another inch higher, but it must have been an illusion, for he never got the full view he longed for.

She boarded a northbound number one train. Headed for Chelsea, no doubt. He had a sixth sense about these things. He stepped aboard one car behind her and stood by the door at the front end, staring through into her car, where he would spot any sign of her exiting.

His instincts proved correct. In less than ten minutes they were at Twenty-Third Street and she rose from her seat to disembark. He abandoned his lookout position in hot pursuit.

* * *

Unlocking the main door of her building with a faded brass key, Lovinia nonchalantly checked her mailbox before climbing the stairs to the second story of the turn-of-the-century walk-up. She walked the length of the dimly lit hallway and entered her apartment. On practically every inch of wall space hung framed record jackets, each one purchased cheap at various second-hand shops, almost all of them jazz recordings. The vinyl itself she had no interest in, since she had digital access to the recordings anyway, but she loved being greeted by the greats when she came through the door: Thelonius Monk, Charlie Parker, Billie Holiday, Miles Davis, Duke Ellington, Ella Fitzgerald. She'd probably never have anything she considered a real home. It didn't jibe with the ever-present need to be mobile—*portable*, she thought with a grin—but she had a knack for making any living space homey.

"Hello, fellas," she said out loud. "And gals." She gave a humble salute to Ella. "No time to lose, I'm afraid."

Stripping naked she made a careful trail of her garments, as if she had drunkenly abandoned them en route to her bedroom, which felt more like a nook than a room, thanks to the open floorplan of the apartment. The stiletto heels were the last to go. These she kicked haphazardly into the bedroom.

Leaving the apartment door unlocked, she slipped into the bedroom to retrieve two long metal skewers, slender and pin sharp, from a drawer in her nightstand. Her Twin Delights. Each one boasted a head, like on a tack or a nail, about the size of a quarter. Etched into the brushed platinum of one of the heads was the image of a woman's lips wrapped lovingly around a cock, her eyes closed in rapture. The other skewer head boasted a vagina being spread by the middle and index fingers of an unseen participant. The bathroom, on the far side of the bedroom, was her next stop. She flipped on the light and started the shower running. Then it was back across the living room and into the dark kitchen to hide, one skewer at each side.

The sensation of waiting for him in the dark was nothing short of arousing. His ignorance and false certainty of the situation were sublime. Part of her wanted the moment to last forever, and she closed her eyes to make it even more complete, more real. But another part of her was growing more curious about her admirer by the second, and anger was pacing not far behind. She was predator, not prey, and this bold young man was going to have to learn that, one way or another.

Gail and Sugar had provided the first clues of his existence, but she didn't need to rely on their drunken accounts. He was a sloppy operator. She'd noticed her phone was missing while waiting for the taxi, and soon after it pulled away, her inebriated friends on board, she'd seen a man with a keen interest in her smoking a cigarette a conspicuous distance behind. He wasn't bad looking, but when she saw him a second time, staring at her through the connecting doors of the subway, she knew she'd picked up a tail. She could only assume he'd overheard her explain how her phone could be used to let visitors in through a link-up with her building's intercom unit. Well, let him come. Let him think he was smarter than Lovinia Dulcet.

A slightly creaky turn of the knob, a click of the latch, and he was in. In her space. Did her anger growl a little as it paced? Bare its teeth? She thought it might have.

Like a marionette, the man crept farther into the room, still unseen but given away by every ancient board he stepped on. When it was obvious that he had passed the sofa, she risked a one-eyed glance past the kitchen door frame. She'd left the bathroom door ajar, and it threw enough light into the bedroom to cast a handsome silhouette of the man. Shoulder-length hair, leather jacket, jeans, boots. This one was a real American classic. Quick, too. It took him no time at all to deduce that she had hastily disrobed and made for the shower. He shrugged out of his jacket and let it fall to the bedroom floor next to her skirt. The light T-shirt he wore peeled away with even more alacrity.

Across the floor in seconds, her thumb pressed firmly against the head of the skewer in her left hand, she reached across her body and swung at him from behind, almost as if executing a backhand stroke in tennis. He howled as the great needle pierced his side and slid almost all the way in. His head shot back. But then he went rigid and his whole body began to quake minutely. His muscles moved under the skin like creatures with their own will, trying desperately to break free of their fleshy confines. Lovinia spun him around and pressed him down onto the bed. Still naked, she crawled on top of him before using the palm of her hand to ram the needle home.

"Is this what you were after, hot shot?" she cooed and flipped her black mane out of the way. "Did you know I used to be a pornographic actress? I'll bet not. Look, I know you can hear me, and see me, even though you can't move. Don't fret, it's temporary. I just want to make things plain, and then, when I remove the pin, you'll be all better. Trust me, it just as easily could have been a killing strike."

Dismounting her hostage, she deposited the unused skewer in the nightstand drawer and squatted to inspect the pockets of the man's jacket. The first one held no phone, but she removed what appeared to be an envelope. She stood up and flipped on the bedroom light. A tingle went through her abdomen. It seemed an odd thing for a thug or rapist to have on him. It was nice paper, though a little dinged. She ripped the envelope away and fell back against the wall.

"Well holy shit and bless my ass. He must be desperate if he's turned to common rapists to run his errands. Or he's too rushed to check backgrounds thoroughly." Her audience lay supine on the bed, motionless except for the quivers induced by the paralyzing needle. His expression was rather horrible as he stared at the ceiling, mouth half open, drool spilling down his cheek. The skewer was in his left side, which she couldn't see from where she stood, but she knew there would be little if any blood there. Even after she removed it there would be no gouts or torrents. She was a professional, after all. "Because I'm guessing this isn't the first time you tried to take a girl against her will, is it?"

She smiled and set Davenport's card upside down on the nightstand.

"I'm pretty sure I have your undivided attention," she said, mounting the intruder again, "so I'll only say this once. I'm going to let you go, only because I don't need the hassle of disposing of your corpse. But if I ever see you again, I will go at you with my needles like a grandmother to a piece of knitting. Lie there with a stupid expression on your face if you understand. Good. Now get ready for some pain."

She reached to his side and worked her fingers between the head of the skewer and his skin. Once she had a good hold she yanked it free and the man beneath her gasped and hitched.

"That's going to hurt for a while, but you'll recover. Mind what I said. This is the last time we meet pleasantly."

"You're ... crazy," he managed, nodding.

"Oh yes. Crazy and mean. It's a potent combination, believe me."

Lovinia stood up and crossed to the bathroom, still clutching the one needle. When she returned she was wearing a dark blue bathrobe and the intruder was putting on his shirt and jacket, reacting periodically to the pain in his side.

"You're really letting me go?" he asked, staring dumbly at her.

"Not quite yet." She grinned.

"Huh? You said—"

"Not until you hand over my phone."

He fumbled for it in his jacket pocket and tossed it onto the bed.

"And that's it? I'm free to go?"

"You're free to go and never come back. Remember, that's part of the deal. You're not as important as you think you are, and you're none too bright. Your dick is the only enemy you need. It'll land you in more trouble than you can dig yourself out of eventually. I have bigger fish to fry. Now get the fuck out of my life, you vicious little puke."

He took her advice, even closed the door politely behind him as he left.

Lovinia took her precious needle to the kitchen and cleaned it off in the sink, all the while wondering what the hell the debonair Davenport wanted with her this time. Whatever it was, it wasn't likely to be boring. She was game. Had some family in Seattle, in fact. A couple of them could even be trusted.

She wiped the needle dry and returned it to the night-stand drawer, admiring her Twins for a moment before sealing them in darkness once more.

CHAPTER 7

Sand raked the visor of his helmet as he rode his Kawasaki through the Outback. The horizon before him was an expansive show of beautiful colors, but it meant that darkness was close at hand. That was fine. He belonged in the dark. But the wind was a pain in the ass. At least road trains, the massive semi-trucks and wildlife killers that crisscrossed the bush, were rare on this particular road. He was several tributaries removed from the Great Central Road. There the combination of high winds and cargo transport had probably scared all other drivers into their burrows hours ago, or slowed them down to the point of retreat.

Still, the truth was that Abel Hazard was going way too fast, pushing a hundred and forty kilometers an hour, wanting to put distance between himself and the mess he'd left behind in a homegrown watering hole a stone's toss from Kalgoorlie-Boulder. Roy's Liquor Lodge was the name of the place. Nothing like truth in advertising. The name didn't lead you to expect much, and that's just what you got. There was a filling station on one side of the road and Roy's establishment on the other. Abel had made use of both tonight. At the one he'd topped off the tank of his bike. At the other he'd settled a score with the Waverly brothers, who couldn't be relied on for much, but by God they were at Roy's every Saturday night like the clockwork drunks they were. He suspected they wouldn't be sneaking onto his property anymore to steal auto parts, but if they did, he knew where to find them.

In well under an hour it was dark, though a cloudless sky provided a staggering view of the firmament. The motorcycle's headlamp didn't so much pierce the darkness as underscore the fact that it lay everywhere, like an inscrutable veil all around him. Even the drama relayed by the twinkling of the stars seemed to confirm that he was alone in the universe. No other traveler's experiences, no philosopher's conclusions, no scientist's theories left any traces that mattered to him now. He was a product of his own will. Even the two-wheeled machine he drove across the loose Australian clay might never have been built if not in order to provide him with a means of transportation on this fateful night. He was the reason the kangaroos and wild boars had so far kept away from the road. And if one wandered into his path after all, he would be the cause of that as well.

But nothing rushed into his path, panicked from a roadside feeding. He didn't even encounter a disorienting blast of bull dust, which might have formed easily enough in one of the dips of the roads he'd been traversing all evening, especially considering how far below normal rainfall levels the area was. There was a lot of loose dirt out there, and it didn't need the help of any road trains to make hell out of an otherwise simple ride.

His strong belief in the power of his will wasn't without justification. When he was living in Germany he'd decided to undergo an unusual surgical procedure. The rumor was that the science of it dated back to the Nazi concentration camps of World War II. He had never bothered to verify the claim. In fact, he didn't want to know. At the time, he'd been afraid to know. Now it just seemed right to remain in the dark, though William Faulkner's assertion that the past wasn't dead, it wasn't even past, did occur to him from time to time, and he wondered ... But he never let the wonder unravel very much.

The surgeon had been a long-faced Austrian by the name of Dr. Schweck. He'd assured Abel that he could remove his amygdala, the part of the brain that controls the fear response. Abel had heard of people losing their amygdalae to disease, and along with them the ability to know fear, but the idea that his might actually be removed through surgery had lit a fire within him, and started him on a journey that took many months, and many thousands of dollars, to realize. Realize it he did. He was seven years amygdala-free, and free of the constraints of fear. If only he could have known this level of power and freedom during his last assignment with the Portable Nine ... Well, things would have been very different. Clayton Barrymore might have been denied his day of victory for pulling the wool over the eyes of the Nine, for one thing. It all came down to trust. Abel had been afraid to distrust the very man who had hired them. He would never fear such a thing again. Or such a man.

He followed a sloping curve deeper into the desert landscape, and then there were lights. Vehicle lights. Encounters were rare on these back roads at night, but not unheard of. Loners dotted the bush country as if exiled from every civilized part of the island nation. Still, Abel took note of the yellow Jeep as it passed, as well as the emaciated youth who sat behind the wheel, staring straight ahead into the vast black night. What was a young pup like that doing out beyond the Black Stump all by himself, without a prayer of getting anywhere meaningful before daybreak? The lad needed a prayer as badly as anyone Abel had ever come across, and as he had the thought, he passed a rusted out pickup truck buried nose-first in a ditch on his right. A common enough sight in the Outback. He figured the owners of such vehicles often looked a hell of a lot like Mr. Yellow Jeep.

"Best of luck, mate," he said out loud and followed it up with a dry laugh.

* * *

Home was a ramshackle dwelling with a sizeable outbuilding situated across a cluttered yard from the front door. Even by daylight it looked a bit like a serial killer's haven, but what more could a man ask for when he didn't particularly want to be bothered? He parked his motorcycle next to the porch steps and removed his helmet. That's when he noticed the tracks. Jeep tracks, at a guess.

"The sonofabitching snake," he muttered, no stranger to voicing his thoughts out in the Great Expanse. Tucking his helmet under one arm, he fished his house keys out of the pocket of his riding pants and climbed the wooden porch steps. "What the hell did he want with me?" And that led to the question —left unspoken—of whether the agitated young man would be paying Abel another visit. If so, when? It was a purely practical question, of course. No amygdala, no fear. But goddamn if there wasn't a funny kind of feeling in the pit of his guts. Maybe it wasn't fear, but something was doing its best to heighten his awareness.

He pulled the screen door open and something fell to the porch.

"Well, what in the hell do we have here?" He bent down to pick up what had fallen. "Sure did come a good distance past nowhere just to deliver a note."

Once inside, he dropped his keys and helmet on an unfinished end table. Switching on the light, he peeled open the envelope and removed the note. He smiled so hard it almost hurt. The Mad Marksman of Malta was back in play. Well sonofabitch, that was fine news. Seattle, huh? Why the hell not? He'd never been there, but he figured if he didn't care for the city or its people he could always stare at Mount Rainier in his spare time. Besides, he only expected to be there long enough for a briefing of some sort. He knew how Davenport operated: efficiently and with great cunning. He wondered how many of the others had already been contacted. Surely Davenport was in need of the Nine in their full glory if he was in need of one. They were a difficult batch of humanity to manage, but if you needed to clear some brush, so to speak, you couldn't hope for a better team of misfits.

The question of whether or not Mr. Yellow Jeep would be returning was also answered. He would not. This errand had not been a labor of love on his part. Davenport would have made the job inevitable, but not lucrative enough to instill an interest in further employment. If the kid had any sense, he'd leave Western Australia before the end of the month and let it become a memory he'd only half believe to be real in five years' time. Yes sir, he'd give Mr. Faulkner's old saw a run for its money if he knew what was good for him.

At some point between crossing the yard and unlocking the corrugated metal door to his oversize garage, he detected the singular insect whisper of a turboprop engine in the distant skies. It wasn't an uncommon means of getting in and out of some of the more cut-off mining communities in the region, but considering the timing, he had to wonder if he of the yellow Jeep had found himself a way out of Dodge even sooner than Abel would have given him credit for. He smiled faintly as he slipped into the storage shed and pulled the thin chain of an overhead fluorescent.

And there was Green Betty, the military-green tank of a truck that would haul him to Perth. It wasn't a long vehicle, but climbing in and out took a little effort because of its height. The deeply treaded tires were about the same distance apart whether you measured left to right or front to back. An angled grill helped with potholes, especially if they were hiding under a lake of bull dust. And everything he could possibly need to keep himself alive was tied to the shortened flatbed. Despite its boxiness, the outfit carried a hell of a lot of cargo. What he didn't want exposed to the elements he bundled up and stuffed in the cubby behind the driver's seat. If either he or the truck needed to rest during daylight hours, he could always unroll the tarpaulin that was tied up above the driver's side window and stake it to the ground for shade. Apart from the underside of her grill, Green Betty was flat-nosed, so the top bar of the grill was festooned with various radio antennas. They bothered his line of sight a little while he drove, but he wasn't about to engage in a form-versus-function debate over it. Anything that helped him get across this great country–continent in one piece was okay by him, and to that end, radio equipment was as valuable as damper and drinking water.

They'd been together for a pretty good piece, but he always knew she was as temporary as the garage, house, and motorcycle. It had only ever been a matter of time before duty called from one quarter or another. The work was what he lived for. He was only killing time in the Outback. That's why he would radio an acquaintance when he neared the outskirts of Perth and arrange for someone to pick up and repurpose Green Betty so that he could make his way cleanly to the airport.

No sense wasting another moment. He unlatched a much larger door that took up almost an entire wall of the garage and swung it inward until he could tie it back. Then he opened the door of Green Betty and pulled himself up into place by using the steering wheel as a handhold. The engine turned over with the roar of life before settling into a trembling idle. He pulled his door shut and eased the vehicle out of hiding. With the fluorescent light still burning forlornly in his side-view mirror, he stepped harder on the gas and was on his way.

"About time for a little fun."

He rounded the turn leading to the main road and left his home of the past three-and-a-half years behind. Soon it was eclipsed by a cloud of red dust in his wake, and a mantle of starlit night overhead.

CHAPTER 8

"**B**ring in another bottle of claret," commanded the fat man as he swiveled a little in his ill-fitting suit and ran a finger across each half of a thin mustache.

The blind man sitting across from him shook his head minutely in an effort to silence him, but he paid no attention. There was only one way to make life in Trujillo tolerable, and that was by drinking to excess. Damn the consequences.

The black servant, dressed in a smart gold-pinstriped waistcoat and tie, nodded sharply and left the room.

"You'll push him too far if you're not careful," said the blind man. "I could feel his temper rise just now."

An electric fan whirred in a corner but did little to cool the place. Comforts were few in the region. The sooner they were done with Venezuela the better, as far as the fat man was concerned.

"Well then he'd better make his purpose clear before the week is out," he said. "I'm not about to swelter to death in this fucking hell hole."

To his credit, the blind man knew when to hold his tongue. He took a spoonful of mousse, then laid down his spoon, pushed the bowl away, and folded his hands together on the table.

Silence reigned after the fat man lit a cigar, until the servant returned with a bottle of vino. The man didn't exactly slam the bottle down, but he set it before his mustachioed master with some force.

"One of the finest vintages in the house, I assure you." His voice itself was like a kind of liquor, smooth at the beginning of each word but with a slight burn toward the end. "Now, Dr. Intaglio, Mr. Bonnet, I have an errand to run. And I suspect the two of you will want to discuss your futures. I will return before midnight."

* * *

The night air was sticky but cool compared to the stifling heat of the tropical days. Trujillo wasn't a large town but it had its comforts. Where the Black Phantom was headed now was one of them. El Aristócrata sat atop one of the town's highest hilltops. Heaping plates of food were available for a good price, as was subpar booze at a ridiculous markup. But it wasn't the generous portions, or the potency of the poison, that brought him here this night. It was the company, and he could smell her perfume as soon as he walked in. If Trujillo could lay claim to a single defining smell it was the reek of dense, trapped exhaust mingled with human sweat. Nothing could have been more antithetical than the scent that now wafted to him from across the small, smoke-filled room. And now he could even make out its source.

He joined the blonde woman at a round table in the darkest corner of the establishment.

"Carmen," he said with a slight nod and brief closing of the eyes as he brought her hand to his mouth for a peck.

She smiled and blew cigarette smoke into the low-hanging light fixture above the table. There was something uncertain about the smile.

"I am delighted to see you," he continued. "Thank you for coming all this way."

"Of course," she said, but they both knew this was a game. It was fear that had brought her here, plain and simple. Working for the Black Phantom came with certain privileges, but they dimmed over time, and in the end all that kept a soul in his employ was fear of his retribution if he perceived himself to be jilted or wronged. To become his employee was to become his slave, and release was granted at his whim and discretion alone. "I've missed you."

Now it was his turn to smile insincerely. "You have news?"

"I have. You know, of course, that Davenport started tailing Max Brindle."

"Yes, I received your messages through the usual channels. I acted swiftly when I learned that he was in Italy to murder our man. But the last message I received only said that you would meet me here. I assume the news you have is of a sensitive nature?"

"It is, I'm afraid. He didn't get the job done."

"What do you mean?" He leaned in a bit.

Carmen stabbed out her cigarette and adjusted the stylish hat she wore. "Brindle is alive and well, which is a good thing, of course. But it begs the question, What the hell was Davenport doing in Florence if he wasn't there to kill Brindle. I had it on the most reliable sources that—"

"I take your point. It is a puzzle."

Carmen let out a heavy breath. It was the sound of a weight being lifted. But when the Black Phantom slammed his fist down on the small table, knocking half the butts out of the ashtray, she jerked away.

"What is it?" she asked.

"Nothing that need concern you, my sweet." He put on the smile again. "It seems I was a little premature, not to mention drastic, in how I dealt with the problem of Davenport. He's not going to be happy with me, I'm afraid. Is there more that you need to tell me?"

"No, that's everything. I just didn't want to take unnecessary risks. I had to get the news to you in person."

"Of course. You did well. But tell me, is that the only reason you came yourself?"

She reached a hand out to him, which he took.

"Of course not." She almost blushed. "There's always an ulterior motive in seeing you."

He kissed her hand again before releasing it. "I'm pleased to know that Mr. Brindle is still drawing breath. That means our plans can go forward. I was living in a cocoon of suspense ever since you informed me that he was marked for death."

"It seemed a reasonable assumption, with Davenport tailing him through Italy."

"Oh yes. Absolutely. I don't blame you, my dear. You shouldn't stay here any longer than you have to, though. This town is a viper pit. Rapists and thugs practically run things in Venezuela anymore, especially in Trujillo state." He gave the open V of his servant's waistcoat a proud tug with both hands. "We may have the Virgin Mary watching over our little town, but she's turned a blind eye to every fashion of depravity. God bless her," he added with a wink.

"I was at the statue yesterday. It's striking."

"The tallest Virgin in the world. What were you doing out there? It's a bit of a drive."

"I wanted to see it. That was the only reason."

"Yes, well, I'd like to see more of *you* before you depart."

"I'm at your service. You know that."

"Fine, then I'll be in touch. You're staying at the Hotel de Misterios?"

She nodded and smiled wryly, as if to say, "Of all the splendid options here in Trujillo, Trujillo, yes, I finally settled on the Hotel de Misterios."

A hard kiss, a lingering stare, and he was gone.

* * *

As he walked along the Avenida Independencia, the main street that wound through the small town like the spine of a felled dragon, he noticed that the jungle felt closer in than usual. A wind was swirling in from the hills, and the trees cast long shadows under a wicked moon as they sang their plaintive song.

Max Brindle, alive. That was good. So why did he feel as if things had taken a very unfortunate turn? His father would have been able to help him sort this out. He wasn't half the man his father had been. Wasn't half the villain, half the paramour, half the thinker. These were his best kept secrets. To the world—especially the underworld—he was spectral, his power without limits. He knew men wouldn't have been surprised in the least if they were told he could disappear from one continent and materialize on another. But on the inside, he felt sometimes like a little boy, frail and afraid, lacking the great Jacques LeGrand's ruthless might and unswerving conviction. Well, not lacking entirely, but he had forever walked in that great man's shadow, which was the germ of his resentment.

But there was Dr. Intaglio, and there was Mr. Bonnet. Yes, he was beginning to think he might be able to trust the two of them, enough to partner with them on a trial basis, at any rate. They'd accepted his offer to come to South America. That was a good start. It was a good distance from jolly old England, after all. And they seemed in need of a sure thing. A little security. The blind Mr. Bonnet, of course, relied on the good doctor for almost everything, and neither of them was young enough to be trotting about the globe in search of one chimerical form of justice or another. They were very nearly in his clutches. He was sure of it. And it had the added advantage of allowing him to get a claw into the fabric of the Portable Nine. If push came to shove with Davenport, maybe it was only a matter of tearing that fabric asunder.

He was crossing the picturesque Plaza Bolivar at a diagonal when a figure caught his eye. Whoever it was seemed to be moving in the direction of the manor house he paid rent on while living in nearby Valera. The very manor house where Dr. Intaglio and his ward were awaiting their butler's return, in fact. He hurried his pace but hung back enough to avoid detection. When the figure turned toward the main entrance to the house, it was obvious he could have no other destination. The Black

Phantom caught up with him before he could reach the door.

"Excuse me," he said in a voice that meant business, though he kept it low. "What business do you have with my master?"

The figure jumped and turned to face him. He was a mere boy, pockmarked and afraid. "I, um, just a delivery," he said with a slight accent the Phantom couldn't place, maybe because of the quaver in the kid's throat.

"A delivery? I don't see a package. What could you possibly have to deliver?"

"You work for Dr. Intaglio?"

"I do." The ruse of playing servant to the arrogant doctor was wearing on his nerves, but it was necessary for now. "Is there something I can take to him?"

"Well, yes. I guess that would be all right." The young man reached into an inner pocket of his jacket and withdrew a cream-colored envelope. "Though the man did say to hand it directly—"

"What's this?" The Black Phantom snatched the envelope from the boy and turned it over. No writing on either side.

"I really don't know, sir. If you can promise to give it to Dr. Intaglio, I'll be on my way. He is home, yes?"

"Hmm? Oh, yes. He's home. I'll be sure to give it to him. And you'll want something for your efforts." He fished a few coins from his trousers pocket and handed them to the boy. "Now vanish."

The messenger must have seen something in the Black Phantom's honey-brown eyes, something that told him not to tarry, for he pocketed the coins and ran like hell in a southwesterly direction. He could have been running to kneel at the base of the great Virgin Mary statue outside of town, for all the Black Phantom knew. Nor did he care. His mind was filled with one overpowering concern: the contents of the envelope.

He ripped it open and read the card within.

A note requesting the presence of Dr. Intaglio and Mr. Bonnet in Seattle. Signed mysteriously MMM. A curious thing. What had he stumbled onto here?

Throwing open the door he announced his presence to his guests.

"Gentlemen, it appears that you are taking a trip."

They had retired to the green room, so called for the pastel color of its walls. The sun–yellow of the dining room must have grown tiring. Dr. Intaglio looked up from a book.

"A trip?" asked Mr. Bonnet, looking a little alarmed. "Where to?"

"Seattle. The doctor will explain." The Black Phantom handed Dr. Intaglio the card but didn't give him a chance to speak. "Do you care to tell me who this MMM character is?"

The doctor studied the note for longer than its terse contents required.

Finally he responded, "The Mad Marksman of Malta."

"The Mad … I've never heard—"

"It's Davenport," Dr. Intaglio explained. "An old nickname."

Bonnet sat as still and quiet as a cat that thinks it's heard something outside.

So there it was, a way forward. Davenport, the very man who had been the source of the Black Phantom's recent vexation, now provided him with the means of winning the next campaign in their burgeoning war. It might even be worth putting his business with Max Brindle on hold, he thought. Or at least altering the terms of the arrangement—perhaps putting Brindle's expertise to use in a different vein.

"We needn't go," said the doctor.

"Don't be foolish," said the Black Phantom. "Do you not see the opportunity that presents itself to us? You must go at once. Both of you. I'll drive you to Valera. From there you'll fly to Caracas, then on to Miami. You'll fly direct from Miami to the Emerald City. I'll have the car ready in fifteen minutes. Meet me around back."

❊ ❊ ❊

"Doctor?" Mr. Bonnet asked, once the Black Phantom had left the room.

"He's right, Bonnet. We need to go. I'm not sure how the Phantom got hold of this, but it's legitimate."

"He wants us to spy?"

"I should think so. Are we in?"

"If you're in, what choice do I have?"

"I'm tired of being a pawn, dammit. We've earned this chance. We'd be fools not to take it."

"Then we take it."

"Good man, Bonnet." He patted him on the knee. "Good man."

CHAPTER 9

He stood atop Peel Hill, watching the autumn sun begin its descent toward faraway Ireland. The castle ruins, just across the inlet, burned with pink-tinged reds and oranges. Soon the castle's amber floodlights would lend their atmosphere to the scene. He had been followed from the moment he left his house, though his pursuer obviously had no idea he'd been found out. It was unwelcome business. No one had sought him out since his retreat to the Isle of Man. That was as he wanted it. Now, it seemed, his life of reclusiveness was at an end. "Nothing is permanent," an old friend had told him once. "Not even the truth." He had bankrupted the man less than six months later.

"If you were told this was a low-risk job," he said loudly into the wind without turning around, "you were lied to." He secured his cardigan one buttonhole higher.

The pause was long.

Then, "Robin Varnesse?"

A nervous voice. Robin was surprised by that. He'd expected brashness. It was the voice of a young man. A boy, practically. Slowly, he turned his back on the Irish Sea, and standing before him, some twenty yards away, was a lad who couldn't have been a day over nineteen. His profuse blond hair swirled about his head in the strong coastal winds.

"You've pinned me down to the city of Peel. Can there really be any doubt as to my identity?"

"I need to be sure."

The accent. Was it Welsh? Hard to tell from this distance.

"Come closer, boy. I'll not bite without provocation."

"I-I was told you were American," the young man said, closing the distance between the two of them, "but you sound British."

"I spent a number of years in London before retiring here. I suppose I've picked up an inflection or two. Now, suppose you tell me a little bit about *your*self."

"I was told not to tell you anything, just give you this and be on my way." The stranger reached into the pocket of his brown bomber jacket and brought out a cream-colored envelope.

Varnesse glanced at the envelope in the boy's extended hand, then back into his eyes. He snatched up the envelope without tearing his gaze from the young man.

"What's this, then?" He gave the envelope his full attention at last. The boy said nothing as Varnesse ripped it open and slid the card out.

His face changed. There had been a sense of fun to the exchange, but now he felt all patience for the game drain from his features.

"Boy!" he yelled and latched onto the young man's throat with one hand. It was a swift and forceful move. Alarm filled the young man's eyes. "Are you aware of the message you've brought me tonight?"

The boy shook his head, his face reddening severely.

"Well, I have a message for you to deliver back to the sender." He let go of the boy's throat but quickly knocked him to the ground with a punch to the side of the head. "Do I have your full attention?"

"No, please. I can't. I don't even know who he is. I don't want to know. This came to me through a friend of a friend. I have no way of getting a message back to—"

Varnesse kicked him in the chest. "I will not accept this. Either you tell him that I decline, or he waits for me in vain. It's all the same to me."

"Same with me, mate." Definitely Welsh. "I don't have a cock in this fight. You do as you please. I've earned my paycheck."

"Okay, you've convinced me. Get the fuck out of here. And not that I think there's much danger of it, but if I ever see you again, I'll be the last person who does. Clear?"

The messenger nodded and rubbed his throat before hauling himself up and walking briskly across the low hill.

By the time Varnesse reached his modest abode on the other side of town, he had mostly changed his mind about things. A cryptic invitation from Davenport was troubling. Frightening, even. But it was above all tempting. The Mad Marksman of Malta wouldn't be calling him out of the woodwork without good reason. And he wouldn't be calling him out alone. If he was in need of Robin Varnesse's services, he was also in need of the other seven. And meeting up with all of them again after so many years was more temptation than a man of Varnesse's temperament could bear. To see the Butcher swing his hatchet again. To hear Lovinia Dulcet spin tales of what her Twin Delights have been up to. To revel in the paranoid delusions of Twitch Markham, the macho adventures of Abel Hazard, the strange synergy of Dr. Intaglio and his seer, Mr. Bonnet. Miranda Gissing …

Ah, Miranda. He had thought much about her over the years. She'd given him plenty to think about. Plenty to miss, frankly. He suspected that she had never been truly capable of love, but that was the adulterated perception of hindsight. In the golden years of the Portable Nine, their love affair could have tied the tongue of the Bard himself. Even learning that she'd been faking every second of it didn't diminish the support her affections had lent him. He never would have survived the exhausting demands of beating down crime and terrorism without her ministrations. Maybe she knew that. Maybe it was part of her contribution to the cause.

Those had been tumultuous times. Did Davenport truly intend to lead them all back into that kind of an existence? Did they still have it in them?

And like that, it dawned on him. These were questions

with answers; they weren't philosophical abstractions. All he had to do to learn the truth about these things, and more, was to answer the call. Of course he would. Even if it meant hanging himself after learning what was expected of him, he had to know.

CHAPTER 10

The Golden Jug was one of Miranda Gissing's favorite spots in Chicago. There were things about the Wicker Park neighborhood that drove her mad, but she could escape all of that with little effort. If it was one of the brightly lit, youth-filled liquor troughs or feeding dens lining Division Street and North Avenue that a girl was after, her options were as wide as the Illinois sky. But for more refined tastes—tastes that valued historic preservation, architectural integrity, and clientele with some character—the pubs off Milwaukee Avenue had more to offer. That's where the Golden Jug, a small, charismatic bar with a God-almighty jukebox in one corner, had staked its claim some seventy years ago.

She was aware of the young man in the brown leather jacket who leered at her from the bar whenever he took a drink from his glass of beer. She expected him to either cause some trouble for her or ask her out before the night was through. But someone beat him to the opportunity. Someone Miranda hadn't even noticed, which was unlike her. This second man gathered up his drink and came to where she sat.

"Excuse me." He smiled and leaned in a little, his necktie swaying in the space between them. "Do you mind if I join you for a bit?"

"Are you for real?" She pushed her drink away from her on the table.

"Do you see something false?"

He was a good-looking man. Mid-thirties, expensive suit, furtive eyes.

What the hell do we have here?

Miranda didn't answer his question, only gestured to the empty seat across from her, which he took without hesitation, blocking her view of the man at the bar.

"I'm not usually this forward," the man said, "but you really caught my eye, so I thought … what the hell?"

"Seems to me that you could probably catch younger prey than me if you put your mind to it."

His smile broadened as he stirred his drink. A white Russian. "Do you see me as a predator, then?"

"Shit, I haven't met a man who wasn't. I don't hold it against you. I reckon a man has to be a little predatory if he wants to get his manhood where it needs to be. It's a long row to hoe from small talk to pillow talk, and women don't tend to make it as easy as pie."

"You're very straightforward."

"Is that a turn-off? It is to a lot of men. Especially white men like yourself."

"You've had some experience with white men?"

She knew that her lack of response was answer enough.

"Do you want me to be equally straight with you?"

"You can be whatever you like."

Metallica faded to black on the jukebox, and the hard riffing of Heart's "Barracuda" screamed out of the speakers to fill the void.

"All right. This is my third drink of the night. I find you attractive, and I'd like to get to know you a little better."

"Took you three drinks to find me attractive, huh?"

"No, it took me three drinks to work up the nerve to approach you."

"You're serious, aren't you? Jesus, son, you don't know what you're biting off."

"Then tell me."

He moved his chair a bit closer, giving Miranda back her view of the younger man at the bar. Yes, that one was definitely trouble of one stripe or another. He was either the most incompetent shadow she'd ever picked up or he was a small-time hood looking for a thrill. She hated to use the hopeful gentlemen before her, but she wasn't about to put up with a bunch of folderol from the greasy-haired punk at the bar, either.

"How about I tell you in the car. You drove, I presume? You don't look like Transit Authority material to me."

"I drove," he acknowledged, "but I take the bus from time to time."

"I'm sure you do, honeybunch. Now this is me taking you up on an offer to give me a lift home. Nothing more. Are we clear on that?"

He nodded.

"If you're a good boy, maybe I'll cough up my phone number at the end of the line."

He gaped as she stood up and removed her parka from the back of her chair. With one arm in and one arm out she ceased her deliberations. "Something I can help you with?"

"I was just wondering if you'd care to know my name," the man said. "I'd love to know yours."

"I'm sorry. I'm not usually so surly, just like you're not usually so predatory, right? The name's Amanda. Amanda Durning."

Why the lie? She hadn't given a false name in years. It carried some risk in a place like the Golden Jug, where she was on a friendly basis with most of the staff and some of the clientele. Old instincts went stubbornly to the grave, she mused.

She offered her hand for him to shake, but instead he brought it to his lips and gave it a soft kiss. "Brandon McGovern, at your service. It's a pleasure to know you."

Oh my, if ever there was a night when she could have used a second pair of eyes in the back of her head it was this one. Mr. McGovern might require his own kind of attention, even as she endeavored to learn what her shady friend at the bar had in mind. But it was times like these that kept her blades from dulling completely, gave her a hint of the old thrills she used to enjoy as a matter of routine. Those days were long gone, but a fire still burned. There was a taste for danger in her gut yet. And longing. Yes, that too.

"Thanks, Eddie," she called to the bartender as Brandon walked her to the door. "Money's on the table."

"Yes, ma'am. I know that. You always pay for your Cape Cods, cash on the barrel. You have a good night, what's left of it."

"You do the same." She always called his attention to the money on the table, not because she feared he'd ever suspect her of skipping out on the bill, but so that other patrons might hear and think twice about employing their sticky fingers. Not terribly likely in Wicker Park, but you couldn't be too careful.

"This way." Brandon turned a corner to where his car was parked.

He let Miranda in on the passenger side and stepped around to the driver's side.

"Mercedes." Miranda nodded approvingly as Brandon slid behind the wheel.

"Investment banking has been pretty good to me. I don't see any reason to pretend I can't afford a decent car."

"It's a shade better than decent, I'd say."

He shrugged and started the engine. The heater was cranked to the maximum setting, which was a relief to Miranda. Autumn had an early grip on Cook County this year. Or maybe Chi-Town had its own weather system. Lord knew, it was unique enough in other ways.

"Where are we headed?" he asked.

"Chinatown." She enjoyed a good adventure, but she wasn't about to give up her real address to this stranger—or to the other man in the bar, should her suspicions prove to be accurate about his intention to follow them.

"Milwaukee to the freeway?"

"That's how I'd do it."

A car door slammed shut somewhere behind them as they pulled away from the curb. An engine churned to life. Miranda Gissing had a feeling she knew who had turned the key.

Maybe Brandon had thrown a few more glances at the rear-view mirror than usual on the way downtown, but he didn't make his suspicions known for certain until they'd crossed the river.

"I'm not the paranoid type," he said, headlights from the car behind reflecting in his eyes as he looked at the mirror, "but I'd swear we're being followed. Guy keeps changing lanes with me and everything. Keeps a polite distance, but he's always right there."

"What's he driving?"

She should have been subtler. He was throwing looks at her now, maybe wondering why she would take a sudden tail in stride. And that was an explanation she had no intention of getting into tonight.

"Some kind of old, low-profile pickup. Maybe a Nissan. Something like that. It's kind of a tan color. You know it? Or the driver?"

"There was a guy at the bar giving off an odd vibe. Kind of creepy. Barely took his eyes off me all night."

"Ah, so that's why you were so willing to entertain my company."

"Look, your timing was convenient. I'll grant you that. But I don't play games. I'd let you have it straight if that's all this was. You get me home and I'll give you that phone number I alluded to. Clear?"

His gaze remained on the road, but a grin played at the corner of his mouth.

"Why don't you get off here." She jutted her chin toward the next off-ramp. "We'll see if he's serious about sticking to us or not."

Brandon veered over a lane so he could take the exit.

"Is he still on us?"

Brandon nodded.

"Okay, then. I'm sorry to involve you in this, but I guess we're going to have to go to the wall with this little puke. Head down this way, to Princeton. Let's see if we can't reverse the game board on our brave little friend."

Something in her voice must have conveyed to Brandon

that question time would come later, if at all, for he obeyed in silence.

"There!" She pointed. "Duck into that alley and pull all the way through to the next street. We'll wait there, and when he turns into the alley behind us, you gun it around the block and get on *his* ass. Surely you can get this hot little piece of German engineering around the block faster than he can maneuver his pickup through the alley."

"Jesus, you've been in a tight spot before, I see. Law enforcement?"

Before she could answer, a delivery truck pulled into the alley ahead of them, hazards flashing lethargically in the cold night air. They looked at each other.

"Shit." Miranda threw a glance over her shoulder. No sign of their pursuer, but was that the bob of headlights she saw back on Princeton? "Better get this thing turned around, like yesterday. Do we need to change seats?"

"No, I'll do it."

He was shaking from nerves, but he set about getting the car turned around. It required a tight three-point turn to reorient the vehicle in the narrow alley, but at last they were facing South Princeton Avenue. Just in time to watch a tan Nissan pickup truck pull slowly to a stop across the entrance, blocking their egress at that end of the alley.

The time for talk was past. Miranda unbuckled her seatbelt, gripped the steering wheel, and jammed her left foot onto the accelerator.

"Hey, what the—"

"Sorry, Brandon. But like I said, I don't play games."

The Mercedes barreled down the alley, narrowly missing the brick walls and dumpsters on either side. They had their follower's attention. His arms were fully extended between his torso and the steering wheel of the pickup, his face a long exclamation of dread as it leered at the oncoming grill of the Mercedes.

There was a bang, followed by the sound of crumpling

metal and shattering glass. Pain as an airbag forcefully pressed her into her seat. Then stillness, almost complete. Something dripped somewhere, and there was a hissing sound. Otherwise, quiet.

She needed to act fast. Windows in the surrounding apartment buildings would be flying up soon. Voices would call out. Lights would turn on. And eventually there would be sirens. It probably only took a few seconds for the airbag to deflate, but it seemed like an eternity. It must have malfunctioned. She couldn't assess the aftermath of the crash, much less extricate herself from the mangled Mercedes, until the damn thing was out of her way.

Something had knocked Brandon out. Maybe the driver's side airbag had slammed his head into the headrest. *What's up with your airbag-engineering squad, Mercedes?* Whatever the case, she was glad for it. She'd been prepared to render him unconscious herself if necessary. A quick search for something to write with, and on, turned up a Cross pen clipped to an inner pocket of his sport coat, as well as business cards in his wallet. Perfect. She jotted down a quick note: *You didn't see me tonight. A. D.* Then she deposited both the pen and business card in one of his outer pockets.

Now the hard part.

She crawled out of the Mercedes and along the alley to the pickup, ratcheting her head back and forth in search of witnesses. So far she saw and heard nothing. The Nissan had been pushed a distance into the street by the impact, so she was able to pry open the driver's door. No airbags in this rust bucket, but there was a hell of a lot of blood. The driver coughed and spit up more, which startled Miranda. He looked as dead as any corpse she'd ever seen. His eyes found hers.

"Fuck," he rasped. "Dear God. What do you want?"

"What do *I* want?"

His ignorant naïveté enraged her for some reason. Why did men like him think they could pull off their little escapades without a hitch? Like it was some kind of right. That the idea of retribution should be so foreign and shocking ...

There was no pulling back now. The switch had been thrown. She reached in and grasped a large clump of hair at the back of his head.

"No!" he cried with a bloody gurgle. "Please ..."

She slammed his face into the steering wheel with enough force to make something snap audibly, either a piece of the steering column or part his head. It required every effort of will she could collect to keep from repeating the action, but she knew that it would stop looking like an outcome of the crash if she overdid it.

Not expecting to find anything of interest, she haphazardly ran a hand through his pockets. A drumming noise distracted her for a moment, until she reached a hand outside the pickup and felt several heavy, piercingly cold drops of rain. Their tattoo on the roof intensified as she continued her search. A distant siren. A woman screaming: *Did you fucking hear that? Can't be good!* There was something in one of the pockets of his leather jacket. Removing the item, Miranda saw that it was a cream-colored envelope. A black sedan slowed as it moved along Princeton, but the driver must have been satisfied that whatever had happened there was no business of his, because the vehicle quickly sped up again and continued on its way.

There was no sense in wasting any more time at the scene. She quietly closed the pickup door, walked in a crouch along Princeton Avenue, and disappeared down an alley across the street. Her left shoulder was giving her some trouble. Must have banged it into Brandon's seat upon impact. But she counted herself lucky. It could have been worse. If she'd debilitated herself, for instance, things could have gotten very sticky indeed. She didn't like leaving things for chance. In fact, she told Brandon a bit of a white lie when she said she didn't play games. There was one game in particular that she positively reveled in. It was the game of cover-up. Few things in life gave her as much pride as her ability to make a murder look like an accident. Tonight hadn't been her best work, but it felt good to have the fires burning again.

As she made her way to the Red Line train on foot, she did a good deal of thinking about the envelope in her coat pocket. Her curiosity was piqued. It seemed an awfully nice piece of stationery for such a two-bit hood to be carrying around with him. But she was determined to wait to satisfy her curiosity until she was on the northbound train that would get her close to home. A cab would carry her the rest of the way.

Pulling the fur-lined hood of her black down parka over her head, Miranda Gissing walked deeper into the chilling Chicago night, as if becoming more a part of it with each step she took away from the scene of her handiwork.

PART II: BEST-LAID PLANS

Glory is like a circle in the water,
Which never ceaseth to enlarge itself,
Till by broad spreading it disperse to nought.
—*Henry VI, Act 1, Scene 2*

What is seen with one eye has no depth.
—Ursula K. Le Guin, *Always Coming Home*

CHAPTER 11

The drive from Abilene to Fort Worth had been a breeze for Max Brindle. He could have done it drunk. Did once, in fact. When he wasn't setting up rendezvous with high-powered clients in exotic locales, he was brooding in his permanent motel room at the Rise and Shine, riding the rails in search of his next bright pupil, or tracking one down to engage in next steps. The cute little piece of ass that ran the Rise and Shine for her aunt and uncle had even taken a liking to him, which not only helped to keep things cool when he fell behind on the rent but gave him something better than his fist to fuck from time to time—usually when he was flush, he never failed to realize, which made her a bit of a whore. That was all right, though. It gave him a little incentive to keep the cash flow flowing. There were droughts, as with anything, but there were also monsoons. It was the nature of his work. And he couldn't blame the girl for wanting a man of means.

But right now he wasn't in his sultry room, or meeting with a client. He was halfway between Fort Worth and San Antonio on the Texas Eagle. And that meant he was working. Amtrak was his office, and he had a feeling he was looking at his first brief of the day. The kid couldn't have been much more than twenty-five. Under thirty, anyway. His hair was average length but greasy in appearance. He wore a black shirt with white lettering that presumably spelled out the name of a metal band, though what that name *was* remained a mystery. Unreadable logos seemed like bad marketing to Max, but he supposed they would have gone out of fashion by now if they weren't translating into dollar signs for someone.

The young man paused in his approach when he was several feet away. He became preoccupied with his phone, reading and tapping in alternating bursts. Slipping the phone into the back pocket of his jeans, he spiraled down the narrow staircase to the lower level. The bistro and lounge, Max knew. He hadn't picked his seat at random, after all. The most worn out, lackluster, abused, and neglected specimens of humanity always found their way to the nearest liquor spigot eventually, especially during an extended Amtrak excursion. And that was the type of person he needed. Weak, hopeless, naive, detached, and angry. It didn't hurt if they were a notch or two lower on the intelligence scale than Max, either. Maybe chess was a less thrilling game when his opponent was beneath him, but the outcome was in his favor and more quickly determined.

Max jotted down a couple of notes in a tiny notepad, wire bound at the top with a dark brown cover, and headed below, his colorful patchwork sport coat the mark of the man.

While he waited to be served at the bar, he scanned the small room. The man whose life he was about to change, if instinct proved reliable, sat forlornly in the far corner. A clear plastic cup of something sat on the orange Formica table in front of him. Vodka sour, by the look of it. Ice cubes floating in greenish liquid. A pink straw resting against the side of the cup.

"What'll it be?" the almost perfectly round black woman behind the bar asked when it was Max's turn.

"Vodka sour with whip." He smiled but it had no effect. The woman only stared. "On second thought, hold the whip."

She turned and fixed his drink without fuss.

"Seven-fifty," She set his order next to the cash register.

The train hit a seam in the track. Max exaggerated the effect it had on his balance, as if he was trying to pick up his drink but could only push it from side to side on the counter. Again, the cashier was unamused.

"Kind of steep." Max pulled a ten spot out of his wallet. "That come with a French kiss?"

This time he got a pair of arched eyebrows out of her.

"Sure thing, let me go get Antoine real quick."

"Okay, okay. Only joking."

She handed him his change and he slid the two quarters her way.

"There's plenty more where that came from," he said with a wink.

"Big spender."

Ah, a sense of humor lurked beneath that spherical shell after all, even if it didn't dare express itself through a smile or chuckle. He suspected that almost everyone had humor in them if you drilled down deep enough. For proof he looked no farther than himself. His line of work, and the types of people it put him in contact with, would have drained the humor out of most anyone long ago. But he had determined early on that if he was going to make a run of this, he would be the person he spent the most time with. His own best friend and worst enemy. It beat the hell out of his previous existence: a budding misanthrope trapped in a job that made his boss rich and kept his own jaw snapping at whatever meat dangled from the hook, like a pathetic Tantalus, too dumb and complacent to move on, trapped in a marriage that had already failed in all but name. He now realized that as long as he kept a sense of humor with him wherever he went, anything was possible. He still had no hope, humanity, or love of country, and he was worthy of the severest contempt, but he felt more at peace with himself than a lot of the fops he encountered in his daily life. Fuck 'em all, he figured. The soulless drones and the middle-class robots. The opportunistic fat cats and the academic snobs. He didn't want wealth, knowledge, or power. What Max Brindle wanted more than anything was to make an impact. If he made a name for himself in the process, that was okay, but the impact was what mattered most. And the young man he was currently sizing up as he approached his table was going to help him along that course.

"Mind if I have a seat."

The man glanced up from his phone and shrugged. "Sure. Looks like there's an empty table over there."

Max looked across the narrow aisle at the empty table to

which the stranger had briefly darted his gaze. The smile that ensued was perfectly natural. He was delighted to discover a funny bone so early on in their negotiations. If he'd been the kind of man who believed in signs, here was one.

He set his drink down close to the other man's, then placed his hat where it was out of the way. The stranger placed his phone on the table and gave an exasperated sigh before making eye contact.

"Look, Shock-O the Clown, or whatever you are, despite your swell comb-over and your coat of many colors, I'm not gay or desperate for cash. The paunch you've got tucked under control by that button-down shirt almost gives me pause, but no, I'm going to pass on the whole fucking thing."

But then he noticed Max's drink. It was gimmicky and overt, buying the same drink as his target, but Max had broken the ice this way before. There was something about the fact that you had a favorite drink in common with a stranger. Somewhere in the neighborhood of astrology, he figured. So be it. Let the rubes have their superstitions, and let him gain from their easy belief. That was the steak and potatoes of his trade, anyway. It's what kept him one step ahead of almost everyone he ever did business with. For his own part, he believed in nothing except the power of belief as a weapon. And maybe the power of a smile, for sales was also on Max Brindle's job description.

"A vodka man?" The stranger nodded at the drinks.

Max also nodded. Sensing that the opportunity wouldn't last forever, he slid in across from the man but turned his attention to the window. Outside, a prairie scene rolled past, punctuated by herds of cattle behind barbed-wire fences, picturesque farmhouses, and stands of oak trees. Sunlight glinted off of everything, wishing it was fire.

"The name's Max." He didn't take his eyes off the rolling scenery. "What do they call you?"

The man forced a single chuckle in the back of his throat. "There's a long list of names I've been called, mister. Jerrod will do." He sipped his drink. "Where are you headed?"

Max turned to face his questioner. "Well, at my age I've pretty well gotten to where I was headed. Now it's mostly a matter of circling back and trying to recapture feelings and experiences I've already had in one form or another."

"I hope that's never my outlook. Pretty fucking sad, you ask me."

Max smiled patiently. "How about you? Where are you headed?"

"Not too sure," Jerrod answered, ably picking up on Max's knack for abstraction. "West, obviously. I'll get off this rolling coach in Los Angeles, which will do for a start, but it's not my final destination."

"You're not much beyond college age, are you?" asked Max.

"Even closer to dropout age."

He liked this kid. Loads of promise in this one.

"You don't think much of me, do you? Or is it just a general disrespect for your elders?"

"I don't have anything against old *people*. It's old *age* I have the problem with. We're all living too goddamn long. There's no point to it. How enjoyable can life be after a certain point?"

Jerrod paused to take a sip, maybe see if Max had any wisdom on the matter. He didn't.

"You said yourself you're basically on repeat. And if your health starts to fall apart, forget about it. I suppose you've got some polished comeback, but I've turned this crystal ball over and over again in my hands." He actually made the gesture, like a mime. "You can't convince me there's life after fifty."

Max took a drink. "Comeback? No, I've got no comeback. Are you ready for some rare truth? It's worse than you could possibly imagine. Getting old, I mean. The pain and humiliation you imagine? All based on your own pitiful frame of reference."

The young man remained coiled but didn't strike, so Max went on.

"The pang of watching the young as they cavort along their joyful paths? That's not just sad. It's gut-wrenching. Depressing beyond compare. The imminent threat of losing sexual opportunity, memory, motor function, equilibrium, cognitive reasoning ... More terrifying than the worst nightmare you've ever woken from in an icy sweat, son. Worse than a month spent watching horror films by yourself while locked in the deepest, darkest dungeon on earth. That's life after fifty. So don't you go pretending it doesn't exist. It's out there, waiting for you, and it'll eat your heart right out of your chest."

The persistent *rick-a-chick-a-rick-a-chick-a* as they rolled along the tracks provided a distraction from their opinions, as did the scenery out the window: all trees and creek beds now. The world that passed by was solid, true, and temporary, while inside it was hard to believe that anything came to an end, including this train journey, which Max imagined might continue into the Underworld, where it would forever circle around and down. So long, truth and solidity.

Jerrod pulled the tiny straw from his glass and let it fall to the table before downing the rest of his vodka sour.

"Whatever you're selling—Max—your pitch needs work. Jesus fucking Christ."

"Buy you another?"

"Listen, I was serious about no monkey business. There's no blowjob at the end of this rainbow, if that's what—"

"Dear God, no." Max laughed a little. "Your pecker's safe with me. So's your mouth. It's just that I'm the kind of man who speaks his mind. My filter wore clean through years ago."

"Anything in particular to blame?"

"No, just woke up one morning no longer able to give a shit. Had no more use for all the rehearsed bull crap people draw on to avoid opening a view onto the vast emptiness within."

"Yeah, I get that. A fellow can only put up with so much before he either wakes up or goes to sleep forever."

"I suppose for you it was leaving school. Was that the break you made with a complacent world?"

"You pay attention. I'll give you that."

"You know," Max said, leaning forward, "I'm not selling

anything. But I do have a pitch."

"What, like a job?"

"*You* pay attention, too. Very much like a job, in fact. But it's the kind of thing not everyone is cut out for."

"I'm listening."

"Jerrod, what are your views on morality?"

"Okay, I get it. You've got something less than savory needs doing. Is that it?"

Max smiled and ran his index finger around the rim of his cup.

"Already we're into semantics. Do you know what that means?"

"I'm a dropout, not a moron."

Max held up his hands, as if to say, "Didn't mean to offend." But what he actually said was, "Let's talk about that word, *savory*, for a moment. It's a curious one. Sometimes a good way to get to the heart of something is to examine its opposite. Can you give me some examples of activities that are *un*savory?"

"Sure. Stealing, cheating ... murder."

There was a pause, during which Max would have lit up one of his cheap cigars back in the good old days, when they let you smoke yourself dizzy on the train. Instead he took a deep breath and closed his eyes as he eased himself back on the bench seat.

"Ah, yes. But are those things always unsavory? Aren't there degrees to all three of those crimes? Surely the poor man who steals a loaf of bread for his famished children deserves more sympathy than the punk who mugs an old woman on a dare."

Jerrod shrugged, but he was paying close attention.

"The man who cheats at cards to win back a little revenge for a wrong done to him isn't deserving of the same punishment as the man who habitually hides an ace of spades up his sleeve for nothing more than personal gain.

"And murder," Max went on. "Is murder just the act of killing a man, or is there more to the word than that?"

"I suppose there are levels ..." Jerrod said.

"Sure there are. Murder implies a kind of viciousness. It's an act of malice. If a man knocks your wife to the ground and lifts her skirt up with one hand while struggling to unzip his pants with the other, maybe you kill him. But that's not murder. That's justifiable homicide. Maybe even self-defense."

"Okay, what's your point?"

"My point is that there are a lot of ways to die in this world, and not too damn many of them are pleasant. Murder can be one of the worst. It can be ugly. But not all killing has to be that way. Some killing has purpose."

"You mean like in a war? That kind of killing?"

The man was hooked through the cheek now. It was only a matter of reeling him in. Max slapped the table, a little harder than he'd intended.

"By God, that's exactly what I mean! Just like in a war, goddamn it. And war is what we're talking about, young man. Believe it."

"What war is that?"

Max took a moment to survey his surroundings. A train attendant had claimed a seat near the other end of the car. That could only mean he was on break, and if there was a creature on earth that could tune out the conversation of strangers, it was the union Amtrak employee on break. Other than that, he and Jerrod—and the humorless bartender—had the place to themselves, and the bartender was even farther behind him than the seated attendant.

"The war you're already a part of. Has the system delivered for you? Have you been cut a fair deal? Or maybe you believe that every jerk in a tailored suit and luxury automobile has worked so much harder than you in life that he deserves everything he's got, and that you, not having worked nearly hard enough, deserve your lot in life, too. But that's not how I see it. You can earn a modest paycheck and shoot it at the corner booze hole. That's one way to scrape by, but there are others."

"Yeah, well like I said, I'm listening. Trouble is, all I hear is a lot of empty talk."

Max reached into the pocket of his sport coat and pulled out a business card. Dropping it onto the table he pinned it down with his index finger.

"I'm not about to show you my hand. Not on our first meeting. You've heard enough about the stakes to know that you won't be filling out a W-4 if you decide to work with me. You have a sense of the risk and obligation involved. What you don't have a clue about is what you stand to gain. Wealth and power beyond your dreams, son."

"What's that, then?" Jerrod glanced at the card beneath Max's finger. "Your business card?"

"That's right."

"Load Control Officer, Pym Cargo," Jerrod read from the card. "Not sure if that's fancy or schmancy, but it's definitely one of the two."

"Got to tell the taxman something every year. Look, if you decide you're ready for phase two of our discussions, give me a call. If you decide maybe you'd rather have the authorities do a little checking up on old Max Brindle of Pym Cargo ... Well, I have no idea how you got my card, and I sure as hell never saw you before. Are we on the same wavelength?"

There was a long pause, during which both men stared into each other's eyes, gauging intent and trustworthiness.

Finally, "Yeah, we're good."

Max lifted his finger and smiled broadly. Jerrod snatched up the card. He didn't bother to look at it further before stuffing it into the pocket of his jeans.

"Look," Jerrod said, sliding to the edge of his bench, "I've got to get back to my seat. Hoping to catch a little shut-eye. Just need to grab a book out of my bag first." He jabbed a thumb over his shoulder toward the connecting door behind him. "I'll, uh, talk to you later, okay?"

"I'll look forward to that. Real nice meeting you, kid." Max knew there'd be restrooms in the car immediately adjacent, and that the baggage car was the next one after that. He stood up and donned his porkpie. "I'll follow you part way. Got to take a whiz."

Jerrod gave him a slightly distasteful look, like he half feared it was going to be no easy thing shaking Max Brindle now that he'd latched on. He nodded as he stood up and pushed the button on the door, whooshing it open. Max followed him into the vestibule and waited for him to engage the next door. As Jerrod passed through to the luggage car, Max ducked into one of the tiny bathrooms, but only for a moment. As soon as he heard the door to the luggage car whisper shut. he stealthily reemerged. In three strides he was at the connecting door, peering through the dingy inset windows of both that door and the one on the luggage car itself. He could make out Jerrod reaching to his right, pulling down a large black duffel bag from the top rack. Not quite at the halfway point of the car. That was all he needed to know. He returned to the restroom and waited for Jerrod to make his way back to the lounge car, where he would climb back to the upper deck and return to his seat.

Whoosh. Boot steps on metal flooring. *Whoosh.* And Jerrod was gone. Max peered out from the bathroom once more, confirming that the coast was clear. Sure as a weasel in a grain bin, he slipped into the luggage car and quickly located Jerrod's duffel bag. He didn't have to slide it very far out before a vinyl-protected address tag revealed itself. Throwing one nervous glance over his shoulder he removed a digital camera from the same pocket of his sport coat that held his business cards. He snapped a picture and double-checked it for clarity. No smart phones for this kind of work. He didn't trust that shit. If hackers were plucking private celebrity nudes out of the cloud, there was sure as hell someone somewhere just waiting for old Max Brindle to slip a fuckup into the works and inadvertently post something sensitive to an open network. His phone had its purposes, but that was mostly for his public identity. His private self required a bit more care in handling.

Lansing, Michigan, he read after enlarging the image on the screen of his Canon. A smile played across his lips. Good Midwestern kid. This was going to be like winning a bare-knuckle fist fight with a gang of toddlers. If he played his cards right, word of this might make it all the way up the food chain to the Black Phantom himself. But it was early to be celebrating any victories yet. No matter how much was at stake, no matter how bright a feather young Jerrod would be in his already well-lined cap, this was no time to rest on his laurels. He was confident that winning the heart and soul of this young traveler would establish an undeniable pattern of excellence on his part, but he also knew that confidence could be a trick of the light—a prerequisite for getting the job done. Reflection after the fact was always truer, though sometimes less flattering.

He didn't like getting caught up in these kinds of thoughts. They got him wondering about the path he'd chosen for himself. Maybe he'd be better off abandoning the whole damn thing. He could stop this. He could make sure that Jerrod … He arrowed the screen of his camera up a couple of notches … Cafferty would never again hear from the eccentric Max Brindle. He could go legit. It wasn't an easy life, but he'd done it before. Surely he'd sleep better at night.

But would he? He thought of his little cutie pie at the Rise and Shine. Donna. She'd be gone like a fart in a tornado if he went the paycheck-to-paycheck route. He was damn lucky he could turn her head at all. She was the best-looking woman he'd ever been with. There was no reason to think he'd find her equal again. It wasn't just the little titties she kept barely hidden in her see-through tops, either. It wasn't just her shapely ass or long, slender legs. Her green eyes and natural blonde hair were a little closer to the mark, but even those didn't fully explain his attachment. He actually liked her company. What was more, she seemed to like his. But she had options. There were plenty of men whose company she might enjoy. If he were to shut off the flow of money permanently, there would be nothing to hold her to him. She was a good kid, but she was still a kid. Hell, she'd be better off without him. That was the cold, hard truth of the matter.

But he wouldn't be better off without her, and he was a profoundly selfish lout. That was also the cold, hard truth. And like that, Max Brindle had talked himself through another brush with moral rectitude.

He pocketed the camera and made his way back to his seat on the upper deck.

CHAPTER 12

S hallot was one of Seattle's poshest eateries. Located downtown, near the waterfront, it appealed to both locals and tourists of a certain tax bracket. The turn-of-the-century brick building the restaurant inhabited also housed a number of condos on the upper floors. The Portable Nine had the opulent but cozy mezzanine all to themselves for an evening of pan-Asian feasting and confabulation.

Davenport sat at the head of the table. His black suit and dark purple tie matched the mostly Thai décor, but his favorite jacket hung on the back of his chair like a security blanket. He pushed an errant strand of dark brown hair across his forehead and scanned the attendees with a wry smile on his lips. His leather fedora sat on the table next to his wine glass. Dr. Intaglio occupied the seat to his right, with Bonnet immediately next in line. The two were, of course, inseparable. *Bonnet the dummy, Intaglio the ventriloquist*, Davenport thought. Next was Miranda Gissing. *Our black beauty*, he couldn't help thinking, though they'd never been together romantically. Not because she was a little plumper than his usual conquests. It just hadn't happened. Yet. The Butcher rounded out that side of the table. Sitting directly across from him was Twitch Markham, who was living up to his name by fidgeting ceaselessly with his flatware while he waited for the games to commence. Next to Twitch was Robin Varnesse, the great man of business. A slightly troubled man, Davenport had always thought. Something about how those sunken, worn-out eyes didn't quite fit with the handsome face and well-built frame that surrounded them. Then there was Abel Hazard. Fearless Abel. Davenport didn't linger on him, for there was something a little disquieting about the way the man stared at him without blinking, his hands politely folded on the table in front of him. Finally, the lovely Lovinia Dulcet. Were her Twin Delights secreted on her person at that very moment? He suspected they were.

It was time to begin.

"Thank you all for coming," he said. "It's been a long time. Maybe too long. I'm humbled by your unanimous acceptance of my request that you join me here tonight. I hope to repay your faith in me with the sincerity of my purpose in bringing the Portable Nine together again."

"I don't mean to be rude." It was Dr. Intaglio's sharp, grating voice. "Really, I don't. But this has been anything but a joyride for Mr. Bonnet and me. We've come a very long way on a great deal of faith, honestly. I think we can do without the niceties, can't we?" Here he passed his gaze from one to the other until he'd made eye contact with everyone at the table. "You have our attention. What the hell is it you want?"

"Riches," was Davenport's disarmingly simple reply. "For all of us."

"Pardon?" said Robin Varnesse.

"Wealth, my friends, beyond your wildest dreams. We've done a lot of dangerous work for a number of reasons over the years. Some of that work has been noble. Some has been … well, of necessity. I propose that the time has come for the Portable Nine to take a slice of the pie for itself for a change. If we do this right, we retire from this madman's—and woman's—game once and for all." He grinned at Lovinia. "Unless everyone here is so satisfied with their current lot in life that there's no room for improvement."

Silence prevailed.

"Yes, I kind of thought so. A nice fat pension wouldn't do much harm to any of you, I suspect. That's what this is about. We've always acted on behalf of the greater good, no matter how unorthodox our measures have been. Tonight I say it's time we measure up to those measures and put ourselves first, once and for all."

Gazes and nods were exchanged, and for a moment Davenport thought they might even break into applause. But before anything so ludicrous could occur, Abel broke the spell.

"None of us is sneering at the thought of having a little more shrapnel in our pockets. I know I haven't been cashed up for a good stretch myself, but you're talking about introducing a whole new level of risk into our enterprise. I assume you mean we'd be going it alone, without the backing of a government or corporate entity."

"Certainly," Davenport said.

"It's madness."

"Then we'll be rich and mad at the end of it all."

"Or dead," added the Butcher.

"Or dead," Davenport conceded. "But that's no new risk. That's always been part and parcel of what we do. 'Death waits around every corner. When it stares you down, only luck, good or bad, will see you through.' Didn't you tell me that once?"

The Butcher nodded, clearly impressed by the ease with which Davenport recalled the words.

"The risk Abel is referring to is something different. Correct me if I'm wrong, Abel, but you seem to be afraid that we run a higher risk of getting caught, or otherwise failing to accomplish our goal, without the aid of an umbrella organization?"

"*Afraid* would be the wrong word," Abel said wryly.

"Ah, yes." Davenport shook a finger at him and smiled. "No amygdala, no fear. I almost forgot."

Abel looked a little startled to have confirmation that his brain operation was common knowledge, though he must have known a secret like that wouldn't be kept from the Nine forever.

"Not afraid, then. But it's a concern of yours. An observation."

Abel nodded once, satisfied with the change in wording.

"Well, we'll have plenty of time to discuss these particulars, as well as the intricacies of the plan I have in mind. I'd like to have one-on-one meetings with each of you to discuss your various roles in the plot. The main purpose of tonight's gathering is to furnish each of you with a communication device."

He reached beneath his chair and brought up a large department store shopping bag. Tipping it over above the table, he let the contents roll out like dice from a cup.

"These are the phones I expect you all to use for any conversations or texts related to this job. They were built specially for me, and they boast proprietary encryption that isn't on the market. The incentive to get this right, ladies and gentlemen, is considerable. The stakes couldn't be higher. If we win the day, we walk with enough dough to disappear forever. My guess is that we'll never meet again after that. But if we fail, there's no telling how many enemies we will have made, or how much trust we will have lost. So don't blow it. Get the simple stuff right. Use these phones, for starters.

"They're all labeled. I've already got all of your numbers in my contacts, and I've texted them to each of you, as well as mine." He held up his own phone to show that it was the same shiny new model that he was doling out to the others. "Bonnet, yours is fitted with additional voice-control features. Dr. Intaglio, would you be so kind as to pass them around."

The good doctor did as he was told, and soon the Portable Nine were equipped with state-of-the-art smartphones.

"Good. I'll be in touch regarding your individual assignments. But first, I'll need to know that you're all in. I can't imagine pulling this off without the cooperative involvement of each and every one of you, but if I can't count on a full deck, I'd rather know now than find out midstream. We may need to adjust our methods and plans according to unforeseen developments as it is. I'd rather not have the added surprise of losing the support of one or more of you along the way. Can I see a show of hands from those who are at least willing to meet individually for more information?"

Twitch Markham's hand was the first one up. Davenport wasn't surprised. The man had spent his entire life inching ever closer to a complete mental collapse. Surely he'd just as soon be out of this line of work and living the life of Riley. Next was Miranda Gissing. That fit, too. Perhaps more than any of the others, she had the potential to lead a more normal life, maybe there was even a domestic streak in her. She had carried out some of the Nine's most important objectives over the years, and he was counting on her heart still being in it. But she wouldn't miss the work. Ten or fifteen years ago, maybe. Now? No. She was smart enough to know that the chances of a major fuckup increased with time. This was not a game for the long term, and they'd been pushing at the edge of that reality for years. The Butcher's hand went up, then Robin Varnesse's. One by one, assent was granted, until at last it was unanimous.

"I thank you all sincerely. Your loyalty is humbling. Now, the two locations I trust the most are this restaurant and our hotel rooms, as they've been thoroughly swept for bugs. I trust everyone is happy with the accommodations at the Regal?"

There were nods but no words of response. It was the silence of the rapt.

"It's close by, anyway. You're an acting troupe, in case it comes up, by the way. I'm your manager. In town for a swanky private show. Sworn to secrecy, et cetera, et cetera. Consider yourselves on call until I've had a chance to meet with you privately. If there aren't any general questions right now, I'll let the staff here know that we're ready to be served. This is a night for indulgence."

"One question," Abel Hazard said with a slight Aussie brogue, the cuffs of his red western shirt rolled up to the middle of his forearms. His voice was a perfectly gruff match for his sideburns and long hair.

Davenport gave a nod.

"We've always worked for an employer in the past, as you said. I get that this is more of an entrepreneurial venture, but it seems like you've put yourself in the boss's seat. Funny thing is, I don't remember taking a vote on that."

Davenport smiled and let his gaze drift around the table.

"I'm not sure what you expect me to say. I dreamt this scheme up and I gathered you here to move forward on it. I guess that does put me in charge, and you're damn right there's no one else to answer to on this. If we play a proper game of cards here, our days of playing lap dog to governments and multinationals are behind us.

"So, can we bring in the food and wine? I want to hear what you all have been up to. Then tomorrow the interviews will begin. Sound good?"

Again he scanned the table, not failing to make eye contact with any of them. There was agreement on their faces as he pressed a button on the edge of the table. It lit up blue, and soon a brisk young waiter strode through the frosted glass doors of the room to present the group with a memorized list of tantalizing specials. As soon as the wine was poured and the water glasses topped off, the Portable Nine were left to reunite, a process that grew louder and more constant with each promptly refilled glass. Soon the table was loaded down with bottles of wine and carafes of water, and eventually, steaming plates of spicy food.

CHAPTER 13

T he knock he'd been waiting for came at last. The first of the interviews.

"Come in, Dr. Intaglio. Mr. Bonnet."

The psychiatrist entered the room with confidence and gave Davenport a friendly handshake. Bonnet, despite his good looks, was more timid as he shuffled forward.

Intaglio turned to his small friend, all smiles. "Where are we today, Mr. Bonnet?"

"A system of caverns. There are different levels, and some rooms are so large I can feel breezes, like the outdoors. Ugly creatures ride strange carts through some of the tunnels. I have to be especially careful not to get in their way. Otherwise the obstacles are all pretty manageable."

"Astonishing," Davenport said. "I'll never understand how it works."

"Hallucinations," Dr. Intaglio said, "plain and simple. It's just that in his case they bear some resemblance to reality. Room service and housekeeping trolleys in this case, no doubt. His eyes appear to be taking in some information, just not in the same way that yours and mine do. For him the information is twisted by the time it reaches his brain. I'm convinced that it's not really blindness at all that plagues the good Mr. Bonnet, but some kind of anomaly of the brain. I aim to prove it."

"Still putting that psychiatrist title to use, I see." Davenport motioned for the two men to have a seat on a small couch, while he took a wingback chair on the opposite side of a glass-top coffee table.

Intaglio tapped his friend's shoulder to let him know he was expected to sit.

"So," Davenport said, "what do you both think of the plan I laid out at dinner last night? Does the idea of walking away from this job as independently wealthy men appall you?" He laced his hands together, except for the index fingers. Those he steepled and brought to his lips.

"Well," Dr. Intaglio responded, fidgeting with his tie, "as a bare objective I think it sounds fine. *We* think it sounds fine. Of course, you didn't go into a lot of specifics, but we're curious what you see as our role in this drama of yours."

"Not *one* role this time. I know that's the usual way with you, but I have something a little different in mind for this. I'll need each of you to take on very separate duties if this is to work. Mr. Bonnet, you're a handsome man. You must have some understanding of that?"

Bonnet inclined his head and grinned in a way that suggested modesty. "I've been told as much, yes, and by voices much prettier than yours." Now the grin became a smile, though Dr. Intaglio didn't look amused.

Intaglio slid forward a little on the couch. "Bonnet can't be expected to get on without me to help—"

"I'd like to hear what Davenport has in mind," Mr. Bonnet said.

"Very good." Davenport nodded. "Then I'll continue. A handsome man like you, Mr. Bonnet, would be the ideal bait for a particular banker's daughter who also happens to be a bleeding heart. But like so many bleeding hearts, Natalie Jackson's charity stops when it comes to romance. Not in your case, though. See, you possess the best of both worlds. Your blindness, and the sad, sad back story I've come up with for you, will surely appeal to her heart of gold, while your looks, we hope, will allow you to … arouse other parts of her anatomy."

"I honestly don't see—"

Mr. Bonnet cut off his partner again. "Well, I'm beginning to. What I see is that Davenport is offering me the kind of role I'd be a fool to turn down."

"But we've never worked apart." Intaglio was nearly whining.

"There's a first time for everything," Mr. Bonnet replied.

Davenport leaned back in his chair, pleased with what he'd set in motion. "Gaining the trust of Ms. Jackson is a vital first step in a complicated plot. Our chances for success are greatly enhanced with Mr. Bonnet's involvement. And of course we have an equally important part for you, Dr. Intaglio."

"Go on." There was no enthusiasm in Intaglio's voice.

"You will be playing yourself."

"I beg your pardon?"

"Well, a version of yourself. A psychiatrist who Natalie Jackson is going to convince her father he needs to see because of a sex addiction she's going to believe he suffers from."

"Will I be the little bird that sings that particular song?" Mr. Bonnet asked.

"Indeed you will, Mr. Bonnet. Indeed you will. And it won't be a lie. By the time Lovinia and Miranda have gotten to Mr. Jackson, he'll be as convinced as his daughter that he has a problem keeping himself to himself. And we'll be well on our way to collecting a lot of very personal information about one very connected Vancouver banker."

"Information collected by me, I assume," said Intaglio.

Davenport nodded meaningfully.

"What if he won't sing?"

"He'll sing. I've seen you in action. You're an adept ... extractor of truth. And if it comes to extortion, I kind of doubt he'd want his wife to know about his newfound proclivities. Miranda's and Lovinia's phones take very nice pictures. What do you say? Can I count on you both?"

"I'm in," said Mr. Bonnet with gusto.

Dr. Intaglio eyed his friend and unofficial patient, then the impenetrable Davenport.

"How much money are we talking about?" he said at last.

Davenport knew he had him in his fist. He slapped his

hands to his knees and rose with a smile. "How does twenty-two million sound?"

"Twent—Each?"

"No, of course not each. Who do you think we're after here, the king of Saudi Arabia?"

"So not quite two-and-a-half million apiece, then." Intaglio bobbed his head from side to side, considering the sum. "Tidy. And who exactly *are* we robbing blind? Who's the banker's big client?"

"A man named Cloft. Archie Cloft. His firm is actively working to bring a raft of his inventions to market, and we're not talking Silly Putty or the hula hoop here. We're talking invisibility cloaks, fully automated flying cars, computerized contact lenses, subcutaneous Wi-Fi. This guy wants to change the world."

"Cloft Industries."

"Bingo."

Intaglio shook his head and stood up wearily. "You're going to get us all killed or jailed, you know that?"

"That's a risk, but it's not the goal. There'll be more details to come, my good fellows." Davenport touched Bonnet's shoulder to indicate that it was time for him and his friend to leave. "We know how to reach each other, so we'll stay in close contact."

"Okay, then." Intaglio opened the door to the corridor. "It begins. I don't want you to think I'm not a little thrilled to see the Nine together again ..."

Davenport gave the doctor's cheek a playful slap. "It was inevitable. We're like magnets on a steel ball. We pull ourselves away with great effort but are inexorably drawn back."

Mr. Bonnet smiled and nodded as he made his exit, and Dr. Intaglio followed.

Davenport closed the door and observed the two men through the peephole as they ambled down the hall. There was trouble afoot in the ranks of the Portable Nine. It was as plain as a crow on a snowbank. For Bonnet there was some hope of reclamation. Certainly he could still be useful to the Nine. But In-taglio was another story, one full of red herrings and unreliable narrators. A tale with twists and turns and subplots galore.

Davenport vowed to make a short story of the man—or write him out completely.

CHAPTER 14

"Please, come in," Davenport instructed Miranda, closing the door behind her. "For you, my dear, I have a special task in mind." He joined her in the main room of the suite.

"You don't waste any time, do you?"

"You were always one for straight talk. Has that changed?"

"No, but I have a question first."

"And what's that?"

"Do you have to be a tall, skinny white girl to get a drink around here or what?

He smiled and crossed to the bar. "Cape Cod?"

"You remember. I'm impressed."

"I received a message from the Black Phantom. This is when I was in Tuscany not long ago. You know the name?" He dropped four ice cubes into a tumbler and filled it almost to the top with vodka before adding a splash of cranberry juice and taking the drink to his guest.

"I've heard of him, sure. So he's operational, huh?"

"I've been reading up on him. His father was a prisoner on Guadeloupe during the eruption of La Grande Soufrière. Came out of it burned nearly to death and meaner than ever. He was in for cutting his brother's arm off, legend has it. With a machete. It's said that he took out his anger over being forced to burn in solitary confinement on everyone he came into contact with once he was free of Basse-Terre."

"Basse-Terre?" Miranda asked.

"That's one of the islands that make up Guadeloupe. It's also the name of the small prefecture where the prison was located."

Davenport poured himself a bourbon, neat, and joined Miranda by the fireplace.

"So, the Black Phantom ..." Miranda said. "He has something to do with the job?"

"He has everything to do with it. Here's where it gets a little difficult. Please, have a seat."

She sat on the edge of the sofa and he took the chair across from her.

"I had to lie to the group at dinner last night. I detect a problem with Intaglio and Bonnet."

"A problem? What kind of problem?"

"I had more trouble tracking them down than the rest of you. It turned out they were in South America. Venezuela. This has been the Black Phantom's stomping ground for years. The apple has never rolled terribly far from the tree, if you take my meaning."

She nodded. "So you suspect they're working for him?"

"It's a possibility."

"Maybe they're playing him. They deserve the benefit of the doubt, don't they?"

"Anything's possible, but my gut tells me he's the one doing the playing."

"And based on a feeling, you're willing to throw them overboard? Even if you're right, we've all worked with unsavory types. The bills need to be paid."

"The Black Phantom sent me a video showing my aunt's house getting blown apart. She was home at the time. An old friend of the family's, Marta, still lives on Crete. I got in touch with her, and she confirmed the whole sorry mess."

"Jesus, I'm sorry. I know how close you were to your Aunt Meredith."

"You remember her name." He smiled and eyed his drink. "Thanks for that. She taught me how to play the piano." He clenched his crippled fist as much as he could and stared at it.

"But why in the name of—"

"It appears the Black Phantom thought I had already taken out a man I was paid to hit. What he didn't know is that I had some technical difficulty with my piece. It didn't go off and my mark lived. They say revolvers never jam, but mine sure as hell did."

"So this is a revenge thing. You want payback."

"Yes, God damn it." Davenport rose and began pacing. "Why not?"

Miranda looked at him with raised eyebrows and stretched out a hand, palm up, as if to say, "Take your pick of reasons."

"Max Brindle—that's the man I was hired to kill in Florence—this guy is connected in the freight business. Like, seriously connected. He moves cargo all over the world. Sets up the deals, anyway. He's kind of a go-between. I don't usually dig too deep when I take on a job. Sometimes the less you know the better, right? But I've done some digging now that I know how much the man's life is worth to the Black Phantom."

Miranda set her glass down on the coffee table. "I'm on pins and needles. What have you learned?"

"We're not just talking about moving illegal goods here, Miranda. This guy Brindle has his fingers in some dark pies."

"Jesus, what? Human trafficking?"

Davenport shook his head. "Not that I know of, though it wouldn't surprise me."

"Terrorism, then?"

"He's a fucking recruiter."

"Jesus."

"Yeah, that was my initial reaction. If you saw him you'd scratch your head all day long over it. He comes across as a pitchman from a bygone era. He's white, middle-aged, balding, overweight. He dresses badly. He doesn't exactly scream Islamic State."

"How do these fucking groups get their diseased ideologies into the minds of outsiders? I mean, I kind of understand how ignorance can be passed on from one generation to another, but to hook a westerner ..."

"It makes for a complicated problem, and a difficult enemy. Like I said, this is personal for me, but tracing the Black Phantom's interest in Max Brindle deepened things. If I get my opportunity, I'll take it, but if we can prevent needless deaths by foiling a terrorist plot, that's the real victory."

"No fabulous wealth, then? No carefree retirement for the Portable Nine?"

"I'm afraid not. I had to come up with something so I can figure out where Dr. Intaglio and Mr. Bonnet's allegiances lie. They're the only other members I've met with privately so far. I spun a yarn for them about a bogus robbery requiring their undercover maneuvers. Really I'm just buying time. Their phones are fitted with trackers and bugs. The rest of us can slowly begin moving on the Black Phantom, but the operation can't take flight until I know what's what with the doctor and the blind man."

"I understand."

"You'll help me, then? To convince the others of my intentions, and how important this operation is?"

"Can you recall a time when you haven't been able to count on me?"

"No."

"And you never will."

"Thank you."

Miranda stood and crossed to the door, then turned to Davenport and smiled. "This isn't going to be a stroll through the park, is it?"

Davenport looked at the floral pattern of the carpet and grinned sheepishly. "No, I'm afraid it isn't."

She nodded approval. "Good. I've been spending too much time in parks lately. Been thinking about buying a loaf of bread to feed the pigeons. It's a slippery slope."

"Shit, you're a spring chicken. Now get out of here. I'll be in touch once I've talked with the others, or *they* will."

"Aye, aye, Captain." She gave a little salute and slipped into the hall, letting the door close behind her.

Davenport swallowed the rest of his bourbon and returned to the bar to pour himself another. The odds had been stacked against the Portable Nine before, plenty of times. But their chances of bringing down the Black Phantom and any terrorist cells he was pulling the strings for seemed exceptionally bleak. At least he'd given up on the idea of abstaining from violence. That would get them nowhere.

CHAPTER 15

D r. Intaglio sat at a desk in the living room of the apartment he and Bonnet had taken, waiting for his laptop to come to life in the limited pool of light thrown from a nearby lamp. He retrieved the phone Davenport had given him from the left pocket of his sport coat. From the right pocket he withdrew a slender device, one end of which he attached to the phone. Once the computer was up and running, he attached the other end of the device to it via one of the USB ports. The Hack-Stick's software immediately appeared on the computer screen, a bank of bouncing green bars showing that it was running a scan on the phone.

A beep, followed by text that appeared as if being typed.

Your device has been fitted with the following: CELL CAPTURE

Who did Davenport think he was, spying on him. Bonnet, too, no doubt. He wondered if the others were having their privacy invaded as well.

Another beep sounded from the computer, again followed by text.

Your device has been fitted with the following: GLOBAL TRACK

What the hell was that? He expanded the details option.

Global Track is a tracking utility that overrides all privacy settings on a supported device and uses global positioning technology to track the device's whereabouts. It cannot be disabled locally without alerting the installer via SMS. GLOBAL TRACK is active at all times, even when your device is turned off.

Well, I'll be damned, he thought. Davenport was more sophisticated than he would have given him credit for. Fine, let him think he had the upper hand. Intaglio and Bonnet would play Davenport's game, at least until they learned more about the operation. The deception did not, however, instill trust.

He'd have to test Mr. Bonnet's phone and let him know they were being tracked. But first he had an important call to make. He untethered the rigged phone from his laptop and carried it with him to the bathroom, where he cranked open the sink faucet and bathtub tap before setting the phone on the vanity and returning to the main room, being sure to close the bathroom door behind him.

Moving to the sofa across the room, he picked up the handset from a land-line phone on the coffee table and dialed Mr. Bonnet's cell. The man didn't like to be disturbed on his solitary outings, but Intaglio needed to test his phone.

"Yes?" Mr. Bonnet answered.

"Bonnet, it's me. No need to say a word. Just come home. We need to talk."

"Okay, I'll—"

"Uh, not another word. Just come."

There was a click as the line went dead.

Intaglio reached inside his coat and retrieved his personal cell phone. He pulled up a contact labeled *Trujillo* and placed a call.

CHAPTER 16

T he Black Phantom lived up to his name as he climbed the stairs in a long, flowing robe. The garment was mostly deep purple, made of a heavy, velvety fabric, but every now and then light from one of the narrow windows caught a flower pattern sewn in with gold thread. The night was cool, but not enough to warrant the use of the hood, which hung between his muscular shoulders. Sweat cooled at the top of his bald head, while the bare-wood floor cooled the soles of his naked feet.

On the second floor he could afford himself the luxury of leaving all the windows wide open. All the interior doors had been removed and taken away. Here was the illusion of freedom, he thought as he glided into one of the most spacious rooms. Moonlight poured in through a large open window. There were situations that called for armed men and brute force, but his preference was to go undetected, to move among the common folk and learn their ways. Power he could buy, and money he knew how to get. But true freedom was elusive, and he was constantly at risk of having it taken from him completely. Whenever he could bask even in a simulacrum of actual liberty, he did so without hesitation.

Like his father, he'd seen the inside of a prison, and he had no intention of making a return visit. Prisons were sewage pits where all manner of failure drained to. Whether you were innocent or guilty, regardless of the severity of the crime that had put you there, prison marked you as a failure. You had failed to stay on the outside. Failed to keep promises to yourself, if not to your loved ones.

But he'd survived the filthy pen outside of Caracas, just as his father had survived solitary confinement, and so much worse, in Basse-Terre. After the Black Phantom had served his time, he survived the deadly streets of Caracas for a time as well. He had been his own man for a number of years, but he could feel the odds catching up with him. A rubber band could only stretch so far before it snapped. He'd been pulling on his for a long time.

No, freedom was not to be taken for granted.

He might one day leave the world of crime behind and never look back, but the timing had to be right. The necessary reserves of cash would need to be in place, his ability to rule by fear assured. If he decided to call it quits, he never wanted to have to return. Once he went straight—which was really just another kind of crooked—it would be for good. And it couldn't happen soon enough.

Too much of crime and terrorism was fueled by ideology these days. There was no sense of gamesmanship to it anymore. Maximum damage, maximum casualties. That's all that mattered. Well, Pierre LeGrand—the Black Phantom of Trujillo, Trujillo, son of Jacques LeGrand—still relished the look in a man's eyes as he stared down death. He enjoyed deciding where on the thread of a man's fate the scissors would make their cut, and he insisted that the man see it coming if at all possible.

There was one man in particular whose thread he wouldn't mind severing. One who had been allowed to grow into far too much of a nuisance for comfort.

"Davenport," he said with a sneer, barely above a whisper.

It was little more than a week since Dr. Intaglio and Mr. Bonnet had enjoyed the Black Phantom's wine, almost directly beneath where he now stood in his dark, breezy, empty lair. They would have made contact by now. He wondered what they'd already learned about the Mad Marksman of Malta's intentions.

He had been standing motionless in the middle of the room but now began moving toward the largest window. Before he could halve the distance, his phone vibrated in the deep pocket of his robe. He stopped to take the call.

"Yes?" he said.

"Mr. LeGrand, it's Dr. Intaglio."

"You know better than to call me by that name, especially over the phone. What is it?"

"Your instincts were good. We're all in Seattle."

"The Portable Nine? All of you?"

"That's right."

"Remarkable. What's Davenport after?"

"Well, ostensibly he's got a major robbery in mind. So major that we'll all be able to retire to a life of leisure once and for all when it's over."

"That's why he's called you all together?"

"It seems that way, Mr. ... Well, it seems that way."

"You sound less than convinced."

"I don't know. It's plausible enough. It involves Cloft Industries, so the take is potentially huge. But he gave all of us special phones that he wants us to use for the operation. He said they can't be tracked."

"Sensible."

"Except that mine *is* being tracked. It's outfitted with a bugging app and a sophisticated GPS tracker. He wants to know our every move."

"Tell me you're not calling me from a bugged phone."

"Of course not. I've got a backup."

"And all the phones are bugged?"

"I don't know. So far I've only tested mine. Bonnet is on his way over with his now."

"Listen to me, Intaglio. You need to get yourself away from the others."

"How am I supposed—"

"Do you have access to an apartment?"

"Yes, that's where I'm calling from."

"Good, then—"

A sound from the adjacent room startled the Black Phantom into silence. The sound of a creaking mattress, perhaps. It was the bedroom, so that would make sense. But who …

"Intaglio, test the other phones and get back to me. I have to go."

He disconnected from the call, despite protests from the other end, and moved with the stealth of a jaguar toward the black rectangle that was the entrance to his bedroom. Almost at the darkened doorway, he halted.

"Whoever's in there, if you don't identify yourself within five seconds, I'm going to assume you're hostile and act accordingly. Let me be clear. The last thing in the world that you want is for me to act accordingly."

"My God, I didn't think I could be any more turned on than I already was."

His guard dropped. "Carmen? What the hell are you doing in there?"

"I couldn't bear the thought of leaving town without … Well, why don't you come over here and let me tell you all about it."

His guard already dropped, he saw no reason to keep the robe, so he let it fall to the floor. He stepped out of the velvety pile at his feet and went to her in the dark.

"I wouldn't have asked you to put yourself in danger by staying in this hole of a town for one more instant than you had to, but I'd be lying if I said I wasn't glad you chose to stay. It's been a long time since we …"

He slid into bed beside her, and the months since their last heated encounter vanished. It was as if nothing had changed in the world and there was no more danger to their existence than the inevitable end that must come to everyone, but never soon. Her lips wandered from his mouth to his chest, where she let her tongue roam in lazy circles, ever downward. She batted him playfully with her hair, fanning the scent of animal passion not quite concealed by shampoo and perfume. By the time she took him into her mouth he was beyond ready. Lifting her away from his cock, he slid atop her undulating form and entered her with the natural ease and certainty that only comes from acquaintance. Familiarity did nothing to quell her obvious approval, however. They kissed passionately, and their lips never left each other, even during the shared climax of their union, when she breathed warm moans of pleasure between his lips.

When it was over, the Black Phantom rolled onto his back and they both stared at the ceiling.

"You've lost none of your talent," Carmen said.

"Likewise. I wish we could live in this room for a week, a month. I'd show you talents then that would make your toes curl."

"Sounds nice. You knew where to find me."

"That damn hotel. Why haven't we been holing up here together?"

"You know how these things are. It wasn't easy staying away from you, but I figured the less we saw of each other the better."

"You know, maybe it's fate that brought you here tonight."

"Why do you say that?" She fumbled for the matches she must have known she'd find in the drawer of his nightstand and lit a slender candle.

She's like a living fantasy, the Black Phantom thought, eyeing her softly lit profile. *Trapped between the unreal and the real. Surely her beauty is only possible in one of an otherworldly makeup.*

"I think maybe it's time you pay our friend Max Brindle another visit," he said.

"Brindle? What for?"

"I need to know who's the best and brightest horse in his stable, if you follow me."

"I don't, I'm afraid."

"His star recruit. Someone young enough to be hungry and new enough to lack curiosity. I've got a job needs doing. I'll need a commander in the field."

"And what, you want me to get a list of names for you? Why would he trust me with that kind of information? Getting close to him to learn as much about his modus operandi as possible was one thing. I've given you some great intel from that, but this ... It would set off alarm bells left and right if I started asking for specifics."

"Maybe alarm bells are just what we need, in the form of a little leverage."

She propped herself up on one elbow as she faced him. "What do you mean?"

"You're right. You've done a very good job for me. I've learned a great deal about Max Brindle because of you. Now you can go to him and tell him it's all been a ruse, and that you need some names or your boss will be most displeased."

"My God, what if he kills me?"

"Didn't you say there's someone in Texas who means something to him? Makes his eyes film over whenever he brings her up, I believe you said ..."

"Donna from Abilene. That's right."

"Women named Donna make excellent hostages."

"Oh, I don't know. It sounds extremely dangerous."

"Well then, I guess I'll just have to make it worth your while."

"You're a convincing pitchman, Mr. Phantom," Carmen said with a smile. "Very convincing." She traced a lazy curve from his chest to his navel with two of her fingers. "I suppose I could don the black wig one more time."

The Black Phantom turned to her with a wry smile and let out a deep, hearty laugh that made his chest rise and fall like the bellows of a great machine.

"No need to disguise yourself this time, love. Let him drink in your natural beauty."

CHAPTER 17

T he street was clear and bright, some of the trees devoid of their foliage, others aflame in their brief autumn mantle. Every house seemed carefully placed for maximum aesthetic effect. A photographer could have made the scene into a cover photo for a real estate brochure without much effort, Max Brindle mused as he turned with a smile and walked up the concrete steps to the front door of the house he'd come looking for. He rang the bell and waited several moments, checked his watch, and gave three loud raps on the door.

A woman's voice from inside hollered, "All right, keep your goddamn nuts in a cup. I'm coming."

The door swung inward and before him stood a woman in her fifties, wearing a conservative dress, her hair pulled back in a graying ponytail.

"That's quite a jacket," the woman said with a sneer. "What are you selling?"

Max had heard them all: fat jokes, digs about his clothes, quips about stature. And though he tightened inside at any kind of insult, he had mastered the art of pretending it was all so much rain in a tempest. Fuck 'em all. That was his guiding principle. His revenge was exacted in the very line of work he attached himself to. Perhaps this homely woman before him would one day find herself murdered at the hands of terrorists. Not only was Max okay with that; he took comfort in the idea.

"Not selling anything, ma'am." He smiled broadly. "Just hoping to find an associate of mine."

"Nobody here but you and me."

She was chewing gum. He detested the habit.

"Ah, is Mr. Cafferty out at the moment?" he asked.

"*Mr.* Cafferty. You mean Jerrod?"

"Yes, that's right. Do you know when he'll be back?"

"I don't know how far you've come, mister, but you're on a fool's errand. Ain't no Mr. Cafferty no more." She said the name in a mocking way. "Hasn't been for several years now. Who the hell are *you* anyway, if I might ask?"

Max had on his tan porkpie hat, which he removed briefly so he could rub his thinning pate.

"Ma'am, this is likely a simple case of mistaken identity. It's not that uncommon a name, after all. See, I'm in shipping. The name's Max Brindle, and I've got a fairly new man working for me. Goes by the name of Jerrod Cafferty. Just to settle my curiosity, could you tell me what happened to *your* Mr. Cafferty?"

She tilted her head to one side and looked him up and down, blowing a small bubble that popped loudly.

"I'm his sister, Isabelle. He left this place to me in his will. Good thing he'd thought to draw one up, too. Wasn't but a couple years older than me. Got murdered in his sleep. Hacked to death with a fucking axe. Are there any more details you'd care to hear about *my* Jerrod Cafferty, Mr. Brindle?"

He replaced the hat and did his best to look recalcitrant. "No, ma'am. No, I think that pretty much clears it up. I'm sorry to bother you."

"Well, you enjoy what Lansing has to offer while you're here."

She didn't quite slam the door, but it closed with enough force to send the same message.

Max turned around on the porch to survey the neighborhood. Middle class America all the way. Neatly trimmed parking strips ran along both sides of the street. Most houses appeared to have been built in the forties and fifties. Not a wealthy neighborhood, but a comfortable one. He wondered if the real Jerrod Cafferty had been murdered in the house at his back.

He also wondered who the fuck he'd met on the Texas

Eagle.

It wouldn't require a private detective to find out, as it happened. The man he thought was Jerrod Cafferty had called him two days ago, surprising Max, who would have bet the farm on having to be the one to pick up the phone, or show up out of the blue, to resume their negotiations. But Jerrod had gone for the bait and wanted to take on some work for Brindle. The trip to Michigan was no big deal for Max. The Texas Eagle had taken him as far as Chicago. There he transferred to the Blue Water, which took him directly to East Lansing. He would have been on one train or another anyway. Why not drop in on Lansing to see what he could learn about his new hire, maybe even make contact.

Not much would have surprised him. When you start nosing around in someone's life—*anyone's* life—dirt of some kind is bound to turn up. But the false identity caught him off guard. It gave his young train traveler some depth. A fed, maybe. Brindle could have misjudged his age some. Hell, the older he got, the younger *everyone* seemed. On an Amtrak train, though? Not the most efficient way to get around if you're doing Bureau work. Besides, there was a careless feel to the way things were shaping up, like the kid's involvement was personal. Max trusted his instincts about such things and quickly convinced himself that if the kid fell to one side or the other of the legal straight and narrow, it was to the criminal side. That was good, but he'd feel a hell of lot better about things if he knew how far he could trust the mysterious fellow. Forget about trust. What were the man's strengths and weaknesses? What did he know? What was he hiding?

Max fished his digital camera out of his sport coat pocket and took a snap of picturesque Wainwright Avenue for posterity before returning to the red Mitsubishi Lancer he'd rented near the depot.

But he wasn't quite ready to leave the Cafferty residence behind. There were a few niggling loose ends that he fully intended to tie in a bow before putting Wainwright Avenue and

Lansing, Michigan, behind him. Why had the young man he met on an Amtrak train bound for Los Angeles taken as an alias the name of a victim of a brutal murder? And why would he want his luggage returned to the address of the real Jerrod Cafferty if it were to go missing? The address couldn't have been any clearer on the picture Max had taken of the man's baggage tag. And then there was the question of who the hell had murdered Isabelle Cafferty's brother with an axe. You had to want someone to suffer as badly as you wanted them dead in order to do it with a fucking axe, the way Max figured it.

He pulled away from the curb and drove down the street, but only so he could turn at the first intersection and double back through the alley that ran behind the house. Sooner or later, either Isabelle would leave or the imitation Jerrod Cafferty would return. If there was one thing that decades of riding the rails had instilled in Max Brindle, it was patience. Finding the ideal parking spot between a ramshackle garage and a wall of juniper, he settled in to watch and wait. It would be almost impossible for anyone to walk to the front porch from the sidewalk—or walk away from the front door to the street—without being seen from his angle of vision. And of course he had the back entrance completely covered. He was prepared for any eventuality.

Boredom quickly set in: an occupational hazard. He did his best to make his line of work look exciting, especially when trying to get laid or silver-tongue an impressionable youth into giving up his life for the cause of senseless destruction, but he spent far more of his time watching the world pass him by than he did chasing down adventure. He was after the golden egg, of course. The gig that would set him up for life. The kind of boredom that came from having more than you needed was a very different kettle of fish than the boredom that had its roots in stakeouts and interminable train rides.

Italy had been a break in the doldrums. It seemed like a lifetime ago now. Max had gone there on official business. A shipping contract with the world's third largest producer of plastic hangers, among other household items, was about to ex-pire, and he had wanted to see to it personally that he didn't end up losing a client in the process of renewing. The hangers were made in China and Indonesia, but the woman who signed the checks—and contracts—had a vacation home outside of Florence. She had no idea that among the closet-organizers and kitchen shelf-helpers that occupied one of the shipping con-tainers en route to Germany was tucked a smattering of human cargo. Not refugees or victims of trafficking, but trained guer-rillas, ready for the commands, and arms, they would receive in Berlin.

The scrape of boots on rough pavement startled him out of his reverie. A man wearing blue jeans and a rust-colored windbreaker walked along the passenger side of Max's rental car. The stranger hewed too close to the vehicle for Max to get a look at his face or hair, almost like he was keeping himself hid-den on purpose.

Gaining the front of the car, the man came into full view, but before Max could react or positively identify him as Jerrod, he quickly spun around and aimed the index fingers of both hands directly at Max, as if they were two separate guns.

"Bang!" Jerrod shouted with an outward thrust of his chin, followed by a slightly sinister grin.

Max could hear him loud and clear through the open win-dows of the vehicle.

"You sonofabitch." Max pulled himself out of the car to face his newest business associate. His breath was short and a little labored from the surge of adrenaline to his heart. "You get points for stealth, son. I'll give you that. And you keep an eye on your surroundings. That puts you several lengths ahead of the average person."

"I hope the firm has more challenging obstacles to throw in my path, frankly, but I accept the compliment."

Keep an eye on this one, Max Brindle, he said to himself. *Do keep a razor-sharp eye on this little laddie.*

"What brings you here so soon after our chat on the

phone?" Jerrod asked.

Max had hoped to avoid a confrontation, at least until after he'd had a chance to rummage around inside the house.

"What do I need to do, run a background check on you? Make sure, you're not on the wrong side of the law? Or maybe you figured I'd call you in for a second interview, in front of a panel of managers this time."

"No, I don't suppose. Still, you're awful quick on the draw. Smells a little desperate."

"I need a good man. Maybe that's you. If not, I'll find another, but that'll take time. I'd rather it be you."

"Okay."

They stared at each other with grins meant to impart more confidence and knowledge than either of them possessed.

"There's a saying in my line of work," Max said.

"Oh? What's that?"

"Conducting business in an alley is a sure-fire way to draw unwanted attention to yourself, especially when there's a perfectly good domicile to converse in not thirty feet away."

"It's a little clunky, but it rings true enough."

"Damn, I like you," Max said with a slight laugh, placing a hand on Jerrod's shoulder and urging him toward the back door of the house. "I don't want to, but I can't help it. You're a likeable guy."

"And you're a sharp dresser."

They walked in silence the rest of the way to a set of concrete steps that led down to a basement door. Jerrod let them in.

"I don't have anything to offer you." Jerrod unfolded a beat-up metal chair for his guest and sat down on the edge of a bed.

"Nothing required, son. This won't take long. You'll meet up with a colleague of mine in Quebec. He'll put you in touch with an operation in Brussels. I'm here to give you all the information you need about your identity and the nature of the work you'll be performing."

"Whoa, tap the brakes, mister. Aren't you forgetting that

I haven't actually agreed to anything yet? I don't want to know another goddamn thing until you've convinced me this is worth doing."

"You refer to money, of course."

"Sure, that's part of it. But if I'm going to go through with this and take on God-knows-what for you, I'll need other re-assurances as well."

"Ah, that's a good word. *Reassurances*. A very good word. A very *apt* word. I could use something in that line myself, as it turns out."

"Could you?"

"Indubitably. Take your name, for instance. Jerrod Caff-erty. It's a good name ... for someone who's been murdered with an axe."

Jerrod rose and stared hard at Max.

"Let's get something straight, Mr. Brindle. I don't like games. I can take just about anything you throw at me, so spare me the bullshit. If my name's a problem for you—"

Max shook his hands at Jerrod. "Now settle down. Jesus, you'd think I insulted your mother or something. I don't need to know your life story, but I like to know who the hell's working for me. More importantly, I like to know *that* they're working for me. Understand? Not *against* me, in other words."

"That makes some sense. And you know how you find out? You ask me straightforward questions, and I give you straightforward answers. I'm in no position to make demands. I know that. I need money, and you have a job. That makes you the boss. I'm cool with that. But I won't be fucked around. Are we clear on *that*?"

"Why don't you sit back down. We got off on the wrong foot here."

"Yeah, that's the truth." Jerrod slowly took a seat.

"My fault," Brindle said with an acquiescent shrug. "I should have played it straight with you. I see that now.

"It's the only goddamn thing I ask."

"Look, I run into a lot of different types in my line of

work. They can't all be handled the same way."

"Fine. And I have a temper. It serves me okay a lot of the time. It can serve you well, too. I do have a little unfinished business of my own, though. I want to tie that off before taking on anything new. Until then, my name is Jerrod Cafferty. After that it can be anything you like. Once I'm yours, I'm yours all the way."

"I don't mean to pry, son, but what kind of business are you talking about? Maybe you could use a little help. I take care of my people."

"This is personal. The butcher who took the life of my namesake also killed *my* brother. I intend to have my revenge."

"I see. Your pound of flesh. That it?"

Jerrod shrugged.

"It certainly puts things in perspective, and I'm sorry for your loss." Shows of compassion had never been one of Max's strengths, but they had their uses.

"That's what you call playing it straight with me? You're sorry for my fucking loss?"

"Okay, okay. But I do sympathize. How did he do your brother, if you don't mind my asking?"

"How else? He chopped him up with a hatchet. Has the Butcher ever done it any other way?"

"The Butcher?"

"Yeah, the Butcher. The Portable Nine, man. You sure you're part of the international crime scene?"

"You're telling me they actually exist, the Portable Nine? I thought they were a myth."

"Nothing mythical about how my brother was killed."

"I didn't mean—"

"Trust me, they're real. The Butcher, Davenport … Miranda Gissing. All of them. They're real, all right."

Davenport. He felt like excusing himself so he could pound his damn fool head against the nearest brick wall for a few minutes. The man in Florence. The man he'd run into twice in the same day and who called himself Davenport and wore a leather fedora. What was more likely, that their meeting—*twice*—had been a coincidence, or that a member of the Portable Nine had intentionally made contact with little old Max Brindle? But for what purpose? Neither encounter had come to anything.

"Did your brain freeze up or something?" Jerrod asked. "What's the prob?"

"It's just ... To think, I'm sitting with someone who knows them to exist ... By God, I know how to pick my people." He rubbed at his mouth and chin.

"Maybe I should ask for a pay raise."

"Jerrod—or whatever your name is—say the word if I can help with your problem. I'm happy to hasten your availability."

"You'd also like to see your name engraved on the Butcher's tombstone."

"Well ..." Max gave a demure smile.

"I tracked the Butcher to Los Angeles. That's where I was headed when you bumped into me on the train. I was too late. He had already split. Every time he makes a move, it's like starting over trying to pick up his scent again. So here I am. Back in Michigan, regrouping. I think he's either in Seattle or Tokyo. Once I zero in on a convincing reason for him to be in one of those two locations over the other, I'll book myself a flight."

"You seem to have a good nose for this."

"My nose is all right, but you can only do so much from a distance. If I can get myself in the same city as him, at the same time, his days are numbered. So far, that hasn't happened. He's a brutal sonofabitch, but he's crafty. That's the Portable Nine for you, from what I hear. Smart and ruthless. Those are the two biggest requirements."

"If half the stories are true, loyalty must be pretty high on the list, too."

"Yeah, I'm guessing there are more than a few qualities listed on the résumé of a Portable."

"Wanted: a self-starter."

"Must be highly intelligent and morally ambiguous."

"Desired: experience committing murder, without getting caught and with a sense of moral superiority."

They shared a laugh over that.

"I'll tell you what, son," Max said. "I'm going to extend my booking at the Ramada Inn. You get this bastard pinned down and give me a call. We'll go after him together."

"The Ramada in East Lansing? What a shithole. Jesus, that doesn't give me much hope for my starting salary."

"My boss is careful where he puts his hard-earned cash. He'd rather spend it on good people than fancy hotels. Along those lines, you have the resources you need for your ... errand?"

"Happy to lighten your wallet."

"I don't have it on me, hotshot, but I could get my hands on an advance if I have to."

"Sounds like a delay to me. I'm okay for now." He nodded at the ceiling. "Isabelle's got some money, and she's happy to put it toward revenge against the man who took out her brother."

"Jerrod, the man I work for ... He's not a patient man. And he's not as fair minded as me."

Jerrod licked his lips, as if they'd gone suddenly dry.

"I think you and I are going to get on just fine, but I don't want you thinking you'll be pals with him. He'll trust you only as deep as he can push you into the ground."

"Cool. Message received." Jerrod stood and clapped his thighs. "Look, Max, I need to tend to some things."

Isabelle crossed the room directly above their heads and left through the front door, as if punctuating the end of Max's visit with Jerrod.

"Don't go spoiling yourself with those luxury accommodations." Jerrod smiled. "I'll bet they even have free color TV."

"Yeah, well, amenities cost money," Max said as he stood up.

"Not all of them. Maybe you'll hook up with some East Lansing floozy and settle in for a night of smack-and-giggle."

Max chuckled. "Maybe so. Keep in touch. If I don't hear from you soon, I'll be back."

"You make it sound like a threat."

It was the kind of exit Max loved. He wasn't what you'd call an imposing figure and he knew it. As a result, he seldom missed an opportunity to strike a little fear in the heart of an adversary. And that's what Jerrod was, at least for the time being. A soon-to-be business associate, yes. But also an adversary. There were no friendships in the criminal underworld, at least not when you were a player on the world stage.

And so Max Brindle folded up the chair he'd been occupying, returned it to its place against the wall, and left Jerrod Cafferty to himself without uttering a word in response to the young man's lingering comment. His smile was all teeth as he returned to the rental car.

CHAPTER 18

E l Pozo. The Pit. It was the only name for the place that he would recognize and accept. Most men would have spent their lives trying to purge all memory of the place from their minds. This was not the Black Phantom's way. He looked back on el Pozo as a beast he had defeated. He was proud to have survived the prison. Not many could claim such a distinction. El Pozo swallowed men whole and expectorated their drained husks, if it didn't kill them outright. In other words, it was a vampire, and so the Phantom had escaped the clutches of the Nosferatu with his faculties intact and proven himself mightier than a creature of the night.

But in his dreams he wasn't always strong. Even though he usually knew when he was dreaming—like now—that sense of weakness was the first indication that he was in a nightmare. He walked through a sludge of darkness, the only discernible source of light a mere off-white blur far ahead. Laughter surrounded him, a constant, sardonic companion on his nightmare travels. Impossibly low in pitch. The devil's laugh. His father's laugh.

He had halved the distance to the light source before he recognized it as *el Pozo*. Now the terror gripped him in earnest. Why would he return to the Pit of his own volition? It was mad, yet his attempts at resistance were met with louder laughter and an increased pace. The prison now seemed to be rolling toward him as *he* continued to move forward, and soon Caracas herself spread like a diseased smile in the background beyond the prison walls. He stopped moving his legs, but it was no use. Something pushed him on. Something with far greater strength than his own.

The particulars of these dreams varied, but the theme was always the same. All of his progress since breaking out of *el Pozo* was a mirage. He hadn't left the cesspool behind. Instead, his path was leading him directly back to its corrupting embrace.

The main gate swung open with the haunted creak of long neglect, and a cloud of stench roiled toward him.

"*NOOOOOOOOOOOOOOOOOOOOOOO!!!!!!!!!!!!!!!!!!!!!!!*" his dream-self screamed as the noxious cloud filled his lungs and threatened to suffocate him.

He couldn't be sure, but he suspected he had *actually* screamed, startling himself awake. His breathing labored and his heart rate elevated, he sat up in the bed, half covered with a thin sheet. A desert breeze drifted in through an open window, along with a wash of moonlight. The solitude was a gloved hand around his throat. It's how he had wanted it. With construction complete, he'd ordered the crew back to Marrakesh to await further instruction. But he could have used a warm body beside him just then, or at least someone to call to in the other room. The plan had been to spend the next few days on his own, gathering his thoughts, but now he wondered if the morning wouldn't be as good a time as any to drive the borrowed SUV back to Marrakesh. He wouldn't have to inform the others of his arrival immediately, but at least he'd be poised to act when the time was right.

The sand-dusted floorboards beneath his bare feet were cool as he crossed the room to look out over the ranging Algerian desert. The new structure was out of sight beyond several nearby dunes, but its presence in the desert was so strong it was as if he could see it. Many games had been played over the years, many of them by a group of do-gooders he was fast losing patience with. If they weren't foiling his own plans directly, it seemed, they were working to thwart the efforts of someone he was at least indirectly involved with. They had gone into a kind of dormancy in recent years, but the Black Phantom never believed for a moment that they had retired. He knew his path would cross theirs one day, and now the intimation was strong that such a crossing had begun. Davenport was getting too close for comfort. He was, frankly, becoming a problem. He would have the support of the others by now, with a couple of notable exceptions.

In fact, the Black Phantom had taken a second call from the good Dr. Intaglio before leaving his Trujillo base for the wilds of Morocco and beyond. Bonnet's phone, according to the doctor, was bugged, just like Intaglio's. He had not been able to check the others yet. Still, there was a decent chance that Davenport was on to the Black Phantom's moles, or at least suspicious.

Well, he had something to show the nine of them, Dr. Intaglio and Bonnet included, and he would bring them to the desert to do so. It was time to finish the Portable Nine's influence in the world. Time to show the world who occupied the throne of the underworld.

CHAPTER 19

"The way I see it, Davenport has this thing about halfway to where it ought to be." Robin Varnesse's English-tinged accent and sharp suit cut like a thin razor in the crisp air as he strode along the Ballard Locks.

The Butcher walked on his left, dwarfing his stature. Abel Hazard, sporting his trademark red-checkered flannel shirt, blue jeans, and work boots, kept up on his right, quiet and attentive as always. A cigarette hung from Twitch Markham's lips, which may have been part of the reason he kept himself off to one side, but he was also a loner, and difficult to peg. Robin knew better than to draw the curtain open too far on the man, though. Not a single one of the Portable Nine was likely to win a social-aptitude prize any time soon.

"What do you mean?" Twitch threw a wide-eyed glance at him, then resumed a nervous tic of alternating his gaze between the ground at his feet and the Salmon Bay Bridge in the distance.

"I get that the bank job on Cloft Industries was a ruse," Robin explained, "but he's not thinking large enough here. I say we can pull this heist and make off with a pretty nice haul. Maybe not as nice as Davenport's rose-colored version, but nice. Then we go after the Phantom. It's risky, but we're no strangers to risk."

"It's gangster shit," the Butcher mumbled. "Davenport wants us to move on the Phantom. I say that's what we do."

"I'm not suggesting anything different, just something to do while we're biding our time. Look, Davenport's fairy tale amounted to larceny. I say we nudge it into the realm of a hostile takeover. We were prepared to collect all this dirt on Archie Cloft's money man. Why not do it for real and use it as a way into Cloft's inner circle? If one of his financial advisors can be extorted, surely the man himself has a skeleton or two that we can exploit."

"Man, I don't know," Twitch said. "Don't you think that's —"

"In keeping with the reputation the Portable Nine have fought tooth and nail to establish? Yes, yes I do."

"I think it's a fine idea," said Abel. "We get our cake and eat it, too. We're going to need money."

The Butcher grunted.

"And how do you plan to sell this to Davenport, exactly?" Twitch said. "We're not a goddamn democracy, you know."

"I think he'll come around to our way of thinking." Robin didn't look at Twitch as he spoke. "The biggest problem he'll see is that it might keep us all in the Seattle area a little longer than planned. A lot depends on chance. That puts us at a higher risk than if we were more spread out. But if we can manage to turn Cloft Industries into some kind of base of operations through which we can funnel money and have access to all manner of resources, surely it's worth the heightened level of risk in the short term."

"The whole purpose of the made-up scheme was to allow us to retire." The Butcher led the group to a picnic table in a small park they had wandered into and they all took a seat. "I guess this would keep things moving in that direction."

"Sure," said Abel. "It's just taking a longer view. Instead of being the perennial hired guns, maybe we could start calling the shots for a change. I think it makes some sense."

"No offense," said Twitch, "but I don't think your vote counts as much as the rest of ours. You've got no fear, so you've got no sense of danger. No sense of right or wrong."

Abel leaned in close to Twitch. "It also means I've got no compunction about a whole raft of activities, so bear that in mind, little hummingbird. And as for a sense of morality ... Well, come at me when you're truly curious and not just petrified by the thought of ending your own inaction. Maybe I can enlighten you." An Australian accent had crept into his voice. The recent acquisition seemed to come and go.

"Boys, let's drop it." The Butcher's baritone command silenced the others immediately. "If we're going to put this to Davenport, the less time we waste, the better. He'll appreciate that, which could work in our favor. I say we catch a cab back to the hotel and ring him up."

Robin removed a writing tablet from an inside pocket, along with a pen, and set to scribbling out a note. The others eyed each other but said nothing.

"Say, that's a good idea." He tore a sheet from the pad. "Why don't you hail us a cab." He quickly started in on a second note. Both notes finished, he used a hand to cover one of the pockets of his suit jacket and whispered, "There's a bug sewn into my jacket pocket. I've been rubbing my arm against it to mask our conversation as much as possible, but I have to lose the jacket. Davenport already knows about it. Three guesses who put a bug on me, by the way."

The Butcher stood like a giant, staring at the steel train trestle known as the Salmon Bay Bridge. It was a bascule trestle, open most of the time to allow ships and yachts of all sizes to move through the locks as efficiently as possible. To Robin Varnesse it seemed as though the only thing stopping the Butcher from hopping on a train and ditching the whole Portable Nine reunion was the fact that the bridge was up, which meant there wouldn't be a train any time soon. As if in resignation to the fact, the seasoned hatchet man turned away from the bridge and his band of reluctant righters of wrongs and made off in the direction of Fifty-Fourth Street. Presumably he would fetch them a taxi, but it was hard to tell with the Butcher. Maybe he'd just keep on walking and never be heard from again.

Abel Hazard rubbed one of his sideburns with the back of his hand, as if coaxing out the gumption to say what had to be said. His screwed-up face supported the idea of some kind of internal struggle, but nothing came. They all enjoyed an uneasy silence as the sun broke out of character to shine a little light on their table, and a small clutch of birds erupted from the ash tree overhead. Soon the Butcher called to them that their chariot awaited.

"Hello," Robin said as he approached the driver's window and handed both of the notes he'd written to the man behind the wheel, promptly following up by pressing a finger to his lips in a hushing gesture. He read along silently over the cabbie's shoulder.

> *My jacket has been bugged. You will take it to the Regal Hotel and deliver it to the front desk. Hand the clerk the second note, which includes similar instructions. Most importantly, ignore everything you're about to hear from us. And kindly burn this note at your earliest convenience.*

He dropped a hundred-dollar bill in the man's lap and said, "So, do you have time to drive four very tired men down to the Regal?"

"Uh, yeah. I guess I could do that. It'll be a little tight. One of you can sit up front, of course."

"Sounds good—" Robin glanced at the man's identification card, which was affixed to the dashboard and featured the same neatly folded blue turban he was currently wearing. "—Ashar. We'll probably nap the whole way anyway. If there's still a decent hard rock station in this town, crank it up. That shit's like a lullaby to me." He peeled off his jacket and tossed it onto the backseat, being sure to open and close the door as loudly as possible. Twitch picked up on the ruse and went around to do the same with the two doors on the other side of the cab.

"You got it, boss," Ashar said, dutifully tuning the radio to KISW, which an instantly obnoxious deejay informed anyone within earshot was at 99.9 megahertz on the radio dial.

Robin gave the driver the okay sign and watched him turn

his Orange Cab around and send it flying down the road. Strains of "Sweet Child o' Mine" drifted from the cab, warped a little by the car's increasing distance. *About time for a* classic *hard rock station*, Robin thought, feeling a little old.

"This is a new path for the Portable Nine," Abel said as they strolled in the direction the taxi had just gone off in. "Or should I say for the Portable Seven? We've never turned on our own before."

"They turned on us first," Twitch was quick to point out.

"True enough," said Abel, "but there is one fact that none of this changes. Unity is our greatest strength. We're nothing scattered to the winds.

"Twitch, it's a miracle Davenport was able to find more than the moldering remnants of you. Your heart's never been in this line of work. I'm amazed you didn't just dry up on your own and roll away with the tumbleweeds."

"At least I know which side of the fence the tumbleweeds gather on." Twitch sounded a little hot under the collar. "I've seen the Devil. Stared him straight in the eye, and he told me I was his, all because of an accident."

"Yes, we all know the story, mate." Abel snickered. "Approached you at a well, did he?"

"He did."

"Probably near a crossroads and everything. You'd killed a girl with a blow to the head using an aluminum baseball bat, as I recall."

"Look, this isn't—"

"An accident, like you say. No need to get all red in the face. Still, the Devil wanted your soul for the deed, the bastard. Well, he got it, one way or the other, didn't he?"

"Dammit, I swear to God I'll—"

Twitch threw a wobbly punch in the direction of Abel's jaw, but Robin was prepared for violence, as always, and he snatched the man's fist out of the air with little effort. No doubt Twitch wanted to respond with a good many things, but Abel's words had cut close to the truth, Robin could see. It must have been the very question, relentless and vexing, that pursued the nervous man every day: *Am I already damned, or am I still one indecent act away from ruin?* Maybe he wondered if it even mattered anymore, as addicted as he was to taking the shortest distance between himself and the next sure thing.

His cigarette discarded, Twitch chewed at his fingers and stared at the ground as they walked on.

"Let's add compassion to the agenda when we get around to discussing morality," Robin said to Abel.

"And then we've got our local Butcher here," Abel went on, ignoring the barb. "Surely you're our biggest liability. My God, the risks you take. That business in L.A. ... That was you, yeah?"

The Butcher grunted and thrust out his chin.

"How we've managed to retain your loyalty is anyone's guess. It's a lust for blood that keeps you going. But you're just smart enough to recognize the strength of numbers, I guess."

"I'm sorry, could you remind me who died and made you pontiff?" Robin asked, getting a little worked up himself.

"And you," Abel shot back. "You were *so* close to having the world in the palm of your hand. You must have been on the verge of selling high and retiring to the tropics. I mean, nothing against the Isle of Man. It's probably more your style anyway. At any rate, things started to collapse around you, like an avalanche of dominoes, before you could so much as pull your fist out of the cookie jar."

Two young women with expensive bags and designer tops crossed the street to avoid having to pass by the unruly men. *Wise*, Robin thought.

"But you learned from your mistakes," Abel continued, "and your financial wizardry has been of undeniable importance to the work we've done. If anyone's going to suffer the slings and arrows of a fiscal landslide, it's generally in your power to see that it's the fellow on the other end of the stick."

Glad to be on the receiving end of a compliment, even a back-handed one, Robin let down his guard somewhat. "And I do my best to make sure the money is fairly redistributed in such cases."

"Oh, yes. It's a wonder you haven't had your surname legally changed to Hood."

"Look, is there a point to all of this?" the Butcher asked. "You're a fearless psychopath with no amygdala and no conscience. There, we've cleared up each other's shortcomings. Can we shut the fuck up for five minutes?"

"Huh. The anvil calls the anchor heavy," said Abel. "Look, all I'm saying is that we need each other if we're going to make a success of this. And I believe there's sense in taking out the Black Phantom. He's been growing in strength and arrogance for years. The world will never be a fairyland, but it will damn sure be a better place without him in it. Besides, I also believe in Davenport. We've had our failures, but never because of any lack of judgment on his part. Danger comes with the territory. We put ourselves on the line by signing up for this kind of work. That doesn't make him responsible when things go wrong. There are plenty of things that could have gone wrong but *didn't* because of his sharp eye and decisiveness.

"And I want to make one thing clear once and for all." He stopped walking and turned to face the others. "You all know about my little surgery. Well just because I harbor no fear doesn't mean that I'm a stranger to morality. In fact, maybe my compassion for others is more pure *because* of my fearless existence. I won't avoid harm out of worry or concern for my own well-being, but I will out of concern for others."

"I'd like an example of that," Twitch said with a sneer.

"Okay, condoms."

"What?" Robin said.

"You know, prophylactics. Hey, he asked. It's what springs to mind. I always wear a rubber when I have sex. I don't fear disease or bringing a child into the world, but my partners might. I respect that. It would be wrong to do otherwise. But as you know, when it comes to business, I assess everything with the cold eye of reason. And if I find you culpable, abandon all hope."

Robin nodded. "Yeah, I've seen that shit in action. No lie. We do get it done, don't we?" He smiled despite himself.

"You're damn right," Abel said. "And whether we're nine in number or seven, we will continue to get it done."

Robin fished the cell phone that Davenport had given him from a pocket and tapped a speed-dial sequence into it. All were silent as they continued their walk into the heart of Seattle's Ballard neighborhood.

"Davenport," said the voice on the other end.

"Varnesse here. The jacket I told you about is on its way back to the hotel for you to finish with."

"Okay," Davenport said. "I suggest you use the time it affords you wisely. I don't need to tell you we're running blind on this. We'll take what we can get, and right now that's a sliver of time."

"Right. We'll put our heads together and report back."

"Robin, I'm pretty sure that Intaglio and Bonnet have set up their own little hideout. I think Bonnet is still giving us the benefit of the doubt, but I'm afraid we've lost Intaglio. Follow the tracking device I placed under his rental car. Something will come of it eventually. Either you or Lovinia are bound to ferret out their schemes."

"Lovinia? What's she up to?"

"Oh, just a little ... detective work. Kind of like you, but she's a little more undercover."

"Okay, good enough for me, boss."

Robin slid the phone back into his pocket, but silence reigned among the four outcasts of fortune. Into the hipster thicket of downtown Ballard they forged. The neighborhood had fallen victim to the same kind of predictable gentrification that was gutting the character of every city in America. Maybe they were so quiet now in part because the pointless commotion everywhere they turned had them wondering what it was they were bothering to fight for anymore. Or maybe, like Robin, they were all a little envious of the ignorant horde of shoppers and wine alcoholics. It was also possible, he had to concede, that they had simply had their fill of chitchat and were ready for action.

CHAPTER 20

"**R**obin," Davenport said to the twenty-something clerk with a wink, which she returned, handing him a suit coat over the counter. Bonnie, her name tag read. Cute smile, but also a hint of depth that suggested she was slightly overqualified for the job. He hoped so. "Jesus, are you all right? You don't look well. Robin, watch out!"

"Oh, shit," Bonnie added, playing her role to suitable effect. "That's going to stain."

"The least of our worries," Davenport said. "Robin, snap out of it. Did you go on a day bender, or what?"

He rubbed his hand violently against the jacket pocket, where Robin's note to the hotel clerk had indicated Intaglio's bug had been sewn in.

The clerk walked briskly to one end of the counter and loudly knocked over a metal pitcher of ice water.

Nice touch, Davenport thought.

"That tears it. This whole suit is going to need to be dry-cleaned. Miss, can you take the jacket. I'll get him up to his room and send the rest of his clothes down."

"Certainly," she responded with another wink. He wasn't so sure this one meant only that she understood her part in the ruse.

He gave a brisk nod as he slid a fifty-dollar bill across to her, then turned in the direction of the coffee service across the opulent lobby.

The coffee was good. Dark and rich. He held the cup under his nose and closed his eyes. The aroma became a fog, but not one that concealed or obfuscated. Instead it transported him to a distant time and place. Crete, 2006. Not his most auspicious hour under God's yellow sun, but one that would put him on a path to earning a reputation—and nickname—to last a life-time. He'd been staying with his aunt. His first visit in over a year. They spent the days wandering the picturesque streets of Chania, but the evenings were filled with wine and song in the comfort of Aunt Meredith's rooms. He would sit at the piano, perfectly situated in a recessed nook. His aunt had a flare for simple but tasteful decorating, a quality he'd admired from boyhood. Bach had still flowed from his fingertips then, both hands working in unison to communicate the urgent and beau-tiful mathematics of what must have been the composer's deep-est thoughts: devotion to his God.

But one of the nights during that two-week visit, every-thing had changed. The thief might have come and gone un-detected, but he knocked a clay pot onto the floor on his way back out onto the balcony. It shattered into a dozen pieces, waking Davenport instantly. Without stopping to check on his aunt, he lunged into the main room in time to see the bandit crawling over the balcony's railing in an effort to regain the nar-row alleyway that wound below and make his getaway.

"Connor!" he heard someone exclaim in a strained whis-per. In the stillness of a Cretan summer night, the voice cut through the air like a blade. "Did you get it?"

Davenport hung from the second story balcony, closed his eyes and dropped. His legs took the fall better than he'd feared. A flare of sharp pain shot through both knees, but he stayed upright. When he looked up the street, away from the faint moon glow off the Mediterranean, he saw the bastard—Connor—spin off into a tight little patch of darkness. He fol-lowed with as much celerity as he could muster.

Which proved unnecessary, for both Connor and his look-out waited for him in the shadows. So did their fists. And boots. And then came the chain.

It caught him on the chin first, knocking him to the

cobblestones, where he rested on all fours, listening to blood drip from his face. His breathing grew labored from anger and fear. A kick to the ribcage turned him over, laying him out, supine and vulnerable. This time he saw the chain coming. Several revolutions were wrapped around the larger man's wrist, which left a good two feet of business end. It came down like a whip on his left hand. He thought of the pot the thief had shattered in his aunt's living room. From the pain that erupted, he imagined that his hand had just suffered a similar fate.

The last he saw of the duo was them running off into ever deepening shadows. The chain dangled at the side of its wearer. What could only have been Davenport's aunt's jewelry box was tucked firmly under the arm of Connor the thief. The sound of the clinking chain hung in the air long after they were out of sight.

Maybe Davenport would have been able to let the burglary go, but the idea that these thugs had cased her home and returned to pull the small-time heist ...

Connor! Did you get it?

Well, that would have been enough to urge him to some kind of action. When he discovered the state of his hand, however, the flower of vengeance bloomed like a time-lapse video in his breast. If he could find them both, great. But he would settle for Connor. He began a series of inquires that very morning, after some kindly ministrations from his aunt, who had been horrified to learn that he went after the culprit, even before she saw the extent of the damage to his hand.

"The value was sentimental, mostly," she'd assured him. "They'll be sorely disappointed if they're expecting to retire on what they hauled out of this old place. But your hand ..."

He'd run some small-time errands before tracking Connor —and his muscle, as it happens—to Malta. He cornered the thief in a corner café and followed him for three days, for no more of a reason than that he wanted to wallow in the secret knowledge of the man's imminent suffering. Opportunity gave its final knock at a popular St. Julian's dance club. While the crowd sweated it out on the strobe-lit dance floor, music thumping from ubiquitous speakers, Davenport approached his target and tapped him on the shoulder.

Connor wore a stunned, stupid expression. Davenport only smiled.

"Where's your friend?" Davenport asked, leaning in to be heard over the bass-heavy music.

"Who the fuck are you?"

Davenport held up his left hand.

"You see this? It's a constant reminder of what's been taken from me."

Connor's eyes darted from the crippled appendage to Davenport's glare. Back and forth. Over and over.

"And you see this?" With his good hand he brought his trusty King Cobra out to play. "This reminds me that no one will ever take from me so easily again."

The crowd parted as if Davenport were a drop of oil that had just fallen into a puddle of water.

"I only asked about your friend to get your attention. I know where he is. Ran into him in the men's room. He's still there. Lying in his own blood. Threatened to kill me when I asked him if he still needs the protection of a chain when he fights. So I shot him in the chest. But I think it was the head shot that did him in."

Connor showed his true colors by turning on his heels and running for the nearest exit.

Davenport put a slug in his ankle, dropping him instantly. The man turned onto his back and writhed like an upended beetle.

"I suppose the decent thing to do would be to put you out of your misery," Davenport said. "But I'm not a decent sort."

Squinting to aim, he put another bullet in Connor's crotch, causing a lake of blood to spread out beneath the man, like wings earned at a heavy cost. The man's arms shot up into the air and wagged spastically, as if he couldn't decide whether to use them to reach uselessly for the pain at his ankle or attempt to stanch the red flow from his groin. To spare him the decision, Davenport shot him once in each forearm.

Leaving Connor to bleed to death, the Mad Marksman of Malta lit a cigarette and walked away.

He might not have been half so brutal if he hadn't learned, in the course of his inquiries, that the two men were involved in the trafficking of young girls when they weren't busy stealing from vulnerable women. Mercy of any degree had seemed unconscionable in light of the discovery.

❋ ❋ ❋

"Let's not have a scene, shall we?"

Davenport held a sip of coffee in his mouth. The voice from behind him was familiar, but he couldn't quite place it. He turned to face a crisply dressed man with a severe goatee and round, frameless spectacles, his hair mostly gray with streaks of black.

He swallowed the coffee. "Gutterson."

Fear should have gripped him by the throat and squeezed the air out of him. Before him stood the man who had hired him to execute Max Brindle. There was no way it was a friendly visit. Someone wanted answers, or worse.

But Davenport didn't feel the squeeze of fear. Maybe it was the fresh trip down memory lane. Maybe it was the fire that blazed within him for retribution against the Black Phantom. Whatever the source of his confidence, he felt it with more intensity in his bones than he had for a very long time. No one had the right to question his standing in the world, even if he had shit-heeled a job for them, as he had for this man. Wrongs could be righted. Negotiations could be entered into. But Davenport's days as the chump were long behind him.

"That's all you have to say?" Gutterson looked as if his face were made of something firmer than flesh, something incapable of spreading into a smile. "I think we can coax a bit more out of you than that. Come, let's have a drink."

Without waiting to see if Davenport would follow—*knowing* that he would—Gutterson glided across the plush carpeting to the darkened hotel restaurant and lounge.

Davenport didn't want to seem too eager to heel, but before letting his recent boss fall out of sight completely, he quickly pursued him to a canopied booth along one wall. He hung his leather fedora and jacket on a brass hook on the edge of the bench and slid in across from Gutterson. In another age he would have lit a cigarette. He wanted one desperately. But of course polluting the airspace in such a manner would have been tantamount to slicing open the neck of a tiger cub in a public square these days.

"I want to know what happened," Gutterson said. "And I want to know why I haven't already heard it from you. I hired you because you're the best. That's why I've come in person."

A slender young man with a neatly kept afro materialized at their table wearing a black waiter's uniform with a red clip-on bowtie. All smiles he asked, "Can I get you gentlemen something to drink?"

"That's all you *can* get us," Gutterson said in his charmless fashion. "We're not having lunch."

Davenport was actually a little hungry and resented being spoken for, but he decided that bearing his hunger would be a greater show of strength than overriding Gutterson's order.

"A glass of Gewürztraminer for me, thanks," he said.

"I'm afraid we don't carry a Gewürztraminer. May I recommend a nice Riesling instead?"

Davenport nodded and gave a dismissive wave of his hand. At least the kid seemed to know his head from his ass. Maybe there was hope for the quality of the wine, which he was really only ordering to give Gutterson a false sense of machismo by comparison, for he was surely going to order something stiffer.

"And for you, sir?"

"Vodka on the rocks," Gutterson replied.

"Thank you. I'll be right back with those."

Both men sat in silence until he returned with their drinks.

"I should have contacted you before now." Davenport ran a finger around the rim of his wine glass. "And I would have ..."

"What the hell happened?" Gutterson stirred his vodka with his pinky, first clockwise, then counterclockwise. An expensive ring he wore on that hand clinked against the glass a couple of times.

"My goddamn gun wouldn't fire. Trouble with the timing, turns out. The damn thing jammed right when I was going to pull the job. By then I was so close to Brindle I could smell his dollar-store aftershave."

"Did he notice you?" Gutterson licked his pinky clean and took a drink.

"Of course he noticed me."

Gutterson tapped his ring against the glass. "*Notice* can mean a lot of different things."

"I was in his space, and he turned to confront me. I talked my way out of it. No big deal. But it affected me, you know? I couldn't get him out of my mind, so I tailed him. The next day I bumped into him at a café."

"He saw you again?" Alarm came into Gutterson's eyes, but also something darker.

"Yes, and again I talked my way through it. He has no idea what almost happened to him. I'm absolutely convinced of that. He marveled at the coincidence of running into me twice and that was the end of it."

Gutterson relaxed a little. "Then that brings us to the question of—"

"Why I haven't been in touch. I know." Davenport leaned in. "Look, you know of the Black Phantom?"

Gutterson's eyes went wide and he nodded slowly.

"Well, he jumped the gun a little bit. Must have got wind that I'd killed Brindle, and apparently he wasn't too happy about it."

"Dear Christ. What did he do?"

"The sonofabitch killed my aunt. Sent me a video of her apartment in Crete blowing to pieces. I was able to confirm that she was in it at the time of the explosion."

He guzzled half of his wine and Gutterson took another swallow of vodka. The burgundy wallpaper and wood paneling of the room practically screamed out to be accented by whorls of exhaled tobacco smoke. Looking across the dimly lit room, he saw that they were the only customers.

"Davenport, listen. What you've just told me makes it more important than ever to proceed with caution. I've seen what you're up to, gathering the Portable Nine together. I've been trying to figure out why. Now I guess I know. But this is bigger than the Black Phantom. Max Brindle is still out there, and the damage he can still cause the world is immense. The Phantom doesn't work in a bubble, either. He sits at the top of a hydra-headed syndicate. You chop off one head, the body lives on. We have an opportunity to dismantle a much larger racket than I was aware of, even when I hired you. A targeted assassination of the Phantom would bungle that beyond repair."

"What are you suggesting?"

"That we work together, not to eliminate the Phantom, but to capture him."

"Capture him? Then what? Torture? That's no way to get reliable information."

"Torture, hell. Losing his freedom is all the torture the Black Phantom will need to start singing like a bird. You know his past, don't you?"

"Somewhat. I know his father was imprisoned on Guadeloupe before he was born. The apple was probably already rotten before it fell from the tree, because the Phantom landed himself in Caracas for a term. But by then he already had his talons in some pretty radical pies."

"That's right. And he's proud of what he's been through, and what his father went through. But he never wants to return to that side of the bars. One of his favorite stories is that his father died a hero's death, slicing his way through a military squadron to free a close friend and spare him a trial he never could have won. Only it's complete bullshit."

"What do you mean?"

"I have it on good authority that the cause of Jacques LeGrand's death was considerably more prosaic than all that. He was napping under a Brazil nut tree when one of the nut-bearing fruits came crashing down on his skull from some hundred feet above. Caved his head in like a honeydew. Killed him instantly. You get hit by a hard, round fruit containing well over a dozen Brazil nuts at fifty miles per hour, that tends to be the outcome."

"Jesus, you're kidding me."

"A close friend of LeGrand the elder was involved. That much is true. He witnessed the whole thing."

With no warning, laughter burst forth from Gutterson's seemingly unmalleable features, but it didn't last long. He drew a folded manila envelope out of his suit jacket and laid it on the table between himself and Davenport. "Have a look."

Davenport's eyes went back and forth several times between Gutterson and the envelope. Finally he pried open the metal clasp holding down the flap and slid the contents onto the table.

"Please, a little discretion." Gutterson propped up a leather-bound folding wine list to block the papers from the view of any passersby.

For Davenport it was like watching a bad traffic accident in slow motion. He didn't want to look beyond the page on top but knew he would. Articles they were, accompanied by photographic images.

Page one: a train bomb in Barcelona. Five killed, seventeen wounded. Who knew how many of the injured ended up dying later? Judging by the picture, probably most of them. A fireball had torn open the gore-slicked carriage before him, derailed it and pitched it onto its side. Two of the heads pictured might have been connected to bodies. One certainly wasn't. It lay on a window, a comet at one end of a blood tail. Davenport turned the document upside down and lay it next to the pile.

Page two: a village burned to the ground in southeastern Syria. The stiffened bodies of charred children lined a road as far as the eye could see. Davenport assumed the lining up of victims to be the work of survivors attempting to emphasize the brutality of an attack, but the caption read, "A row of children snatched from their parents' arms lines the street, all of them burned to death after being dowsed with gasoline and set on fire." The text of the article explained that family members were forced to watch before being summarily dispatched themselves. No building in the small village remained standing.

Page three: a terrorist plot thwarted in Vancouver, British Columbia. Nine Arab students were arrested when a bomb-sniffing dog happened to detect their large-scale operation. Working out of an entire floor of art studios in a downtown high rise, the operatives had planned to level an unspecified hotel during peak tourist season. In the photo, they stood facing the camera, their hands obviously cuffed behind them. Not a hint of sentience or joy behind any pair of eyes.

"Jesus, Gutterson. How many of these are there?"

"Oh, this is just a sample. And this kind of thing is only the scorched earth the Black Phantom is happy to turn a blind eye to, or even help along whenever expedient. This kind of attack often sets the stage for a more Machiavellian scheme, usually involving profit. He was always a bad egg, and he's getting worse."

Davenport added the pages he'd looked at back to the pile, which he straightened out before returning it to the envelope.

"Okay, you have my attention. But capturing a man like the Black Phantom is a much more difficult undertaking than tracking him down and killing him. How do you expect me to pull this off? And what's in it for me?"

"I don't have much to offer you, either in the way of assistance or compensation. But you have the Portable Nine. When have the Nine ever failed when they set out to accomplish something? I could never pay you all what you're worth for this, but it could open doors for future operations. It could, in fact, get the economy flowing in the right direction again."

"You said you don't have much. Do you have anything?"

Gutterson removed a single Polaroid from another pocket in his blazer and placed it facedown before Davenport, leaving an index finger on it for a dramatic beat. Davenport turned it over and stared at the grisly close-up of a black man's face. The top of his head was either missing or bashed in. Beside him lay a large circular pod of some kind.

"What the hell is this?"

"That is a snapshot that was stolen from Pierre LeGrand's prison cell in Caracas. It's been in my possession for several months now. When it comes to the Black Phantom, any personal article is of potential interest, so when I saw an opportunity to own a photograph that must have been important to him in some way ..."

"I'll be damned," Davenport said, sliding the Polaroid back toward Gutterson. "It's proof of how his father truly died."

"Well, I don't know if I'd go so far as to say proof. But almost certainly a weapon that can be used against the Phantom. He can't want this to get out. Keep it, by the way. It's yours."

"Mine?"

"If anyone can find a way to use it against the sonofabitch it's you, and the rest of your portable compatriots."

Davenport pocketed the picture. "I'll take the picture, and I'll go after the Phantom. But I can't promise we'll take him alive."

"Ach, what's a promise? It's like a kiss in a whorehouse: a pleasant surprise but ultimately meaningless. You take the picture. Pull it out from time to time and study it. Imagine that it's *your* father lying there. And see if it doesn't start to hold a strange power over you. Imagine the power you might hold over Pierre LeGrand with such a weapon in your pocket. Either you'll come around to my way of thinking or you won't. But I think we're running out of chances. Hell, not to sound too grand about this, but I think the whole damn world might be running out of chances."

"There is one other small gesture you could add to your payment," Davenport said.

"Go on."

"Don't ever use Jaggert or his sidekick for anything more serious than jacking a car. They're going to get themselves killed, and they're stupid as hell, careless."

"I'll take your suggestion to heart," Gutterson said.

"Fair enough. Now, I could tell you that I have to use the restroom, but really what I'm going to do is get up from this table, walk away, and not come back. Either you'll hear from me or you won't."

Gutterson nodded, but the smile that might have accompanied such a gesture naturally enough never came. His face had sealed itself back up. All traces of mirth had fled the scene. Davenport slipped into his jacket and donned his hat. Tugging lightly at the brim, he took his leave.

CHAPTER 21

This was a new low for Carmen. She had plenty of reasons to be less than proud of her easy acceptance of bad men, and her almost-as-easy participation in bad business, but she'd never had to take a hostage before. She'd watched from the sidelines, even kept a gun trained on the abductee while the main perpetrator ran an errand or took a shit. But she'd been careful to get involved only in activities that she could plausibly deny responsibility for. Not just legal responsibility, either. It was important that she not take on any great moral conflict. You could take the girl out of the church, but getting the church out of the girl was another matter.

Yet here she stood in a one-room church house in The Middle of Nowhere, Texas (maybe it wasn't so easy to remove the girl from the church after all), watching a young motel clerk cry herself dry as she hitched and squirmed on the hardwood floor. Donna's hands were bound behind her back and tied via a constrictor knot to her ankles, which were also bound together. She wasn't going anywhere until Carmen said so.

"I'm not a terrible person," Carmen said. "At least you can rely on that. You won't get any macho threatening bullshit from me. I'm just doing what needs to be done. I don't intend to be any meaner about it than I have to be. Of course, you don't do as you're told and keep your yap shut, then I'll have to *get* mean. Are we reading from the same book?"

The wet-eyed girl from Abilene looked up and nodded. Maybe a little hope of surviving this ordeal had seeped into her system. Or maybe her body was simply getting tired of sobbing. Either way, Carmen welcomed the calm. It made her less anxious.

"Your job here is easy," Carmen continued. "You just need to keep your shit together until our friend gets here, and *while* he's here. You're an object in this transaction, nothing more. I realize that may not appeal to your feminist sensibilities, if you have any, but sister, there's a time and a place. Take a few bullets when you're young, and you might just live to do the shooting yourself in old age."

"You told me you know Max," Donna said in a sodden voice, "but you didn't say how."

Carmen eased herself down onto a nearby pew. "We knew each other in Florence. That's all you need to know. More than you need to know, actually. Now, let me ask *you* a question, and this is an important one, honey. The question of the day, easy. How much do you mean to old Max Brindle?"

"What do you mean? I don't know. He stays at the motel whenever he's in Abilene, but mostly he's not in Abilene."

Carmen leaned in closer. "You're misinterpreting the question, dearie. Have the two of you ..." She made a circle with the thumb and forefinger of her left hand and slid the index finger of her right hand in and out of it. "You know, fucked?"

It was hot in the small church. Cloying. Maybe she shouldn't have been so soft with the girl, about her kind and giving nature, because she felt the pinpricks of anger beginning to stipple her insides, and the last thing she needed was to screw this up in a fit of rage. Why couldn't the little bitch get her head around the balance of power in this situation? It would be so much easier if it didn't need to be spelled out.

Donna nodded.

"Does he love you?"

"I don't know. He gives me money sometimes. I mean, not like that. Just out of the blue. To help me out."

"Sounds like love to me. I never let him within a Canadian mile of my musty grotto for that very reason. He strikes me as the kind of man who could fall in love with an ocean clam if it was fresh and moist enough. But I didn't speak to him the way

I'm speaking to, either. Somewhere in between is my comfort zone when it comes to handling men. Talk nice, keep hope alive, but deny, deny, deny. That's how I operate." *Unless the man in question happens to be the Black Phantom.* "Anyway, good. I think this will be a quick roll of the dice and you'll be on your way back to the Rise and Shine Motel before you know it."

The main door squealed open and a shaft of sunlight cut through the aisle to Carmen's right, catching Donna in its shine.

"Max Brindle." Carmen turned in her pew to face him. "I didn't even hear you drive up. I suppose you parked half a mile away. That's my cautious Max." She had to admit—to herself—that the silly man had an inexplicable appeal. No sense of how to dress himself, and no real merit in the looks department, but he carried himself with a certain air. A confidence. She didn't know quite what the hell to make of him half the time.

"Carmen." He recognized her instantly, even without the wig and sunglasses, but his attention soon turned to Donna. "This is unpleasant. Let's get to the bottom of it and see how we go about clearing things up."

"Very good. We share a preference for expediency. And I don't think we need to ask Donna if she agrees."

Max's footsteps creaked and echoed in the confined space as he stepped to within a couple rows of where Carmen sat and took a seat across the aisle from her. Donna returned his gaze with adoring eyes. Carmen was legitimately moved by the surprising reaction. Max was as unlikely a knight as you could ever hope to meet, as far as she was concerned. Different strokes.

"She's fine," Carmen said. "And she'll remain fine, as long as we keep this neat and civil."

"I'm in no position to behave otherwise," Max responded. "How do we untie those knots?"

"Simplicity itself. The Black Phantom is interested in you. He has been for some time. Mostly he just wants to keep an eye on you and see what he can learn about the movement of certain cargo around the globe. But he's recently taken an interest in some of your side operations."

"So we both work for the Phantom."

She ignored the observation. "He approves of you. Erase any worries you may have in that regard. He appreciates what you do for him. In fact, he needs your help." She paused, expecting him to probe, but he only stared at her, expressionless as a deep-sea fish. "He wants to hire your top gun on a temporary basis. Someone young, hungry, and imaginative. By the way—" She gestured to Donna. "—it's up to you to see to it that this little slice of ham doesn't sing about any of this. Are we of a piece on that?"

He nodded. "I don't suppose I need to bother asking what the Black Phantom needs with one of my associates."

"Not so. He was very clear that as an act of good faith I can inform you that he needs help taking care of some business involving the Portable Nine. You've heard of them, I gather?"

"The Portable Nine?" He snorted, then chuckled several times and eventually burst out laughing. "Well isn't that the son of all bitches. I think I might just have the man for the job, yes. Can I assume there's more in it for me, and my employee, than the freeing of Donna here?"

"A million for the two of you. Half up front, half when it's done. But this isn't a mass assassination we're talking about here. They need to be taken to the Phantom, alive."

"Alive? That's fucking—"

"I believe the answer you're looking for is, 'Yes, ma'am. It won't be easy, but consider it done.' Besides, the job's half done already."

"How so?"

"All nine of them are in Seattle as we speak. When do you suppose we'll have an opportunity like that again?"

"Okay, okay. Fair enough. I'm in. Now let her go."

* * *

Carmen didn't respond but went to Donna and bent over,

presumably to undo her bonds. Max slipped his hand into the pocket of his multi-colored sport coat and brought out a six-inch lock blade. He opened the knife and stared at it. He wanted to cut Carmen's throat wide open and watch her blood flow across the floor of the house of God. Wanted Donna to see how much power he held in the world, and how impervious he was to the power of others. Wanted to sweep her up in his arms and carry her away from the whole mad scene and make her eternally grateful to him. Instead he closed the blade and pocketed it as he stood up.

"This wasn't necessary," he said. "Kidnapping Donna. I would have listened to your offer without all of this."

"You needed to know how important this is to the Black Phantom, and how far he's willing to go to make sure things turn out to his liking. He won't be trifled with."

Something caught his attention. He craned his neck to try to see behind Donna.

"What's with her hands?" he asked. "Why are they still tied?"

"Okay, now I want everyone to keep things in perspective and remain even tempered for me."

"What the fuck are you trying to pull here, Carmen?"

"Nothing. I was up front with you. It was her I told a little white lie to."

"What's going on?" Alarm swept the color out of Donna's face. "You said I'd be home soon."

"Yeah, well, I'm afraid that was the lie. You and I are going to have to be roommates for a while."

"God dammit." Max wished he'd given in to the urge to end her life several moments ago. "This is some low shit."

"Oh, come on. It's insurance, plain and simple. You'd want some too if the roles were reversed. And it won't be long. Just until the Black Phantom knows he can trust the situation. This can move as fast as you want it to move. Our insurance policy should make things move pretty quickly indeed."

He glanced at the hand that was tucked into her jacket

pocket, figuring it was a little hot for her to be wearing a jacket in the first place—and that she might just have a piece in that pocket. Her smug look as good as confirmed it, and so he turned, a shadow in the sun, and walked down the nave, such as it was, to the exit.

It sounded like Donna stood up and followed, likely with a little prodding from that gun in Carmen's pocket. He could practically feel the bitch smiling at being in the driver's seat.

CHAPTER 22

Jerrod had a window seat in the Roastrum Café on Seattle's Capitol Hill. He flipped through the contacts on his phone until he found what he was looking for. After a pause to finish off his caffeine fix, he tapped one of the numbers.

"Hello?" said the voice on the other end, flat and cautious.

"Max, it's Jerrod."

"Good God, I've been waiting for you to get back to me. How many messages did I leave? Weren't they fucking urgent enough?"

"I haven't exactly been sitting on my thumb here, you know. I've been doing some digging, and I've found out plenty. You'll be pleased. I know I am."

"Spill, dammit. The fate of a rather special young lady hangs in the balance."

"So you mentioned, about three voice mails back. I thought you understood that I have a certain piece of business to tend to before you can consider me yours."

"Yes, yes, but things have … intensified. Surely you appreciate that?"

"It changes nothing for me. I'm after the Butcher. Once I've dealt with him we can move on."

"You don't understand. I couldn't go into detail in a message, but the Black Phantom wants the Portable Nine alive. All of them."

"What? That's insane. How are we going to forcibly move nine lethal operatives halfway around the world?"

"How? By accepting that it's the only way to set Donna

free and collect a million dollars. That's how."

"Jesus, how do I get myself mixed up in this kind of shit? Okay, listen. The Butcher is here in Seattle, so at least we're not looking at a side trip to Tokyo."

"Yeah, well guess what? The rest of the Nine are there, too."

"What?"

"I'll fill you in soon enough. But it means we're halfway there, Jerrod. We can do this."

"It still leaves us with the problem of the Butcher. I want that motherfucker. His head, anyway."

"Look, maybe we treat this as a deferment, huh? He keeps his head for now, but it's yours eventually. Shit, maybe you'll have the Black Phantom's blessing when he's done with him. This really isn't the kind of thing we can say no to."

Jerrod watched a gay couple walk past the window, laughing and exchanging light, playful touches. He couldn't remember the last time he laughed at the world.

"Yeah, okay," he said. "I see your point."

"Yeah? That's great. I knew you'd see the sense of it. You're a smart kid. You'll go far with them smarts."

"Better to be a smart feller than a fart smeller." A dumb joke he used to hear his dad say. One of the few things the old bastard didn't regularly punctuate with a knock to the side of the head or a punch in the rib cage. Jerrod suspected the childish humor would play well for Max.

"Ha! You're goddamn right. Sounds like it must be about time for me to get on a plane to Seattle, huh?"

"Yeah, I guess maybe we'd better turn this into a proper partnership. I'll need some help if I'm going to take this on."

"If? Still with the *if*."

"A figure of speech. I'm in."

"Thank you."

❉ ❉ ❉

The brisk late afternoon breeze blowing in off of Elliott Bay filled Jerrod with a sense of inevitability, that the tarot cards had been laid and his fate was sealed. It was already dark, but the evening lay before him. Maybe there was some fun in his immediate future. He figured he could use some, because the long term might not be such a joy ride.

Halfway down the hill he found a club that had a warehouse look to it. Techno music thumped from within. Along a side street a neon sign advertised DRINKS—LIVE JAZZ. That was more his speed. The business with Max Brindle was officially on hold. Jerrod Cafferty's number one priority was to unwind.

As he crossed the entrance to a dark alley that reeked of piss, a blur shot out from behind a dumpster and took him by the hood of his sweatshirt. Before he could react, he was being slammed against the brick wall of the bar he had almost made it to. Two hands were at the front of his hoodie, balling it up and pulling him deeper into the alley.

"What the fuck? Get your fucking hands off me!"

But he was no match for the other man's strength. A fist came at him fast, connected with his jaw. He felt blood and spittle fly out the other side of his mouth as he went to the pavement. The man was on top of him in an instant, both knees drilling into Jerrod's biceps. He was pinned.

"Okay, punk. Q and A time. I Q and you A. Got it?"

Jerrod nodded, dazed. The man wasn't what he'd expected from the brutality of the attack. He wore a suit, and sculpted facial hair adorned his chin. What the fuck *was* this?

"You've been doing some digging, and it's led you to some interesting places. I want to know what your interest is in the Portable Nine. You seem to be especially concerned with one member in particular. And let's skip the part where you ask me who the Portable Nine are. I'm asking the questions, remember?"

"I … remember. I've been hired to get in touch with this Butcher. I don't know much about why. I just know that the person who hired me wants to know where the Butcher is. That's all

I know. I found him, that's it."

The man stared down at him without saying a word for a long time. Then he twisted his knees deeper into Jerrod's arms. Jerrod grunted in agony and gagged on blood.

"So far so good. Two more questions, and these are important, so take your time answering. Who's asking for this information, and have you reported the Butcher's whereabouts yet?" He bent forward and widened his stare before adding, "Don't lie to me."

"Grammit," Jerrod said.

"What?" The man leaned in further and turned his head slightly to one side.

"Grammit, idjididdleoffen …"

"What the fuck are you saying? I can't—"

Gauging his moment to the second, Jerrod slammed his head into his attacker's. The result was immediate. The man slid off of Jerrod's arms, his knees meeting the pavement with what seemed to Jerrod like a crack but was probably only a thud. Regardless, a stunned look spread across the man's face as he brought one hand up to check for blood. Jerrod launched a volley of punches that had blood spurting from cuts all over the man's face in seconds. Then he grabbed hold of his throat and squeezed. The man's eyelids fluttered, but before they could close, Jerrod was pulling him across his chest in a fluid motion that ended when the man's head collided with the brick wall behind Jerrod. The sound was both satisfying and ugly—probably a death blow, but to be sure, Jerrod rose to his feet and, taking his attacker by the lapels, slammed the back of his head into the pavement of the alley, over and over. Until there could be no doubt.

No mercy for assholes.

A quick search of the man's wallet revealed that his name was Samuel Gutterson. Jerrod was surprised to know the name. He was connected to Davenport, the leader of the Portable Nine, in some way. That gave him all the sense of urgency he needed. He fished his phone out of his pocket and took several close-up pictures of the corpse before him. Maybe he'd share them with Max. Maybe he'd send them to Davenport. Or maybe he'd keep them to himself. But at least he'd have them if he needed them.

Leaving the body of Samuel Gutterson—minus all manner of identification, which he pocketed—to the vermin of Capitol Hill, Jerrod ran deeper into the alley, hoping a plan would occur to him by the time he reached the next street. A plan for evasion of capture, if nothing else.

CHAPTER 23

"I really don't understand how you manage it," Lovinia said to Mr. Bonnet as they strolled along Post Alley in search of their next watering hole, or whatever came their way.

He didn't know he was walking with Lovinia Dulcet. She disguised her voice with a soft southern twang and wore a peachy fragrance she wouldn't have been caught dead with as her real self. She'd also avoided her trademark stilettoes in favor of a pair of low-profile pumps, which not only made her seem much shorter but also altered her gait.

"Every blind man I ever knew needed a cane at the very least. Most have dogs. But you … Why, you're like a wizard."

"Do you wish to test my inability to see again?"

"No, no. That was only a little fun. I hope you didn't take offense."

"Natalie, what would you say to having our next drink at my place? It's not far by taxi, and I have a well-stocked bar."

"I'd say that is a most appealing offer, Mr. Bonnet. Would you like me to hail—"

"No, I see a dragon coming in for a landing."

She looked at him in disbelief, wondering if she'd heard him correctly, but before she could formulate a question he was stepping off the curb and waving his arms. The very cab she'd planned to hail pulled over to where they stood, and they both slid into the backseat. He was a good-looking man, she observed, not for the first time. His hair was as white as Leslie Nielsen's, but the change had come prematurely, so he still had a somewhat youthful air. And he wasn't tall. These things, taken with the blindness, gave the impression of harmlessness. Mr. Bonnet wouldn't have seemed a threat to anyone. Lovinia knew it was a mistake to believe in that assumption. Behind the lids that Bonnet kept closed for longer intervals than the average person were gears and switches and dials and gauges. He was the easiest kind of man to underestimate. A clockwork mannequin.

"Did you say you saw a dragon?" she asked after he'd given the address to the driver.

"Um, yes. You see, I navigate the world through a series of unpredictable hallucinations. They must somehow be based on reality, whatever that is, because I get by almost as if I were sighted. But there are limits, and frustrations."

"Tell me about the frustrations." She cared about this man and actually wanted to know. It wasn't a ruse to keep up appearances. She hated the thought that he and Dr. Intaglio might be working against the Nine, on the side of the storied Black Phantom. But if they were, they had drawn a line that could not be undrawn.

"Oh, you don't want to know about my problems." He placed a hand on her knee, just below the line of her skirt.

"Please tell me you're not the condescending type. That ain't how I had you figured."

He cocked his head a little as the taxi rumbled its way through the downtown core, headed northwest toward Elliott Avenue. "Okay, fine. You want to hear, you'll hear. But I'm afraid I'll bore you." He removed his hand from her knee. "The hallucinations, they take on a certain mythological aspect. For a week or more I might see nothing but images related to hell, for instance. Then one morning I'll wake up and the world will seem like a fairytale. Another week might pass like that, and then I'll find myself in a world set in the heavens, where I move from cloud to cloud, never setting foot on solid ground. Setting can influence what I see, too. If I'm hot or wet or in a closed-in space."

"Remarkable. I've never heard of such a thing."

"I don't know if anyone has it to the extent that I do. Total blindness is rare enough as it is. To be plagued by detailed hallucinations is exceedingly uncommon. To have such an extreme case as mine ... Well, I've never heard of such a thing, either."

"Were you born without ..."

"Was I born blind? No. My condition would border on the miraculous if that were the case, wouldn't it? No, surely my visions are related to a buried memory of how things are, how they look ... how they sound. I was in my twenties when I lost my vision. But we'll leave that for another time, shall we?"

"Yes, of course. I didn't mean to pry."

"Not at all. Some doors will open when you knock. Others won't. That's all."

They arrived at their Salmon Bay destination and Mr. Bonnet paid the driver, who left them to the mild drizzle that had developed. He led her across the street by the arm and let them into what appeared to be a walk-up apartment, repurposed from something far more utilitarian. Perhaps the steep staircase had led to the offices of a boat repair shop in another lifetime, or to a fishmonger's countinghouse if you went back even farther.

The rooms he was renting at the top of the stairs were more than livable but not extravagant. The design was symmetrical, with two closed doors in each far corner and an open kitchen layout, which was separated from the living area by a bar-style counter. Square-paned windows took up most of the east wall. She assumed the corner rooms to be bedrooms. One for Intaglio, one for Bonnet, no doubt. A cozy lair for them to plot their treason.

She had to reel in her resentment, though. Tonight her task was simple: Keep Bonnet convinced of the plan to extort money from Cloft Industries and sow as many seeds of doubt as possible regarding any claims Intaglio was likely feeding his partner about the Portable Nine's real goals. Everything beyond that would have to wait.

"What'll you have?" Bonnet asked.

"Oh, gin and tonic, since you asked."

While Lovinia assessed her surroundings, Bonnet tended to mixing drinks at the bar that stood at one end of a designer sofa.

"It's quite a place you have here." She wondered if it was something he and Intaglio paid rent on even when they were away. More likely they had a friend in Seattle who was able to hook them up. All she knew was that not wanting to stay at the Regal Hotel with the rest of the crew didn't win Dr. Intaglio and Mr. Bonnet any plausibility points.

"Is that just an observation, or are you informing me, in case I'm unaware?"

She eased herself down onto the sofa. "You know, your blindness really isn't an issue with me. I wish you'd stop trying to make it into one."

He handed her the gin and tonic she'd asked for and sat down beside her with a black Russian for himself.

They sat in uncomfortable silence for a while, sipping occasionally at their drinks.

Lovinia added after a moment, "I guess that wasn't entirely true, what I said."

"You mean about my blindness not being an issue?"

"Yes. I do have one question. Then I really would like to put it to rest for the night, though."

He was looking over at her and now he shrugged. His expression said it was of no consequence to him whether they went on talking about his condition all night long. She had to admit to herself that it was a little eerie how sighted he seemed, as if *blindness* wasn't the right word for his condition. He *saw* the world, just ... differently.

"What am *I*?" she asked.

"Pardon?"

"You said the taxi was a dragon. What am I?"

"Oh, that's an unfair question. The correlation between what I see and what—"

"I ain't trying to decide if I want to walk out that door and never return. I'm just curious."

"I'd rather not say, to be honest. It's not a reflection of what you truly are. I've learned to ignore the tendency to draw parallels. But you'll want to."

"Well, now I really am intrigued."

He sighed and set his tumbler on the coffee table.

"You make it difficult for a man to make his move. Do you realize that?"

She smiled and took a drink.

"There's no polite way to put this, I'm afraid. You're a goblin."

"I beg your pardon?"

"I warned you. Look, if I paid any attention to these things, why would I be as interested in you as I am?"

"Maybe you have some kind of weird goblin fetish."

"May I look at you? For real?"

"You mean ..."

His hands came to her slowly. For a moment she had the comical idea that he was going to paw at her breasts, though she knew he wasn't. It was her face he was interested in, for now. She barely had time to notice how elegant his hands were, the fingers long and slender: deft looking. And then they were upon her, probing her features with an uncanny lightness of touch. He dabbed at the ridge of her nose with a thumb, and the next thing she knew, a pinkie was running along the hollow of her cheek. Two fingertips brushed along her forehead. Her eyes closed as a pleasant thrill ran through her, settling between her legs.

"Oh, you're no goblin," he said, barely above a whisper.

She opened her eyes and saw him swallow a lump in his throat. What were people like them doing in such a violent and dangerous line of work? She wished Davenport's ruse—the one she was here to hard-sell on his behalf—were true, that she and the rest of the Portable Nine were within striking distance of lasting retirement from their life above the law. That they were close to putting all their killing ways behind them and living out the rest of their years in well-earned comfort.

Still, she didn't let her reverie prevent her from making a mental note never to let him touch her features when she was plain old Lovinia Dulcet.

It was her turn to sigh. And then she leaned in for a kiss, running one hand through Bonnet's full white hair and with the other removing his glasses and setting them aside. His body hitched a little when their lips met. She'd startled him, which only turned her on all the more. He repaid her kiss, and she swung one leg across his lap so she could straddle him. She wished she could have had a painting of the moment. The two of them locked in this primal embrace. The storm before the storm. It was an odd thought, but it didn't diminish her enthusiasm. Or his, she noticed as she undid the fly of his pants and handled what throbbed there.

❋ ❋ ❋

Twitch, Abel, Robin, and the Butcher stood in the shadows along Salmon Bay Marina, keeping watchful eyes on the apartment building across the street. Their extreme patience and cunning would have been apparent to anyone who noticed them, but no one did notice them. Nighttime revelers passed within ten feet of them at times, but they were more likely to be seen as shadow or flora than humanity.

They felt it themselves: the old feeling, the good feeling. Their talents were unique, and tonight they were being put to good purpose. Robin felt sure he wasn't the only one of the four who suddenly longed to put to use other skills that had been languishing for too long.

A metal door opened across the street, throwing a shaft of light in their direction. Lovinia Dulcet stepped out and immediately scanned the area for signs of her compatriots.

Abel stepped forward and called out in his acquired Australian accent, "Hey, beautiful! You going our way?"

Her shoulders sagged in relief as she hurried across the

street to join the others.

"Well?" Robin prompted.

"Well," she said, brushing hair behind her ears and grinning a little, "I think I've got him hooked."

"He fell for it, then?"

"Yeah. He did. Sorry you guys had to go to such lengths to keep an eye on things, but safety first, I suppose."

"No joke," he said, looking down at his phone. "If you'd have stayed up there much longer, you would have had company."

"What do you mean?"

He held the phone up for her to see.

"You see the blinking red dot?"

She nodded.

"That's Dr. Intaglio. His car, anyway. And it's fast approaching, as we suspected. He'll be here any minute."

"You're tracking him. Clever."

"He goes out a lot without his phone, so we've had to go a little old school on the surveillance."

She smiled and the five of them wandered off toward Leary Way, where they hoped to blend in with the masses.

* * *

Dr. Intaglio fumbled with his keys, hunting for the right one. What the hell did he have so many keys for? He was always on the move, and he couldn't remember what half of them were for. Thumbing to the key to the apartment, he twisted it in the lock and let himself in.

No lights. It was early for Bonnet to be in bed, but he had said he'd be here waiting for Intaglio. Switching on the lights, Intaglio crossed to Bonnet's bedroom and knocked lightly with a knuckle. No response. He knocked a little harder.

"Mmm, what is it?" Bonnet asked, his voice groggy.

"It's me. I thought we were going to talk. I've arranged for our privacy."

"Oh, sure. I just got a little tired. Thought I'd take a nap while I waited. Let me throw something on."

"Leave a little chest hair exposed, would ya? You know how that turns me on."

"Very funny. Be right out."

Intaglio took a seat on the couch under the window, his posture expansive with both arms stretched out along the back. He crossed his legs—which should have been more difficult than it was with his paunch—and smiled, cock-sure of himself and his standing in the world, for no particular reason.

Then he saw the drink glasses on the coffee table. His posture remained the same, but the smile vanished. He was expecting to learn from Mr. Bonnet that there was no Natalie Jackson, that Davenport had set him up with a wild goose. But here on the coffee table, doubt took the unassuming form of two—not one—empty glasses.

He leaned forward and took up one of the tumblers, inspecting it for the tell-tale signs of lipstick. No dice. He picked up the other glass, and there it was: the unmistakable curved smudge of magenta at the rim.

"Sonofabitch," he said, just above a whisper, and set the glass back down.

"So, the others are out of our hair for a time?" Bonnet strode confidently into the room, hardly like a blind man at all.

"Yes." Intaglio looked askance at his friend. "They're back at the hotel."

"Excellent." Bonnet sat across from Intaglio in a designer armchair. "I have good news to impart."

"I gather." Intaglio nodded to the glasses on the table.

"Ah, yes. Well ..." Bonnet couldn't contain a smile. "You must be referring to the fact that there are two empty glasses on the coffee table. I have to admit, I left them out for you to see."

"So there *is* a Natalie Jackson? Are you telling me that Davenport is on the up and up with his plan to extort money from Cloft Industries?"

"It would appear so."

Intaglio glanced toward Bonnet's bedroom.

"She's not still …"

"No, she needed to get back to some friends, but we had an interesting time, I assure you."

"I'll be damned. Still, why all the suspicion toward us?"

"I've been thinking about that. My guess is that Davenport does suspect that we're running something on the side with the Black Phantom, but it would be another leap to think that we might actually be working against the Portable Nine."

"The Portable Seven is how I've come to think of them."

This caught Mr. Bonnet off guard. He sat back in his chair and tilted his head to one side, considering the remark.

"Did her father come up?" Intaglio asked.

"No, it's a little early for that. I need to build up some trust. But we'll get there."

"How can you be so sure?"

A wistful air came over Mr. Bonnet, and Intaglio wondered if the man was seeing one of his hallucinatory vistas, or was this a deeper vision, something closer to the truth?

"We made love, if that's troubling you."

"And you equate a good fuck with trust-building? Dear God."

"Doctor, I don't mean to be complicated, but here's how it is. I admire you, and I place a good deal of importance on our friendship. But your days of lording it over me and keeping me under your thumb are past. I have a job to do, and I've begun doing it. The rope I've been given may hang me, but by God, it's my rope to hang from."

"Jesus, the naïveté! You see a lot for a blind man, but there's much you remain utterly blind to. You don't exist in some kind of protective bubble, you know. Your actions and effectiveness are closely tied to the success of this entire operation, and the success of the group."

"Yes, and Davenport has shown that he trusts me with that responsibility. If it's good enough for him, it should be good

enough for you. Whatever we may do in the future that discon-
nects us from him and his causes, we know his strengths and his
virtues. We can honor those, even as we seek to exploit them."

"You *are* making things complicated."

"Things *are* complicated."

"I'm not sure what that means, exactly, but it's been a
long day and I'm tired to my bones. I don't have the energy to
spar with you into the night."

"You know, the Dr. Intaglio I used to know wouldn't have
betrayed the Portable Nine unless he could leverage a certain
amount of free agency out of the deal. That was our original
plot. But somewhere along the way you got caught up in the
Phantom's spell, and now you're as beholden to him as you ever
were to Davenport. What happened to the idea of us striking out
on our own? 'A little competition is oil to the machinery of free
enterprise.' Do you remember saying that to me?"

Intaglio nodded slowly, looking down at the hardwood
floor. "I remember. You and your fucking idealism."

"Me and my—I can't believe what I'm hearing. Where's
your fucking idealism? A real tribute to your profession, you
are. Both professions, actually: psychiatrist *and* self-appointed
secret agent."

"You've never spoken to me in this fashion before."

"Is that the problem? Is it only under conditions lacking
dissent that you're able to function? That's sick. You should
really see a shrink about that."

Intaglio's head remained bowed, but his gaze slid up to
Bonnet's smug face. "You've made your point, Mr. Bonnet. The
compassion associated with my profession has its limits in me."

"I can see you glaring at me like a reluctant suicide. Must
be one of my more exaggerated hallucinations. I guess we've
chatted enough for one night, though. Let's get some sleep.
Things will look fresh in the morning."

"I suppose you're right." Intaglio straightened up. "We'll
pick this up over coffee."

"Now you're talking."

Words were one thing, of course. But Dr. Joseph Intaglio did not like the boldness that was surfacing in his trusty sidekick. Not one little bit. He said no more than goodnight, however, as he readied himself for bed.

Mr. Bonnet reciprocated the reticence.

CHAPTER 24

Miranda heard something at the door of her hotel room. A shuffling. It was too late in the day to be housekeeping, and Davenport wouldn't have been so timid. Same with the others. Maybe it was just a snot-nosed kid who had wandered too far from his family's room. Or maybe someone was waiting for their significant other before heading out for a stroll. But there were other maybes. Like maybe someone who didn't have any goddamn business outside her room was up to something she wouldn't approve of.

She took a step forward but was stopped cold by a large envelope being slid under the door. What was it about the act that seemed intrusive, almost violating? The thing to do would have been to throw open the door and see who the hell had done such a thing. Chase them down the fucking hallway if necessary. But she didn't do either of those things. Instead she bent down with an almost cautious slowness. By the time she had the envelope in her hands and had ripped it open, the deliverer might have been halfway out of the hotel.

Sitting down at the writing desk in the main room of her suite, she slid the contents of the envelope out into a neat pile. They came out upside down, but she could tell they were sheets of photo paper. In among them was a sheet of regular stock, which she discovered was a typewritten note when she turned it over. She set the note aside and flipped over the pile of printed photographs with some trepidation.

One hand went to her mouth while the other held the first of the photos with a slight tremble. When the first image in a pile of printouts featured the bloodied face of a dead man, it didn't bode well for the uplift potential of the rest of the pile. But she managed to flip the first photograph over to see what lay beneath. Another shot of the same face, only bloodier and from a slightly different angle. The third was from an angle that showed the man's head to be caved in severely at the back. She was nauseated by the time she turned over the seventh and final glossy.

The note seemed to glow at the periphery of her vision as she stared at the overturned pile of photographs. She didn't want to read it, wasn't sure she wanted any part of this whole damn business, suddenly. She'd almost forgotten how dark her dealings with the Portable Nine could get. But then she remembered how many of those dark moments were the direct result of her own actions. It was far too late to extract herself from blame, and therefore past any point of withdrawal from the business at hand. She had invested heavily in the code of the Nine, and she owed them her loyalty. Most of them, anyway.

She snatched up the note and held it to the lamplight.

Dear Ms. Gissing,

I'm sorry to have to disturb you with such blunt pictures. They're really not meant for you. They're for Mr. Davenport. I'm sure you can appreciate the need for caution. He's being watched more closely than you, and I really can't risk capture at this time. He'll no doubt recognize the poor sucker in the pictures, but in case there's uncertainty, it's Mr. Samuel Gutterson. He'll know who that is, even if you don't.

The only other message I have for Mr. Davenport is that he should keep his goddamn hounds at bay. Games will only lead to more misery.

Oh, and if he's interested in meeting with me, it's easily arranged. In fact, I insist. Tell him to be at the front desk for a phone call at 7:00 p.m. Next steps will be made clear.

Many thanks,

J. C.

A car horn sounded in the street below, followed by the squawk of rubber on pavement. Miranda wondered if it was her mysterious photographer/delivery boy making his getaway.

She stood up and leaned on the desk with both hands. Davenport was likely still in his room. They had talked not long before. He needed to be made aware of this immediately. She knew who Sam Gutterson was, and she knew that his brutal death would not please Davenport.

Pausing to pick up her room key from a nearby table, she hurried to the door and pulled it open. But before she could cross the threshold, a knee came up into her stomach, hard. It took the breath from her, and she chided herself for falling for the ruse.

An elbow came at her face with wicked swiftness and she heard something break. Her nose, presumably. Down she went, only to be kicked back into her room. The next thing she knew, she was being picked up and carried to the bed as the door swung shut behind her and her attacker.

J. C.

She assumed it didn't stand for Jesus Christ.

Clever bastard. The ruse may have been simple, but that didn't mean it had been stupid. She had damn sure let her guard down, though. She wouldn't underestimate this one again, if he did her the courtesy of letting her live.

"Please tell me I don't need to bind you to this fucking bed." He stood at the foot of the bed, waiting for a response.

She shook her head and backed into a sitting position, as far away from him as possible.

"Good. I have handcuffs with me." He patted his jacket pocket. "But I'd rather just have a conversation. I want to know that I have your attention because you want to hear what I have to say, not because you're trying to tell me whatever will get you freed the quickest."

He drew a thicker line than she did between captivity and freedom, but she kept the thought to herself.

"Davenport will receive a very similar package to the one I slipped under your door." He sat down on the corner of the bed, his manner suddenly avuncular, despite his being quite a bit younger than Miranda. "The photos are exactly the same. The note's a little different. See, I'm going to need you as leverage for the next phase of operations. That's what this is all about."

"Are you saying you're taking me against my will?"

"That all depends."

"On what?"

"On the nature of your will."

His stare was devoid of mirth, almost of humanity, but then he let out a laugh, forced and ugly, following it up with a tap to her foot which sent a wave of repulsion through her body.

"Seriously," he continued, "if you play along, this will go much more smoothly, for everyone. I mean, I need Davenport to think you're in grave danger, but you don't actually have to be."

"You know, I wish I could say I don't have a problem with any of this, but I think you deserve more honesty than that. Think about it, would you pack your bags and step in line if the shoe was on the other foot?"

"The shoe is not on the other foot. It is on this foot, you see. And on this foot it shall remain. There is only one foot you need to be concerned with, in other words."

He had an affected way of speaking that added to his overall lack of appeal. Until she had the upper hand in some way, this man was best treated as a coiled snake.

"So," she said, "what was the plan if I had decided to call Davenport about this instead of walk down the hall to talk to him in person? You seem to know that was my intent."

"I don't trust to the intent of anyone." He shook an index finger meaningfully at the ceiling. "Leave nothing to chance. That's my way."

Personalities swam in and out with this guy. What the fuck had she gotten wrapped up in this time?

Moving to the desk where she had read the note, he turned over the pile of photographs and briefly admired his work.

"This is the only phone in the suite. That's not a question. I was in here earlier. I know. Being able to sweet-talk maids is an essential skill, by the way. She's also going to deliver Davnport's envelope. Anyway, if you look down here ..." He squatted and peered under the desk. "... you'll see that the line has been disconnected from the phone and tucked very neatly under the carpet." Standing again, he added, "So, you might have tried calling your friend, Mr. Davenport, but it wouldn't have done you any good. At the lack of a dial tone, you would have been out the door and into my waiting arms, only three or four seconds later. I know the Portable Nine wouldn't be dumb enough to use cell phones. You're already vulnerable enough just being in the same city."

Good, Miranda thought. His smarts weren't infallible, since he hadn't considered the possibility of modified phones. "You mind if I ask what the J. C. stands for?" She needed to learn something about this lunatic, preferably a weakness of some kind.

"Let's start with the J. The name is Jerrod. Now it's my turn. Can I count on you to walk out of this hotel with me, and around the corner to my car? Or will we need these?" He patted the jacket pocket again, and this time she could hear the distinctive rattle of metal.

She nodded and he offered his hand to help her off the bed. Declining, she stood up from the opposite side and walked ahead of him to the closet to retrieve her coat. When he caught up to her, she closed the closet door and quickly slid into her coat before slamming him backward into the bathroom wall, her right forearm pressed across his throat like an anvil.

"We're going to get one thing nice and clear before we take another step, yeah? The easiest thing in the world right now would be for me to run you across this fucking room and toss you through the sliding-glass balcony door. From fourteen floors up, you could pretty much count on an untimely death, and I would have no trouble blaming it on the goddamn maid.

That's point number one. Point number two is that I don't take kindly to being kidnapped. It happened to me when I was a little girl. Only lasted the length of a block or so, but it left a scar. So that brings us pretty roundly to point number three, and that is that my will is in your court, for the time being. I'll go on this little outing of yours. You'll tell me a little more about what's going on and who you're working for. But this is only because I'm concerned about what you may have in store for Davenport if I don't comply. Your type doesn't understand that kind of humanity, I know. That's why I'm spelling it out for you.

"Now, I know that talking is out of the question right now. That'll be true of breathing before too long. So why don't you just go ahead and blink three times if we're on the same team, or at least playing the same sport."

One blink. Two, this one a little fluttery and longer to undo itself. Finally, three.

"Good."

She backed away and let Jerrod catch his breath, which was a little like watching a caught fish try to make sense of life outside its usual watery world. *He should count his blessings that he isn't dangling from a hook*, she thought. She'd considered using a hanger from the closet for a similar purpose.

What he wouldn't realize is that she had made sure his head had banged into the wall with enough force to leave an impression. She saw the impression now, and a small streak of blood. It was the kind of thing that might go unnoticed, or unaddressed, for months by hotel staff, but if Davenport happened to make his way into this room—and she had every reason to believe he would—it would not escape his notice. If he was thinking clearly, he'd realize that it might be an intentional clue. And if there was a real miracle of luck in this otherwise crap situation, maybe he'd wonder if he could get a DNA sample of some kind from the indentation.

Long shots, Miranda Gissing had learned long ago, were well worth the trouble of a little investment. Every goddamn time.

CHAPTER 25

There was, of course, an Archie Cloft. He was known the world over, and his tech empire was centered in Vancouver, British Columbia. Robin had half assumed that Jackson would also turn out to be real, but apparently he was a construct of Davenport's imagination.

Still, every Archie Cloft had a Mr. Jackson. Maybe it was a Mr. Radcliffe, or a Ms. Heddley, or a Mr. Crawford … But every Cloft had a Jackson.

With his vast experience moving and shaking in the corporate world's loftiest heights, it didn't take Varnesse long to learn that Cloft Industries' Jackson was one Elaine Rafferty. She funneled, laundered, invested, and grew the company's deep coffers. And like all Jacksons, she was at constant risk of becoming the fall guy for some inopportune discovery. It was no small part of her job to ask herself, of every transaction that passed under her purview, whether it put the corporation's American operations at risk for charges of embezzlement, fraud, or tax evasion. Intentional Ponzi schemes and shady real-estate buys were likely someone else's bailiwick, but otherwise the buck stopped at the desks of the Jacksons of the high-finance world. It was a steam-pressure existence that paid just well enough to make the likelihood of suicide a reasonable substitute for early retirement.

He'd hit it off with Elaine the first time he barged into her palatial Seattle office. Her trust was easily gained, to the extent that a woman in her position ever really trusted anyone. But his initial hope of wooing her and achieving the lion's share of his aims in that manner were quickly dashed. She was very married, judging not only by the gaudy rock on her left hand but also by her intermittent mention of the lucky man. And even though Robin Varnesse wasn't without ego, he couldn't have pretended to be in Elaine's league.

None of which meant he couldn't continue forging a friendship. Either way, their relationship was bound to end in betrayal on his part. He needed to wheedle enough information about Elaine's inner workings from her to develop a plan for extortion of some kind. Only then would the details of his operation begin to fall into place. It wasn't the kind of work that could be planned too far out or you'd end up reinventing the wheel at every turn. The financial machinery of the world was simply too complicated for that. Robin's goal was to reduce the complication factor as much as possible, turn some of the question marks into exclamation points, and formulate a plan of execution from there.

At that point, he would likely need the help of Miranda, another woman who had proven immune to his charms, despite an illusory fling many years ago, for which he had readily taken the bait. He sensed a pattern forming but refused to admit to himself that he was contemplating her involvement based solely on the lingering feelings that he harbored, or that his attraction to Mrs. Rafferty was adding fuel to the fire of his clandestine ambitions.

"Mr. Vale."

Her voice was more mellifluous than he remembered, and he remembered it to be plenty mellifluous. Her smile was the perfect match as she rose from her green leather chair and extended a hand across the mahogany desk between them. He took it and laughed lightly.

"Mrs. Rafferty," he said with a polite nod. "I don't suppose we need to be this formal every time we meet."

"Next you'll tell me it feels as though you've known me all your life."

He didn't know what to say to that. It was a little close to the mark.

"Please," she went on, "have a seat."

He did as she instructed and they enjoyed a comfortable silence for a moment. She was the kind of woman who could amass lovers as some women collect jewelry or shoes. Maybe that was why the most successful people in business tended to be very extreme in temperament and very easy to look at. They simply chose to put much of the energy that might otherwise be expended on philandering into the art of war. It was a shame he'd had to use a false name with her. It was the kind of subterfuge that all but negated the possibility of a real friendship between them, let alone a romantic relationship.

If only he could be as hard hearted as so many who worked with numbers and dollar signs. But then, weren't all of the Portable Nine marked by a deviation from accepted norms? A blurring of the lines between the crime they fought and the means they employed to do so? If any of them made it into old age with their sanity intact, they'd be able to count themselves victorious, as far as he was concerned. Adopting the occasional false identity was simply one more occupational measure carrying the risk of existential displacement.

Besides, they'd have to make it into old age to begin with, and that was no sure thing. Robin wasn't much of a believer in sure things to begin with, in finance or in life.

"You were characteristically vague about the nature of this appointment," Mrs. Rafferty said.

There was no lift at the end of the statement, no sense that she was being interrogative. Surely her patience was an illusion. Every second of her time could be assigned a dollar amount. She probably knew exactly what that amount was, too.

He crossed his legs and brushed an imaginary crease out of one pant leg. "I happened upon some information—completely by accident, mind you—that put me in an awkward position. I saw that a large sum of money is marked for transfer to an overseas holding account for no other reason than that it has yet to be claimed. There are two choices before me, as I see it. I can do nothing and almost guarantee that this money never makes its way to the rightful parties anyway, or I can take the entrepreneurial view."

"Sounds like a pretty nifty accident. How much money are we talking about?"

"Now see, that's not the expected answer when you drop a bomb like this. I would have thought you'd want to know where I was nosing around when I made this discovery, or who controls the accounts in question. Maybe even who the money actually belongs to."

"Sorry, Lieutenant Columbo. Life isn't always as tidy as it is in the storybooks. But if it makes you feel better, who controls the accounts?"

"Funny you should ask. It's almost impossible to tell."

Something changed in her eyes: a passing flare of ice.

"Almost?"

"Almost." He waggled an index finger with meaning. "Very few things are impossible. I was able to trace some of the flow of money to a PIN."

"I see."

"Turns out it's a PIN associated with a couple of Cloft Industries accounts. I could do a little more digging, but I thought I'd check in with you first."

"What is it you want, Mr. Vale?"

"I want to know what my next steps look like."

"I'm listening very carefully. I suggest you choose your words in a like manner."

A quick nod and a smile. "Of course. Here's what I think. Someone's out to get rich, or richer, from the accumulation of illegal fees that have been charged to some twenty thousand innocent consumers, clients, what have you. Those fees have been collected into several corporate accounts and readied for transfer to a temporary haven. If I may engage in just a bit more conjecture, I'm guessing that you're the one doing this dirty work, but not on your own behalf."

"This is beginning to sound an awful lot like extortion. If that's your intent, I highly recommend that you stop right now."

"It's not, I assure you. I come to you with a sincere offer. Whoever planned this thought it through. It's neat and it's clean. The victims have no idea what's been happening to them. They probably saw a modest monthly fee spread across several accounts, for some indecipherable service, and shrugged it off with a few muttered curses directed at the free enterprise system before returning to the slog of their daily lives, if they noticed at all. Or, if they were former employees, maybe they grumbled at a revision to their pension before having a nap. I say we keep them all in the dark. What I take issue with is the idea that all of this cash is fated to line the pockets of someone who didn't lift a finger to redirect it."

"You're suggesting that I skim a little off the top for myself, maybe fudge the numbers a little so no one's the wiser."

Again, no trace of uncertainty in her voice.

"You're not thinking big enough, El—Mrs. Rafferty. Do you really think I would have brought this to you if I was talking about skimming?"

"What, then?"

"Why shouldn't you take the whole fucking thing? The entire goddamn pot of gold at the end of the rainbow?"

"Oh, that's good of you, Vale. You're awfully generous with other people's money. Or maybe you have an undisclosed motive."

"I'm getting to that. I can help you convince the nameless orchestrator of this plot that things started to heat up. The plan wasn't as airtight as you originally thought, and you're worried that the FDIC may have been flagged. You have no choice but to redirect the money to the victims."

"But I won't redirect the money to the victims, will I, Mr. Vale?"

Robin extended his hands and shrugged. "Each of us could live very comfortably on half of that stockpile."

"Half? I thought you said you weren't out to extort me. By what bizarre logic do you deserve five million dollars?"

"Oh, the cat's out of the bag now, isn't it?"

"Spare me the bullshit, please. Why should I cut you in?"

"I was hoping we could avoid discussing—"

"Well consider your hopes dashed. I can't imagine it's the first time."

"Ouch. No, it's hardly that. Okay, let me lay it out in plain English. I want half of the haul because the diversion is my idea and I'll have a lot of work ahead of me to make sure it's believable that the money is being funneled back to where it belongs, and not into the pockets of a couple of thieves. If you decline my offer, I'm afraid I'll have no choice but to push for the entire sum. I'm willing to share with you. I like you, and you've earned it. But if push comes to shove, I will have you killed and claim every last penny for myself. If you want to call that extortion, fine. I prefer to think of it as business. And frankly, the longer we debate this, the less inclined I am to share the spoils with you anyway. This is the most important decision of your life. I suggest you make it quickly."

She rose like a cobra and slithered to the nearest window. Her back to Robin she said, "You filthy little shit of a man. You're asking me to risk my entire future for five mil. It's an insult."

Robin also stood up, crisping his suit as he addressed her. "I'll expect an answer before I walk out that door. You know what happens if I don't have one."

He turned to leave and covered half the distance to the door before she stopped him cold with a single word.

"Death."

He turned. She was facing him.

"What did you say?"

"I choose death. My Christmas bonus will be more than five million dollars. And if you want the full ten million, you'll have to kill me for it."

He'd overplayed his hand. *Shit.*

"What's *your* plan for the money, then?" he asked.

"My plan, Mr. Vale, is to let it absorb into Cloft Industries."

"That's not *your* plan."

"Let me clarify. *My* plan is to enforce *the* plan."

He stepped to the door but paused with his hand on the knob. Turning his head only slightly he said, "You'll be hearing from my attorney."

And he was gone, knowing that his parting words would sow a seed of confusion in Elaine, and also a seed of worry. He had taken her advice and chosen his words carefully. They were designed to make her doubt his place in all this, give him the air of authority. Maybe even the law.

Despite the unfortunate, though undoubtedly temporary, collapse of the bargain he had hoped to strike with Mrs. Rafferty, a grin stretched across his face as he waited for the elevator. He had no intention of sending a real lawyer to visit her, of course, but Miranda Gissing had played roles at least as challenging. She'd be perfect, if it came to that. But he didn't think it would.

CHAPTER 26

D r. Intaglio and Mr. Bonnet sat patiently in coach, waiting their turn for takeoff. Intaglio had insisted on coach, as usual. It was less conspicuous than business class, and it reminded him that he was not yet where he deserved to be in life. He would get there, but until then, coach it was.

"Davenport is going to miss us," Bonnet said.

"You worry too much, my friend. Far too much. Sometimes the end of a thing presents itself. If it's within your power to throw the switch, you do it. Forget about permission. Hone your knack for apology. That's what I say."

"Yes, well, I get the distinct impression that the Black Phantom has had it up to here with mea culpas."

"Our options are as open as ever. Besides, we helped that young man—Cafferty—learn more than he would have on his own. It's not like we're letting the Portable Nine go free. The Phantom will have his captives."

The plane rolled into position at the head of the runway, and soon the engines throttled up, rushing the aircraft toward liftoff. Turbulence hit as soon as they were airborne. Intaglio couldn't have cared less, but he knew it would bother his travel companion. Bonnet had gotten enough of a grip on his fear of flying not to be bothered too much by random pockets of rough air at cruising altitude, but when it started in during takeoff it unnerved him. He likened the feeling to one of precognition or a sense of foreboding.

"Does it have an impact on your vision?"

"What do you mean?" Bonnet asked, his voice a little on

edge.

"The turbulence." Intaglio studied the man, curious and amused. "Does it figure into your ... vision-scape?"

Bonnet nodded.

"Would you care to fill me in?"

"I'm at an amusement park. This is one of the roller coasters. I'm being dragged to the peak of an enormous incline."

"Nothing so bad about that. Nothing to be scared of, eh?"

"How long is this flight? Fourteen hours? Fifteen? If it's like this all the way my heart will explode in my chest."

"It won't be like this the entire way to Marrakesh. The captain would divert under conditions even approaching that kind of prolonged trouble. Use your head, man."

"But you consider turbulence to be a sign of trouble?"

"No, I don't. You know I don't. You're reading into my words. Now why don't you wait this out. We'll be out of the ascent soon. Things usually stabilize at that point. Then you'll be able to get yourself some sleep. This was a worthwhile trip, Bonnet. We learned how far we can trust our old friend, Mr. Davenport. And we've earned major points with the Black Phantom. This was a great show of loyalty. Surely it won't go unrewarded."

"Okay, just don't expect me to raise my hands above my head."

"Pardon?"

"If this tubular can decides to take a dive, it might still feel like a roller coaster, but I won't wave my hands in the air like I'm enjoying myself."

Dr. Intaglio let out a snort of laughter but it was forced. He didn't like Bonnet's mention of crashing. The man had odd gifts. Who knew how far they extended. God help the little bugger if he ended up instilling a fear of flying in the doctor, who had never dreaded taking to the skies a day in his life.

Doing his best to settle in for the lengthy trip to Morocco, Intaglio stretched one leg out so he could fish his keys from his pants pocket.

"Ah," Bonnet said, "time for a nap?"

"Huh? Oh, you hear the keys. Yes. Is that okay with you?"

"It's an extraordinary talent you have."

"Something I taught myself as a youngster to escape the tirades of my father."

He slid the keyring onto his index finger and hung his hand over the armrest between himself and Bonnet. The keys dangled and he closed his eyes. In fifteen minutes exactly, the keys would fall from his finger and he would wake, as refreshed as if he'd slept the whole night through.

* * *

The roller coaster stalled at the crest of a bend, Bonnet stepped out of the carriage and made his way up the track to a power box, behind which he could relieve himself without being in anyone's line of sight. Finishing his business there, he returned to the carriage and stepped over Dr. Intaglio to his own seat and buckled himself in. Someone had apparently repaired the ride, because moments later it resumed its bumpy course. Bonnet stared ahead at the track that occupied his mind's eye, wondering when the inevitable drop would come.

Davenport had called him aside for an illuminating conversation recently at a seedy sports bar on Capitol Hill. In Davenport's view, Dr. Intaglio had decided which bed he meant to lie in. Bonnet, in that same view, was at a crossroads, every bit as important as the one where legendary blues man Robert Johnson had made his deal with the devil. Davenport was prepared to accept Intaglio as an unfortunate casualty in a much larger campaign to turn the tide of the Black Phantom's influence throughout the criminal world.

"But you, Bonnet," Davenport had said to him in sweet but seemingly sincere tones, "you're another bag of dice altogether. You have potential we haven't even begun to tap into, and you saw for yourself, if you'll excuse the expression, how Intaglio responded to that realization in my hotel room the other day. He doesn't want to see you rise in the estimation of the Portable Nine, or the Black Phantom. Either bed you choose, my friend, will end up being the bottom bunk as long as you continue to tether yourself to that paragon of self-interest."

Not a bad description of the doctor, Bonnet had to admit to himself. *Not bad at all.* That wasn't to say that Bonnet wanted the same role for himself. He didn't need to be a paragon, but he sure as hell could use a little more self-interest in his life. Helping Davenport and the rest of the Nine take a slice out of Cloft Industries might been a step in that direction.

That particular ship had sailed for him, but there were other boats on the ocean. He had told Davenport of his and Intaglio's plan to regroup with the Phantom and bring him up to speed on the Portable Nine's plan to embezzle enough money from Archie Cloft's fiscal surplus to set them up for life. Davenport was surprisingly pleased by the news. He encouraged Bonnet to make the most of the trip by finding out what the hell the Black Phantom was doing in Morocco. Even though it had seemed to Bonnet that the Phantom already held the winning hand by knowing about the Cloft caper, he acceded to the plan without complaint or hesitation. He would gather intelligence for Davenport, he assured the man, and get it to him at the first opportunity.

It had been a lie, of course. Bonnet and Intaglio had already been embroiled in the Phantom's plan to capture the Portable Nine by the time Bonnet met with Davenport.

A dip in the track made his stomach weightless for a moment, but it was not a sign of initial descent. That was still hours off. Knowing he wouldn't sleep a wink in the air, he donned a set of airline headphones and plugged them into the arm rest of his seat. A pedestrian recording of the fourth *Brandenburg Concerto* assailed him. Bach's genius would survive the clumsiness of the interpretation, though. It was better than nothing.

CHAPTER 27

Robin Varnesse pressed play on the digital recorder that Davenport had left for him at the hotel's front desk. Lovinia, Abel, Twitch, and the Butcher sat around the small round table in Robin's room, rapt and barely able to contain the questions they had. The envelope Davenport had stuffed the recorder into also contained a brief note, stating that it was best if everyone except Miranda, Bonnet, and Intaglio were present for the listening, and that the storage card be destroyed when they were done. Destruction of such media, and accompanying notes, was standard procedure for the Nine, so the fact that Davenport felt it necessary to point out the obvious gave the matter additional weight.

Davenport's disembodied voice soon had the floor.

"Hello, friends. Robin, I know I can trust that you have followed my instruction to have everyone present before you listen to this. It eliminates a lot of potential confusion and vigilantism. I want you all to know that my only interest is in keeping things from unraveling further. To do that I will need the help of each and every one of you. Not just a single mercenary on a hero's mission.

"Miranda is in some trouble. I had a note under my door, along with some disturbing pictures, that prove Sam Gutterson is no longer among the living. Whoever delivered these images wants to meet with me, alone. I can't be sure he's the one responsible for Gutterson's death, but it's clear the man was murdered.

"The note also indicated that Miranda has been taken prisoner. I requested card keys to all of your rooms when I checked in. I hope you can overlook the lapse in trust, but it had been a long time since we'd all worked together, and I already suspected mutiny among

us. Anyway, I let myself into her room with my card key. Immediately I noticed an indentation in the wall between the bathroom and the entryway, right about head level. There was a small amount of blood, too. An unmistakable sign of struggle, and one that had Miranda's signature all over it.

"If one of you is inclined, you might find some DNA on that wall. Feel free to avail yourself of the equipment I have locked in the safe in my room. The combination is 32-06-12. I've left instructions at the front desk that any of you can request a spare key to my room. For those of you who aren't tied up with the DNA trace, I'll be in the utility shack near the main parking lot of Discovery Park at seven o'clock tonight. That's where our friend wishes to meet. I expect Miranda will be there as well.

"Stealth is the name of the game, folks. Strike only when it's a sure thing, and let's take this punk alive if we can. At a guess he isn't a trained professional, but he's a loose cannon. Sometimes that's worse. Isn't that right, Butch?"

All eyes shifted reflexively to the Butcher, but he only went on staring at the recorder.

"I guess that about covers it, but it bears repeating: destroy the media card and return the recorder to the safe in my room. Maybe I could handle this one on my own, but I don't want to leave anything to chance, not when there's so much at stake. Let's find out who this reckless fucker is, shall we?"

Robin reached for the recorder and switched it off with an air of calm resignation that he didn't actually feel. He would have much rather flung the goddamn thing across the room while loosing a string of profanities, but that was not his way, not in the company of the others. He would have been out the door already if he'd listened to Davenport's message by himself, which is exactly why Davenport had taken steps to ensure that it didn't happen that way.

Lovinia, clearly sensing his inner struggle with the news that had just been laid on their doorstep, jumped in to fill the awkward pause.

"Listen, Robin, why don't you and I team up on the DNA.

I can run the samples easily enough, but you and Davenport are the only ones who understand how to open the back door to all the federal databases."

"It's a good idea," Abel said. "I should be at Discovery Park when this goes down. I have a lot of experience with night work, and it will be well dark by seven o'clock these days. Of course, I'm not afraid of this little puke, either."

"Sure," Twitch said, "but that's always true. You're not a one-man wrecking ball just because you walk through life un-afraid. And we sure as hell don't look at you as expendable just because you're willing to take on things the rest us might not exactly relish. Besides, this isn't like taking out an Islamic State cell. It's someone who has overestimated his leverage and abilities."

"That's probably true," the Butcher said. "It seems like an overt, clumsy piece of extortion. We might even be able to scare the piss out of him. I say the three of us reconnoiter at the park while Lovinia and Robin chase down the bastard's identity."

"I'll do what the rest of you decide is best," Robin said without looking at anyone, his voice low. "I only have one re-quest. If he's harmed Miranda in any way, I want the Butcher to bring me back his head. I don't give a damn about taking him alive."

He stood up, retrieved the recorder from the table, and left them to their plans. After a moment's awkward silence Lovinia followed him out of the room.

CHAPTER 28

"All comfy-cozy, then?" Jerrod asked, his voice reverberating in the confines of their new location.

Not a trace of mockery in his tone, only in the words. Miranda had no answer.

He rushed at her and bent way down so that his face was mere inches from hers. A caged bulb shone down on them from the ceiling.

"*I asked you a fucking question!*"

"I don't know what you expect to get out of this," Miranda said, unwilling to bend under his scare tactics. "Davenport isn't going to give you any more than I can, just because you have me squirreled away like a damsel in an episode of *Mighty Mouse*."

He stood up straight and gathered his wits. "You have me pegged as a real small-time loser, don't you? Well you might just find out that there's more to J. C. than meets the eye. Turns out I have a *couple* of objectives here tonight. I'll explain them to you, but first things first."

He tossed a set of handcuffs down to her.

"I agreed not to bind you on our way over here, but this isn't going to be much of a hostage situation if I don't have a hostage. Click 'em up."

She secured one of the cuffs firmly around her right wrist and started to do the other one when Jerrod interrupted her.

"Uh, uh, uh. Let's go behind the back, if you don't mind."

It had been worth a shot. Always test the waters. That was Miranda's philosophy. Situations like this had a fairly wide range of possible outcomes. Why let your adversary determine every nuance? But you also had to know when to dig in your heels and when to give in. She reached behind her back and secured the second cuff. She had been handcuffed and tied before, but it never got easier. It was like running down a hallway and having a barrier slam down behind you, and then another one right in front of you. All priorities vanished in an instant, except one: get free.

But she had decided to ride this out. She could have taken him out a hundred times between the hotel and the dingy utility shack serving as her temporary jail cell, but she had decided it was better to learn as much about his motives as possible, even if that meant waiting for Davenport to show up so that Jerrod C. would start spilling some serious beans.

"Okay, that's better. So, like I said, I have a couple of objectives here tonight. One of them is to let your friend in on the wishes of my employer. The other is more of a personal thing. On the first point, Mr. Davenport's cooperation is non-negotiable. On the other, I have a little wiggle room. Not my choice, mind you, but circumstances dictate that now is not the time to be overly selfish."

"Why are you telling me this? It seems to me that I'll find out soon enough, along with Davenport."

He put something to his lips that she assumed was a pinch-hitter of dope. Not an encouraging sign of how the night could turn out. But then he blew into the pipe, hard. She felt a sting at her neck and wished she could rub it.

"What the fuck?" she said.

"A mild neurotoxin. You have a few minutes of consciousness ahead of you. Then rest."

"Why?" she asked, her neck beginning to itch a little.

"Well, that's between Davenport and me. You don't need to worry your pretty little head about it."

He picked up a rock that must have been used by service workers to prop open the door and hurtled it at the overhead fixture. The bulb shattered from the impact, plunging them into darkness.

The condescending shit. She had misplayed this, and her last thought as she slipped from wakefulness was how deeply she regretted not having put her hands around this twerp's throat and squeezing until he ceased to draw or expel breath.

* * *

Davenport paced before the entrance of the utility shack, scanning for any sign of what might be going on inside. Seeing and hearing nothing, he wandered around to the back of the small structure. Nothing there but a couple of high windows of block glass. He completed the circuit and approached the only door. The knob was stiff but clicked free with enough pressure. He pushed the door inward and entered the pitch-black interior.

"Mr. Davenport, I'm guessing?" came a male voice from somewhere in the dark.

As he'd expected, the voice was young.

"Who am I speaking to?" Davenport closed the door behind him to avoid being backlit for the bastard. If one of them was going to be blind, they both were.

"You can call me Jerrod. Your friend is here at my feet, but believe it or not she fell asleep."

"Miranda?" Davenport whispered before realizing there was no need for quiet. In a louder voice he added, "Are you in here?"

A penlight flashed on about ten feet from where he stood. It took his eyes a moment to adjust, and when they did he saw Miranda's slumped form. A few black curls hung across one eye. The other was closed. There was no obvious sign of violence, but Davenport refused to believe she'd simply fallen asleep. She was comfortable in situations that would send the average grizzly bear into a permanent breakdown, but no one was *that* comfortable.

"What have you done to her, you little shit?" He found a light switch, but it didn't do anything when he toggled it.

The penlight flicked off and Davenport could hear the man shuffle across the concrete floor (over broken glass?). Miranda's kidnapper wasn't as dumb as Davenport had hoped. He was moving around to make it difficult to pinpoint his location in the small room. He'd probably been here during the day, too, studying the space to get a feel for any advantages that might be had in a confrontation. It wasn't the first time Davenport had found himself at a disadvantage, however. Experience was going to have to make up for the imbalance in preparedness. That's all there was to it.

"Mr. Davenport." The voice hadn't come from the corner Davenport was expecting. Damn the acoustics in the small room. "I understand you can be a bit of a hero, so I want to start there. I was joking about your friend taking a nappy-poo. She's been injected with a slow-acting neurotoxin. Now, before you get all excited, the antidote is hidden nearby. If our little conversation goes the way I want it to, I'll wake her up and send you both packing. Otherwise ... Well, you understand how these things go."

"Understood," Davenport replied, struggling not to grit his teeth, which might have been viewed as a lack of self-control. "Now what's this about?"

"This is about someone called the Black Phantom." He paused, but Davenport said nothing. "He has a very strong wish to see you."

"I suppose it finally dawned on him that he forgot my birthday."

"The Phantom wishes to see you and the rest of your merry band. In person. In Morocco. Soon. I'm here to facilitate that meeting."

"That wish of his had to trickle down over quite a few stones to reach the likes of you. Can you give me the name of a rock or two above you? Just curious."

"Then stay curious. Will you make this easy for me, or does it need to get challenging? I need the Portable Nine in Morocco. I'm the first to admit that it will be a hell of a lot easier with your cooperation. It's also the quickest way to satisfy that curiosity of yours."

Davenport liked the desperation that had crept into the man's voice. This was a hell of a thing. If not for the fact that Miranda lay dying on the floor, it might have been amusing.

"Before we go any further with this, can I have your full name at least?"

"Oh, fine. Why not? Jerrod Cafferty. Ask around, you might learn something about me."

Cafferty. It didn't ring any bells, but Davenport didn't have long to ponder the name before the door at his back came banging inward. He spun around and saw the silhouette of a large man in the doorway. A snapping sound, followed by the shaking of something containing fluid of some kind. Then the eruption of green light as a light stick arced to the floor.

"Sorry, Davenport," the Butcher said, closing the door and stepping deeper into the room. His hatchet hung at his side. "Pussyfooting is not my strong suit." He turned his attention to Jerrod. "What the fuck's going on here, punk? Where did you hear that name?"

The effect was startling, even to Davenport: Butch standing there in the midst of all that sudden, eerie light, like a hired scare at a small-town haunted house. It was clear that Jerrod was impressed as well. He was slow to respond.

"The Butcher. I wasn't expecting to see you just yet."

"I get a lot of that," the Butcher responded.

"Davenport," J. C. said, all nerves, "explain to your friend about the situation with Miranda. Now!"

The Butcher turned to Davenport, as if to say, "Well?"

"He claims he shot her full of some kind of neurotoxin," Davenport said, pointing to where Miranda lay. "He's got the antidote hidden somewhere around here. If we don't do as he asks, she'll die."

The Butcher leveled his gaze back on Jerrod and took a step in his direction. "You know something? I was given a special request involving this woman's well-being. A friend of mine asked that I separate your head from your neck if it turns out you've laid a hand on her. What do you think about that?"

Jerrod backed into the rear wall. "I think you'd better listen to Davenport. If anything happens to me, Miranda dies. I can bring her back."

"Where's the goddamn antidote?"

"I can't tell you that. It's my only insurance policy, for God's sake."

The Butcher laughed, and it carried an unpleasant reverberation in the confines of the shack. His head swung from side to side and Davenport thought he might be reconsidering his course of action. But then the laughter stopped, and the Butcher said, "You're young, but I would have thought you'd outgrown fairy tales. There's no such thing as an insurance policy, young man. They're a myth."

He brought the hand axe up over his shoulder, took aim and let it fly. End over end it sailed toward Jerrod Cafferty. Davenport tracked its trajectory, swearing it had lapsed into slow motion as it buried itself in the wall inches below Cafferty's crotch. In an instant the world sped up to normal speed again and Jerrod clutched at his privates, his face a mask of shock and dread. It stayed that way even after the Butcher retrieved his weapon, with some effort, and pee spread across the front of Jerrod's jeans.

The Butcher slid his axe into the loop inside his jacket and picked up Miranda to move her outside. He paused at the door. "If there's really an antidote somewhere around here, we'll find it, but my guess is that he's bluffing. She'll come out of it on her own."

"I didn't know you were a gambling man, Butch," Davenport said. "Would you be so quick to risk your own neck?"

"I think you know I would. Now, if we're going to pay the Black Phantom a visit, I say we do it on our terms. We don't need puffed-up pukes like that calling the shots for us. In fact, maybe we *should* kill the little bastard."

"That would narrow our options, for damn sure. Maybe

we wouldn't have to go to Morocco, but we'd sure as hell need to get out of Seattle."

"Might as well be Morocco, though, huh?"

Davenport dropped his head and gave it an exasperated shake. When he looked up again the Butcher was smiling.

"So the kid lives?" Davenport asked.

The Butcher left without another word on the subject.

* * *

"You got him?"

The voice was a whisper in the dark, coming from a patch of trees to their left. The Butcher laid Miranda down in the grass as Davenport went to investigate.

"Jerrod, that you?" the same voice asked.

"Yeah," Davenport whispered, hoping to buy a little time.

"Everything copasetic? Did he fall for it?"

"Did he? Shit." Davenport was in full voice now, and he lunged at the speaker, grabbing him by the lapels and pushing him against a cedar.

The two men stared at each other in equivalent, stunned recognition.

"Davenport."

"Brindle. I'll be a sonofabitch." He let go of the man's multi-colored sport coat.

"Well, fuck." Brindle's eyes darted over Davenport's shoulder. They were the unpredictable eyes of a frightened raccoon.

Davenport didn't dare check to see what, or whom, Brindle had glanced at.

"Okay, Davenport, look. I need to show you something. I don't know what Jerrod did to upset things, but this is all very straightforward. He and I are just messengers." His hand went to one of the pockets in his coat.

"You'd better pull that hand out a good deal more slowly

than you put it in," Davenport said.

Max nodded and slowly removed something from the pocket before glancing over Davenport's shoulder again.

This time Davenport couldn't resist the bait. He turned to have a look, but Butch and Miranda were still out of sight, and Jerrod didn't appear to have emerged from the utility shack. It had been a ruse. He turned back to Brindle in time to see that he had something up to his lips, through which he now blew, sharp and hard. Something stung Davenport's throat. His hand flew up to rub the spot.

"Dammit, what the hell?"

That was all he had time to utter. The poison acted quickly, sending him first to his knees and then onto his side. The dim light of the hovering moon eventually blurred and faded to black.

* * *

Max Brindle stepped over Davenport's limp body to find out what the hell had gone wrong inside the small structure. Several yards on, he almost tripped over the woman's body.

"Who the fuck are you?" someone nearby wanted to know.

Brindle spun to his left, and before him stood a large man with deep-cut features.

"Max Brindle," he said, sticking out his hand, which still held the blow pipe.

The large man seemed thrown by the invitation to shake hands, which had been the point. Max shrugged and brought the pipe to his lips. With a sudden burst of air, another dart had found its mark. The man went for the axe at his side, but fell to one knee before he could free it from its loop. Then the other knee struck the ground and he fell backward. The pressure on both knees looked like it must have been incredible, but Max wasn't about to alleviate the man's discomfort. He wasn't a registered nurse, for fuck's sake, and this was presumably the one and only Butcher that Jerrod had mentioned. Fuck him. Max Brindle's only job was to get the Butcher, Davenport, and the other members of the Portable Nine to the Black Phantom. It was enough of a job.

A scream came from above, and for a brief moment Brindle wondered if the sky had cracked open, letting a fallen angel drop through to the earthly realm. A straggler from the great rebellion, perhaps. Of course, the truth was more prosaic. He got himself turned almost halfway around when the full weight of a man fell upon him. Someone had jumped from the roof of the utility shack, and now they both slammed to the ground and rolled as one across pine cones and loose rocks.

"One of the Nine, I presume?" Brindle managed as they struggled.

"You'd better hope the next thing out of your mouth is a good reason for me not to end your life," his attacker responded, turning Brindle onto his back and pinning him.

"You have a problem on your hands. Your compadres ... They've been poisoned with blow darts. I have the antidote. Without it they die. You and the others will need to play ball with me. And we have to think in terms of minutes, not hours, unless you want to become the Portable Six. Please, let me up, so we can talk like gentlemen."

After a pause, the man pinning him down said, "Okay, there's a picnic table over there." He nodded to a point outside of Max's field of vision. "That's our conference room. Let's talk."

* * *

Twitch Markham stood behind a knotty old poplar, a vantage point from which he had watched as Abel flung himself from the roof of the utility shack onto the other man's back. It was the first piece of action he'd been able to make much sense of since the Butcher and Davenport had hauled Miranda out of the structure. Everyone seemed to be dropping like spiders with their silks cut. He was eager to step into the action but knew to bide his time.

Sit tight but stay alert.

Practically the story of his life. At least it had started to feel that way toward the end of their run together. The Great Collapse. Of course, it hadn't been a final collapse. Here they were again: the Portable Nine, fighting for justice in a world where all moral judgments were relative, all progress fleeting, and all sense of accomplishment false.

God help us all.

"We all have our place in things," the man in the sport coat said to Abel, who sat across from him at the picnic table. "I shouldn't have to tell you that. Allow me to explain mine."

"You can spare me the fancy talk, mate," Abel said back to the man. "I know you're only using it to conceal your fear. Let me explain something to *you*. There is no lasting hierarchy in this life. Right now, you have me at a disadvantage, but the worm will turn, and you will suffer for your choices. So let's leave philosophy out of this, and why don't you tell me what it's going to take to revive my mates."

"Just a little cooperation, I assure you. Cigarette?"

Abel shook his head. The other man shrugged and leaned to one side so he could dig into the pocket of his patchwork sport coat. What he brought to his lips, however, wasn't a cigarette. Not a regular one anyway. Maybe French, but it was too dark to be an American cigarette, and too small to be a cigar. It was the man's smile as he took a deep breath that raised the alarm.

"Abel!" Twitch shouted, stepping out from behind the tree.

But his warning only served as a distraction. Abel turned toward Twitch's voice, exposing his neck to the man who sat across from him, and the man blew. A moment of stillness followed, but no more. At the end of it, Abel began swatting at the air in front of him, as though warding off ghosts, before falling straight backward. His legs caught on the picnic table, leaving him in an awkward position until gravity at last pulled him all the way to the ground.

"Motherfucker!" Twitch yelled as he charged at the man who had risen and backed away from the table. *"I'll tear the tongue out of your head!"*

"I'd be more concerned with keeping a civil tongue in *your* head than in removing his."

The voice, which had come from behind him, stopped him cold. Of course there'd been two of them. One in the shack and one on lookout. How careless they'd been. It was a rusty machine Davenport had embarked upon oiling up to full speed. Twitch only hoped they were able to get the kinks worked out before one or more of them paid for a stupid mistake with their lives, if it wasn't already in the cards.

A sting at the nape of his neck. "Damn," he said, rubbing at the spot. Before he could turn far enough around to see his attacker, he was down.

❊ ❊ ❊

"That was some splendid timing, young man," Max said as he took several steps toward Jerrod. "I do believe I could learn to rely on you."

"I'm still not going to suck your dick," Jerrod said.

They shared a brief laugh.

"Listen," Jerrod went on, "we need to get these poor slobs in the van."

"True enough. Why don't you sort of … group them together while I get the van and back it in between those large trees over there."

"Yeah, cool. But, uh, Max?"

"Yes?"

"You going to tell me now? Where's the antidote?"

"Ah, yes. You'll like this. It's secreted on the aircraft, waiting for us at Boeing Field."

"On the plane? Why?"

"I figured most of them would turn up here, despite your instructions for Davenport to come alone, but I wasn't sure we'd have to incapacitate them all, or manage to. I figured if push came to shove and I had to tell any of them where the antidote is, they'd see how pointless it would be to resist flying to Morocco at the Black Phantom's request. But we can have the rest of this conversation on our way to the airport, no?"

"Yeah, yeah. Absolutely. Let's finish this."

Max started off toward the parking lot, but stopped, remembering something. With a snap of his fingers he said, "Once you've got them in a pile, use one of their phones to text the other two. They must be back at the hotel. Tell them to meet us at Boeing Field in forty-five minutes or their friends don't wake up. Include a picture of the bodies."

"Sure thing, boss. Now that I realize they do have cell phones."

Max didn't ordinarily like running around in the dark, endangering his life and risking capture, but by God he felt good tonight. By the time he opened the rear doors to the van, he was whistling "Wouldn't It Be Loverly?".

He'd never felt more certain that it would be.

PART III: JUST DESSERTS

When I looked down, I saw what had become of my blackbird. It lay dead next to the trunk of the oak, its beak open as if the fall had taken it by surprise.
—Joe R. Lansdale, *Cold in July*

The desert was a school, a school where each day, each hour, a final examination was offered, where failure meant death and the buzzards landed to correct the papers.
—Louis L'Amour, *Shalako*

CHAPTER 29

L a Tarte was the apotheosis of the Black Phantom's dark objectives and flawed philosophies. He walked its perimeter like a panther circling its prey. The Pie, in English, though from the outside its name was meaningless. It was simply a circular building. But there was no other man-made structure in sight, so its very presence was odd to begin with— to the outsider, not to the Phantom. To him it represented the inevitable completion of a goal that had had him in its iron grip for too long.

He let one hand drag lightly along the rough stucco wall as he completed his circuit. At the strange building's only means of ingress he paused to gaze inside, patting out imaginary wrinkles in his white silk shirt, which flowed over meticulously pressed dress pants. After buffing the tops of his burgundy Westons along the calves of each leg, he strode into the heart of *la Tarte* like the emperor of the very desert itself.

"Ah, Dr. Intaglio," he said, nodding to a cell on his left. "And the good Mr. Bonnet," he added, addressing a cell on the opposite side of the enclosure.

And here is where *la Tarte* earned its name, for on the inside it was divided up into wedge-shaped cells that left a small circular yard in the center. This is where the Black Phantom now stood. The structure comprised nine cells, in fact, but neither the cells nor the prisoners they were constructed to incarcerate were portable. This is where the so-called Portable Nine were to become his caged birds.

"You sonofabitch," was Dr. Intaglio's dry-throated response.

"Oh," the Phantom said, clapping his hands together and returning his attention to the psychiatrist with a look of mock sadness. "The last refuge of the hopeless, cursing." He took a step toward Intaglio's cell and replaced the sad look with one of rage. "Don't think for a goddamn minute that locking you up in the desert is the worst I can do, you treacherous bastard!"

The sun was oppressive here in the center of the Pie, where even the hot desert winds provided no relief. The cells were fifteen feet high and there was only a wire-mesh ceiling covering them. Wooden door frames at each cell held metal bars that ran eight feet from top to bottom. A rough cement floor blanketed the cells but not the central yard or entrance. If ever there was a more primitive, more brutal, prison than *el Pozo*, he had created it here in the Algerian desert, not far from the Moroccan border.

"You will be joined soon. You have decided where your loyalties lie, so you will share accommodations with those you serve. Until they arrive, might I suggest that you cogitate on the wisdom of your alliance?"

"You've got this upside down, Phantom." Intaglio gripped two of the bars of his cell and pressed his face closer. "Nothing has changed. I serve no one but you. Everything I've done —everything Bonnet and I have done—has been to further your ends."

"That's not what Max Brindle tells me, and he's a pretty reliable bird. But there will be time enough to prove what you say, if it's provable. For now, I'm afraid you will suffer some. My court differs from all civilized courts in one key respect: here you are guilty until proven innocent. That doesn't mean I'm incapable of reason or mercy, but they won't come easily.

"Maybe you could steal a play or two from your friend here." The Black Phantom stepped aside and gestured across to the other side of *la Tarte*. "Mr. Bonnet seems content enough with his lot. Perhaps he senses that it needn't be a permanent one."

Bonnet sat in the center of his cell with his legs crossed,

his eyes closed, and something like a smile on his lips. *The ascetic personified*, the Phantom thought with a chuckle. Maybe you had to get blind in this life before you could truly see. Funny how that kind of advice generally came from those who lived in fear of the dark. The thought ended up troubling the Phantom a little and he focused on Dr. Intaglio once more.

"You have enough food and water to last for days." He glanced at the covered plastic barrel and metal bin in Intaglio's cell. "But I'll return this evening. I suggest you enjoy your peaceful solitude in the meantime. It's a rare gift, and who knows what the future holds?"

The Black Phantom turned his back to the doctor and, winking at the blind man across the way, exited *la Tarte* with a low gurgle of laughter.

* * *

"Joseph?"

The doctor stared across the prison yard at his companion of many years. He didn't feel like answering right away, though he wasn't sure why. Then it dawned on him. He was scanning the warehouses of his mind for a trick he could pull on his hapless friend. Why, he didn't know. Was it a need to lash out at something—anything—that drove his sadistic urge? Had the new reality of their relationship to the Black Phantom pushed him into a state of true loathing for the sidekick he'd carried for so long? Or was it simply the thought of being double-crossed by Max Brindle that brought out his vindictive streak? The answers to these questions didn't trouble him much. The desire to work mischief was in him, and giving it rein was all that mattered.

He decided he'd stand a better chance of pressing the right buttons in Mr. Bonnet if he had an idea what visions were currently standing in for the man's connection to reality.

"I'm still here," Intaglio said at last.

"We chose our side, I suppose." Bonnet said, his voice unsteady. "And we chose wrong. I don't think we're going to come out of this with a friend between us, if we come out of it at all."

Max fucking Brindle.

"Where are you?" Intaglio asked.

"Where—oh, that. It's not worth talking about."

"I want to know."

Bonnet rose to his feet and let his head hang as he shook it slowly from side to side.

"It's … not a nice place."

"Well, okay. It has that much in common with reality."

Bonnet's head came back up and he appeared to be staring directly at Dr. Intaglio. It gave the doctor a chill, despite the suffocating temperature.

"The heat you no doubt attribute to the blazing sun is for me the output of a billion flames and rivers of molten brimstone. The sizzling upright snakes I see are bars. Had the Black Phantom not spoken to you I would have assumed him to be the towering devil I beheld in his place. So yes, there is commonality between my perception and yours. My hallucinatory view of the world isn't always so far from the mark."

"Hmm, perhaps."

Intaglio wanted to know how he appeared to the blind man across the yard, but he didn't dare ask. There was such a thing as too much truth, and he'd been paddling through an ocean of it for weeks, especially the last two days.

"What if you've got things backwards, Bonnet? What if you're the one who sees things clearly and the rest of us are running blind?"

"I don't follow."

That was a laugh. All the man had ever done in his life was follow.

"You seem to be describing hell," Intaglio went on. "What if that's not an illusion or hallucination but reality? What if you've died and wound up in the eternal furnace?"

"Oh, I reasoned such nonsense out long ago. If hell was all

I ever saw, maybe your question would give me pause, but the variety of my helpful visions has kept me on this side of lunacy. This, too, shall pass."

Dammit. Intaglio wished he could wipe the dirty smile off the man's face. He had never felt more alone in his misguided life.

CHAPTER 30

The Black Phantom paced through the rooms of his Algerian hideout, completely naked. His luxuriant midnight-blue robe lay draped over the footboard of his bed. Soon he would hear the roar of a Jeep or Land Rover or some souped-up SUV as it crested the great dune to the northwest of his temporary residence. Then he would know the man was close, for there was no other destination in this part of the desert. It would be the man and his driver.

His nudity wasn't only for effect. It was often his preferred state in private, especially in hot climes. But he knew it could be used to emphasize his power over others, too, maybe even to establish that power. In this case, the dynamic was long established, but men got foolish notions in their heads when they traveled great distances. Something about seeing new lands deluded some men into believing there was more to them than in fact there was. In such cases a little gentle reminding of the order of things never hurt. It was the same reason he hadn't gone himself to retrieve the fellow for whom he now waited. A show of influence.

And so the Phantom stopped at a window where a warm breeze whispered through, tousling the sheer green curtains as it entered his dominion. The sky pressed down on the desert at the horizon, threatening to make fragile glass of the sandy redoubt. But here, in the shadow of his shelter, he could see the sky for what it was, and how it respected and feared the sand beneath his feet. He sensed, in turn, the desert's aloofness toward the heavens. And he could now hear a rumbling in the distance that could only mean one thing: his guest would soon arrive.

He resumed his pacing, which slowed in proportion to the crescendo of the vehicle's engine outside. Exiting through a back way, he waited for the driver to come to a stop on the opposite side of the building before sauntering into view around a corner.

"Jesus Christ," Max Brindle said, stepping down from the Jeep, which had pulled alongside the Phantom's mode of transportation.

"Not quite," The Black Phantom replied.

"I get that times are tough," Brindle said, "but surely you could wrangle a set of clothes from someone."

"This is a naked land, Max." He spread his arms out on either side of his muscular torso. "It has no respect for anything hidden or disguised and will devour what it perceives as false."

"You're as flowery as the man you want to bring down. So much talk in this trade anymore." Max gave his head a shake. "What does any of it mean? You're as false as they come, and I don't see you bursting into flame."

The Phantom took several steps toward the man.

"You refer to Davenport, yes?"

Brindle nodded, a little nervous, whether at the over-step of his words or at the Phantom's closer proximity it was hard to say.

"You don't have enough faith in your own work. Davenport and his gang of do-gooders are as good as got ... if you've come here with the news I'm expecting."

"Um, yeah," Brindle said. "I was able to get the Portable Nine as far as South America. They're in a safe house. Hardly what I'd call a *fait accompli*."

"No, you did well. You're too modest. Now you and I, we take a little ride."

He jerked his chin in the driver's direction. Whoever was behind the wheel reversed out of the paltry shade of the building and turned to pursue the far side of the dune he had crossed to get to this remote location.

Another show of strength: Brindle and the Phantom were

alone in the desert. There was nothing the American wouldn't do now if promised guidance, water, or recompense in return. Or if threatened in some way.

"Come. Have a drink while I get dressed. Then I have something to show you."

* * *

The interior of the dwelling brought welcome, if slight, relief from the Algerian heat. Max's first impression was that the place was a thrown-together dump, but as he ambled through the main room, he realized that the Phantom, or someone, had applied a minimalist hand to the design of everything, from the rustic furniture to the African tapestries to the carved tiles of the fireplace. Gazing more intently at the tiles, he saw that they featured intricate figures engaged in what might have been joyful dancing, but for the terrible frowns they all wore.

He'd risked life and limb to make sure every member of the Portable Nine was sequestered in an undisclosed location amid the jungles of South America. Well, okay, he'd only physically collared five of them, with Jerrod's help. Two had fled before he could get to them, but the remaining two had come along willingly enough for the sake of their friends' safety. It had all gone off like a perfect soufflé, as far as Max was concerned.

So why did he harbor the feeling that the Phantom hadn't called him here to present him with a reward for services rendered?

"I want you to see for yourself what's possible with a little vision and hard work," the Phantom called from an adjacent room. "Sometimes we accomplish more than we realize." Then, stepping into Max's line of sight wearing a black silk shirt with mother-of-pearl buttons down the front and a pair of sharp slacks, he added, "Such moments must be celebrated to buoy us up for the dark days of defeat. Come."

The Phantom strode out into the blazing sun, across to

where his own SUV waited.

"Really?" Max said, nodding toward the black vehicle. "Black, in this heat?"

Glancing over his shoulder at his guest, the Phantom replied, "Observant. Good. Black is my color. It is the color by which I have been judged all my life." Here he held up his hands to emphasize that he was referring to the color of his skin. "And it is the color by which I intimidate. So yes, a black mode of transportation, even in this desert heat."

He opened the driver's-side door and slid behind the wheel as Max passed in front of the grill to the other side.

"I will park some distance from what I wish you to see," the Black Phantom said as he steered the SUV away from the structure and into the vast sameness that stretched in all directions. "You can walk?"

"I can walk, at least until I drop."

At that the Phantom laughed harder than Max thought the little joke warranted, and despite the cloying heat that his driver refused to combat with air-conditioning—only the fan and rolled-down windows—he felt a chill climb up his arms and across the nape of his neck. He'd known he was playing a kind of chess match with a ruthless gamesman, but it had never before occurred to him that he might be in league with a madman.

CHAPTER 31

L ovinia Dulcet had never held with meditation. Not for herself, anyway. She had no doubt it served a purpose for those who truly needed to escape the realities of their tedious lives in order to maintain a healthy perspective, but in her line of work the opposite was the case. If she wanted to remain not only healthy but alive, she needed her wits about her at all times. There was no room to embrace distraction or flirt with the appeal of respite. Calm was always an act, and not always an easy one to pull off.

They were in real trouble here. Maybe more than they'd ever known. They'd been drugged repeatedly on the way from Seattle to the African desert, only to awaken at last in these cages. The nine of them had never been taken prisoner en masse before, and it had frightening implications, for them and the world. But there was nothing to be gained from the bickering that currently worked its way back and forth across and around the circular enclosure in which they'd been locked. Her companions would come to their senses eventually. She had no doubts on that point, but there was no time to lose at the expense of their temporary unwillingness to grasp the urgency of the situation. If they were in a discipline that demanded the assiduous use of every minute during a job, it had now been reduced to seconds. Water and food were one thing, and she wasn't sure they had enough of either to get them as far as the Black Phantom claimed. But perhaps just as dangerous was the psychological impact they would start to endure before long—all of them except maybe Abel Hazard, anyway.

And so while they hollered and blamed and conjectured

and theorized, she went to work with her Twin Delights. The implements weren't accustomed to such strenuous activity. The flesh they were designed to pierce always gave way with ease. The concrete that had been hastily poured to serve as a floor to this circular prison, on the other hand, came away in chips and wafers that seemed awfully small payment for the amount of effort she was putting in.

Mr. Bonnet occupied the cell to her immediate left, which is where she had first noticed a fissure in the corner, near to where the floor met the wall. That would have been reason enough to begin there, but there was also some sense to joining up with Bonnet first. He might need more help navigating an escape than the rest of them. Why save that dilemma for last? Also, the option to her right was Twitch Markham. He would have his role to play in coming events, as they all must, but she didn't favor the help of a nervous man until sturdier stock had been freed from its cage.

On the other side of Mr. Bonnet was the Butcher. She could actually catch glimpses of him when he came right up to the bars of his cell and wrapped his powerful hands around them as he argued with Dr. Intaglio and Abel Hazard across the way. It seemed to Lovinia that he could have ripped the cage door free of its moorings with those simian fists. She feared him as much as she valued his strength. All of the Nine feared him a little—again, except for Abel. Abel and Bonnet were the Portable Nine's resident freaks of nature (surgery, in Abel's case, but it amounted to the same thing). But as long as the Butcher had something productive to focus his energies on, his closest allies would remain safe. She had to have that much faith.

Clutching the Twins with a thumb on each head, Lovinia continued to chip away at the crack in the floor. The lack of immediate results discouraged her, but instead of giving up, she hammered away with more force and speed. Then, as chips of poorly mixed concrete began to fly from her strikes, her intensity increased again, out of hope instead of doubt. Tunneling under with the Twin Delights wasn't her goal. She aimed to carve out enough of a trough beneath the wall to allow her to pull pieces of it inward with her hands. Getting the job done before the Black Phantom returned to make the next move in his demented game of desert chess was a long shot, but trying had to be more productive than the arguing the others were engaged in.

It wasn't until she paused in her work that she noticed they had fallen silent around her. If they hadn't all been locked up like rats waiting to be experimented on, she had no doubt they would now be huddled together, peering over her shoulder to see what she was up to.

"Lovinia?" It was Twitch.

"No, it's the fucking sand snake," she replied, half joking, half irritated.

"What are you playing at?" Dr. Intaglio asked.

"She's digging out," Miranda Gissing said from her cell on Intaglio's right. It was one of two that flanked the entrance to *la Tarte*. Davenport had been deposited in the other. "Isn't that right?" she called to Lovinia in a slightly louder voice.

Lovinia stood, wiping sweat and several strands of black hair from her forehead. Davenport sat far back in his enclosure on a narrow wooden bench that rested against one wall. He had been in that position since his arrival, refusing to involve himself in the disagreement the others only now took a rest from. But he was paying attention. Oh yes, even with his eyes cast down to his feet, he was listening and thinking. She'd have tossed him a penny for his thoughts, if she'd had one on her. His mind was never idle, never off, and more than a handful of times he'd saved the ass of one or another of the Portable Nine as a result. His austere presence suddenly emboldened her. They were the Portable Nine, goddammit. Not some group of chumps the Black Phantom could kick around however he saw fit. He'd be sorry he'd ever taken it into his head to make prisoners of them, if it was the last thing she ever changed his mind about.

"Yeah, I'm digging. Maybe it's not as effective as yelling my damn head off, but it's all I can think to do."

Her skirt was black and made of leather, but at least she had decided against one of the pairs of leather pants that were hanging in the closet of her hotel room back in Seattle. As uncomfortable as she was in the merciless Algerian heat, at least she didn't have on a pair of leather fucking pants. And she'd managed to trade in her high heels for more sensible shoes in Venezuela. Getting through your day was often a matter of counting your blessings. It may have been her mother who had taught her that once, probably on one of her alcoholic tears.

"And what's your plan once you've broken through to Mr. Bonnet's side of the wall?" Abel asked. "That's where you're digging, isn't it?"

She had to look through the bars on the very left side of her cell to be able to see him. Robin Varnesse's and Twitch Markham's cells lay between Abel's and Lovinia's, and she could see nothing of either of them.

"I don't know. Strength in numbers? I noticed there was already a crack on the floor, leading right up to the wall, so I figured that's where I'd start."

"We're not going to get anywhere by turning our individual cells into one big one."

"What do you suggest?"

"The back."

It took her a moment to figure out who had spoken. It wasn't Abel. She pinpointed the direction the voice had come from before she identified the timbre as belonging to the Butcher. His fists still gripped two bars of his cell and he pressed his face between two others.

"What did you say?"

"The crack on your floor. How far is it from the back wall?"

Unsure of the answer, she turned to examine her handiwork. The end of the crack was closer to the wall she shared with Bonnet than it was to the back wall of her enclosure, but between that beginning point of the crack and the shared wall, she had chipped out a triangular expanse that she was hoping would soon allow her to start prying pieces of wall away. Two of the triangle's vertices were located where the floor met the interior wall, of course, and one of them was also quite near the back wall.

"Part of it's close, but that's not the direction I've been digging in."

"That's my point. Maybe it should be."

Of course. The entrance to this absurd prison had no door or gate. It was completely open, so there was no need to tunnel under the bars to access the central area. She only needed to break out the back and run around to let herself in through the entrance. But what good would it do? There she'd be in the middle of the prison, and there the rest would be, still captive in their cages.

She could hide, she supposed, and hope to jump the Black Phantom when he returned. Catch him unawares with her Twin Delights. A risky proposition, especially if he didn't come back alone, or if he spotted the damage at the back of the prison when he approached and therefore entered suspecting a trap. But the one advantage that tunneling out the back had over staying put, or joining forces with Mr. Bonnet, was that it would allow her to hand off her weapons-cum-tools to one of the others, perhaps the Butcher himself, in case sheer brawn ended up being called for. She could toss them from where she stood and let him do all the heavy lifting, but that was no sure thing. What if they glanced off one of the bars and twirled away, forever out of reach for any of them? Besides, the bars would complicate the act of throwing, whether she stood back and gave the needles an overhead toss through her own bars—sacrificing long-range accuracy in the process—or reached her throwing arm through the bars first, thereby sacrificing force.

It was equally improbable that she'd be able to pass her Twin Delights around, first to Bonnet, who would then relay them to the Butcher. The walls between cells didn't strike her as particularly strong, but they were thick. Plus, there was the added thickness of the door frames. Even to pass the Delights to a next-door neighbor would require some kind of toss. There was no way to hand them directly to the person. No matter how she thought it through, throwing felt like a last resort.

"Okay," she called to the Butcher, "now we're talking. That's how I'll proceed. I'll tunnel out the back of my cell and bring the needles around to you."

"Are they going to survive this kind of abuse?" Robin Varnesse asked. She couldn't see him, but his smooth voice and subtle accent were instant tip-offs.

"The Twin Delights? Let's hear it for Japanese steel, baby. They could break us out of this overheated joint and help us build twelve more like it before they'd so much as need sharpening."

And like that, the time for talk was over and Lovinia was hunkered down once more: poking, digging, scraping, and excavating with renewed hope that she would not die like a dog in the bleak Algerian desert.

CHAPTER 32

L ike many aspiring despots before him, the Black Phantom struggled to reconcile his feelings of immortality with a sense of reason that assured him he was, if anything, marked by his mortality at least as much as he was by any claim to power or privilege. The threat of death was a sea surrounding his island of one, and Death itself could appear—scythe in hand —from as many quarters as it could in any actual sea he'd ever sailed. Would he drown, starve, or be taken by a shark? Only God knew for sure, and He was keeping shtum.

One way he didn't anticipate having his mortal coil sprung was as the result of a traffic accident while driving the only vehicle visible in a very large desert, but he couldn't resist showing off to his passenger. He bounded over the last major dune before they would arrive at *la Tarte*, not by straightening out near the top to descend the other side in a straight line, but by continuing the high-speed diagonal of his ascent. At the crest, the SUV took to the air briefly before coming down hard on the shifting sands. Two things might have happened. The SUV might have tumbled its way to level ground, which more than likely would have been the end of him and Max Brindle. Or it might have corrected itself enough to allow for a continuous descent on all four wheels.

Luckily for them, the latter transpired.

Even after they came to rest on the desert flats, whorls of sand fogged around them. They might as well have been on Mars for all they could see of the world in that moment.

The Phantom smiled. "There are many lessons for us in the desert. Here is one. This little drama is over now, so let it be over. We have work to do, and I brought you here for a reason other than to show you fear. You think the desert gives a damn about five minutes ago, or yesterday, or the decade before last? Of course not. And why? Because time comes along and carves its changes into us and then disappears. We carry some of the scars with us into the future, but then they belong to a new present, never the past. The past makes us what we are but has no value to us in the now. If you can accept that, you can accept just about anything."

Max hadn't taken his gaze from the windshield. His expression was inscrutable, but the Phantom needed no facial tells to know that the man was terrified of having come so close to perishing in a foreign land.

The engine had stalled, but LeGrand got it running again, and soon they were heading for another dune, this one much smaller than the one that had almost gotten the better of them.

"We'll approach on foot," he said to Max, "but we can get a hell of a lot closer than this."

"I hope this trek amounts to more than another lesson," Max said in a low, quiet tone.

"Maybe there are only lessons, Mr. Brindle. Nothing more, nothing less."

* * *

The Phantom parked alongside the dune and stepped out of the SUV. He went to one sloping edge of the dune and stared to the southeast, as if he would wait forever for Brindle to join him if he had to, as if time truly did mean nothing to him and so he was willing to use up as much of it as the situation required. Max wouldn't have chosen this godforsaken spot as a destination, for love or money, and the Black Phantom's company was hardly a thing to covet. Taken together, they provided a steady undercurrent of unease. He knew there was anger in the Phantom. It was the stuff of legend. Yet he seemed loath to display it without cause. Was it a game with him? Perhaps. Let your quarry try to guess when the blow would come, or the harsh word. Drive the adversary out of his mind with suspense, which was far more crippling in real life than in the paperback novels Max enjoyed from time to time.

Finally, he stepped out of the vehicle into the airless heat. Rocks now poked out of the sand in places, creating a sense that they had come much farther than they had. He took up a spot beside the Phantom.

"Well?" he said.

"You don't get thirsty?" The Phantom didn't turn to face him.

"What's that supposed to mean? Of course I get thirsty."

"Then why don't you get us some water for our hike. There's a jug in the back."

Still no eye contact had been made, but the Black Phantom's tone was different than before. There was something in it—something guttural—that invited no further conversation and would brook no disobedience. Max dutifully went to the rear of the SUV and procured a dusty plastic jug of water. Only as the Phantom rounded the sand dune did Max dare to follow. The leader's sure gait granted him permission.

CHAPTER 33

The Butcher handed the implements back to Lovinia after he emerged from the back of his cell.

She slid them into the custom sheaths on either side of her skirt. Almost all of her skirts and pants were similarly equipped. A hard flap, one-and-a-half inches long, was left unsewn at the top, allowing for quick access to the paralyzing steel within. A casual observer would mistake the ribs of leather for decorative piping.

They stared at each other for a moment, a little proud of the progress they'd made.

"It's a big desert," she said to him. "Any thoughts on which way we go once the others are free?"

"I'd say we get the others free before we worry too much about that. Give your Delights to Abel and then you and I will take a little walk. There should be some tire tracks in this depression we're in. They'll disappear as we get into the windier areas, but they might give us some indication ..."

He let the thought trail off, so she walked around to the entrance of *la Tarte*. They weren't out of the woods by a long shot, but even if the Black Phantom were to return just then, his expression upon finding her and the Butcher free of their cages would be worth every inch of effort put into the plan so far.

"Be careful with these." She handed the Twins to Abel. "They're sharp."

"I'm not afraid," he said with a smile.

"That's why I mention it. You're liable to carve yourself up out of that lack of fear. It'll be the end of you one day. The question I have is how did you ever work up the courage to have your damn amygdala removed in the first place? I wouldn't elect to be without mine for all the sprouts in Brussels."

"Story time later, huh? Let's get the hell out of here first."

"Always for another time. Is this why we never truly get to know each other?" She turned to address everyone. "We only come together when duty calls, and our line of work doesn't really come with social hour, does it? What do you all say we plan a friendly get-together after this is over? Maybe Mexico or South Africa. Someplace where we can actually get to know each other, maybe even plan for a future that doesn't involve saving the world."

"How about a destination that doesn't fry the leather off an iguana?" Miranda said.

"Fair enough. You name it."

"Scandinavia."

"You're on. Everyone else in?"

She saw Davenport rise from his bench, something ghostly in how he stood up so suddenly, claiming her attention before saying a single word.

"Aren't you forgetting that there are a couple of mutineers among us?" he asked Lovinia. "A rat and his flea."

The funny thing was, she almost *had* forgotten. The Nine had been oaring the same boat for so many years, it was difficult to accept treason among their ranks.

"Okay, okay," she replied.

"Let's just keep the details of future plans to a minimum, huh?"

He should have looked as ridiculous in his black leather fedora as she felt in her black leather skirt. Not exactly dressed for the desert, either of them. But he didn't look ridiculous. He looked resolved to see this situation to its conclusion, whatever that may prove to be. He looked like a leader.

"All right." She turned back to Abel Hazard. He was hard at work and needed no words of encouragement. She followed up with, "Good," rather lamely, and clapped her hands together as she left the prison again to reunite with the Butcher.

"Looks like this is as far as the tracks get us," the Butcher said, turning to survey *la Tarte* from the slight rise he had climbed. "And they look old, almost like fossils."

She soon joined him and kicked absently at one of the tire impressions. "We haven't heard a vehicle, either, so the Phantom probably hasn't driven this close to the prison for a while."

"Well," he continued, "the tracks do appear to lead toward this dune. Maybe we should check out the other side of it before doubling back to look in on the others."

"After you, *Herr* Butcher."

CHAPTER 34

The Black Phantom stopped as he and Max arrived at the edge of a depressed part of the desert. Max held out the water bottle, misinterpreting the Phantom's reason for stopping. The Phantom smiled at the obeisance.

"You see?" The Phantom looked out across the desert.

"See what? I see more desert. Flatter than what we've covered, but still des—"

He saw it at last, as the Phantom knew he would.

"Now that you've spotted it, it seems obvious, yes? How could you have missed it?"

"Yes." Brindle struggled to make out what he was beholding from this distance. "But what it is it? I mean, it's a structure of some kind, but ..."

"Max Brindle, I give you ... *la Tarte*. The Pie."

"The Pie?"

The Phantom resumed walking down the slight incline toward the plain on which *la Tarte* had been hastily constructed. Over his shoulder he called out, "See where there's a piece missing? That's the entrance. Come, have a look."

* * *

Max hadn't been crazy about the idea of paying a solo visit to Pierre LeGrand to begin with. As they approached the odd building—seemingly the *only* building in this entire fucking desert, except for the humble rambler from which they'd embarked on this excursion—he questioned his sanity. He had never before been so entirely at the mercy of another man, let alone one with the trail of violence that LeGrand took such pride in. It was an idiotic situation to be in. Yet there was the potential for advancement here. Like so many things in life, Max's predicament was a trial. To fail might mean death, sure, but to pass ... Well, to pass might mean that one Max Elliott Brindle, lately of Abilene, Texas, would soon find himself in a situation several stages above what he only could have dreamed of several weeks earlier.

The Black Phantom wandered a little to the left of the entrance they had been heading toward, as if proudly inspecting his Pie. While he was distracted, Max could have sworn he caught movement from within the enclosure.

Like a white flash inside his brain, a possibility grew very distinct. *La Tarte* might not be some kind of treasure trove or museum or redoubt or any of the other things Brindle had been telling himself it might be. *Dear God, it might be some kind of prison.*

And if it was a prison, he wouldn't need three guesses to name its most likely occupants. LeGrand could have transported them here by now, if that had been his goal.

Movement again. Someone, or something, had definitely stepped across the field of vision the entrance afforded. If it was some kind of prison or jail, what kept the inmates inside? Whoever he'd seen, twice now, seemed to have absolute freedom of movement within the enclosure, with nothing to prevent them from walking out.

Maybe there was more to the situation than met the eye. Max slipped past the entrance to have a look at the opposite side of the structure from where the Black Phantom roamed. His gaze quickly fell upon a small pile of rubble and, behind it, a jagged hole in the wall—large enough for a person to squeeze through.

Okay, he had to think fast. He knew something LeGrand didn't. That was a gift. A treasure. He dared not squander it. But how to put the vague knowledge to use? And what, exactly, was to be gained? Did it outweigh the risks?

"I've seen enough," he called out to LeGrand, loudly enough for anyone inside the Pie to hear as well, and started back toward the SUV.

The choice had been made in a split second. Not enough time even for him to realize what it meant or why he'd done it. But as he walked away from the Phantom and his prison, he realized what he'd done. He had given the Portable Nine an edge, and thereby sided with them in whatever campaign was being waged. Would they see it that way after he'd gone to so much trouble to make sure they ended up here? There was no way to know, but it didn't really matter. He had made his decision and there was no turning back. Maybe his bread was now buttered on both sides. And maybe he was toast.

"What do you mean, you've seen enough?" the Phantom responded, more incredulous than angry, though Max doubted he could count on that remaining the case for long.

He wanted to stop before the Phantom's temper forced him to. That was the seasoned bully's power: his reputation went before him, and the foreknowledge that rage and violence were in the air was enough to bend most wills. But Max needed time to think things through. If he gave in now, any ground he'd gained would be lost. At the very least, steering the Phantom's attention away from *la Tarte* gave the Nine time to react, or for something to happen and take some of the onus of orchestration off of Max's shoulders.

"God damn you, get back here!" The Black Phantom yelled, but Max could tell he was following. The distraction had worked.

"No, I see how this is. You want to lock me up in that thing, that Pie. Well I'd rather die."

He could only get the words out by keeping his eyes forward and shouting over his shoulder so the Phantom could hear. Eye contact would have reduced him to the subservient drone he'd been on the way out here.

"No one's going to die, you fool. And I'm not going to lock

you up!"

"If I get to the SUV without you stabbing or strangling me to death, I'll wait for you. I won't leave you out here to die, but I don't like the look of that place, and I'm not going in."

"Why does the world conspire against me these days? From a worthless hatchling in the dirt I've risen to be the most feared overlord in the criminal kingdom. And now, when all I aim to do is rid the world of a handful of low-rent soldiers of fortune—if they can't be turned to more useful purposes—I'm fought at every turn!"

There was rage in his voice, but also an undertone of regret, maybe even sadness. Certainly frustration. But it was possible in life to travel so far down the wrong path that it would be a weakness for any foe to show the least sympathy toward you. Max wasn't quick to sympathize, anyway. He certainly wasn't about to waste such precious currency on Pierre LeGrand.

He kept walking.

CHAPTER 35

"**H**ow long do you suppose it's been here?" Lovinia asked.

"It's damned odd," the Butcher responded. "This desert'll fry you to the ground in no time if you're on foot."

"It didn't drive itself here."

"No, that's true enough. Let's have a closer look."

They walked around the black SUV in opposite directions, not needing to tell each other they were searching for booby traps.

"I'm a New York City girl," Lovinia said. "I don't know from cars." She laid a hand on the hood.

"Good instinct, but you won't be able to tell anything from the warmth of the hood. Not in this heat. It was running not long ago, though."

"How do you know?" she asked, removing her hand.

"Listen. Hear that ticking noise?"

She tilted her head and listened for a moment.

"Yeah. Yeah, I do."

"That's the sound of things cooling down inside. Whoever drove this here isn't far."

"Do you think they might have passed around one side of the dune, headed for the jail, while we were making our way around the other side?"

"I can't think of a better explanation."

"Okay, so what do we do? Rush back to help our compadres or hole up here, maybe crawl under this damn thing and wait?"

"I say we wait under the SUV for a quarter of an hour. If we don't have any visitors by then, we charge."

"You noticed that the keys are in the ignition, I presume?"

"I did. But I don't want to alert them any sooner than we have to."

"So back on foot, then, after fifteen minutes."

He nodded.

She lowered herself onto her belly and wiggled under the SUV. The Butcher did the same.

CHAPTER 36

"**N**ow can we talk, for God's sake?" The Phantom was trying to make himself sound patient, but it was a clear falsehood. They had arrived back at the SUV and he was exasperated. "What is this all about?"

"I had a bad feeling about that place. That's all. Why can't we just go back to your pad and discuss our plans for the future? That's what I thought I was here for."

"It *is* what you're here for, dammit, but I wanted to show you *la Tarte* first. You're right about that place, you know. It is a prison. But I have no interest in locking *you* up there. I wanted to show you who I already have locked up there."

"I could probably guess."

"Sure, now. But why couldn't you have played along? Crime used to be different. It used to be enjoyable. People operated by a code. There was an appreciation for theatrics. Now it's all about getting your cut in the shortest amount of time possible and moving on to the next dumb adventure."

"I'm happy to drive."

Without saying another word the Black Phantom went to the passenger side and climbed inside. Max felt like he'd won something here, but he wasn't sure what.

"They'll be fed, I assume, and watered?" Max said as he turned the key in the ignition switch. The engine shook and rattled to life.

"Of course. I've hired a band of outlaws from Oum El Assel. Met them at a tea house in Marrakesh a couple of years ago. They'll do anything I ask. And you want to know what their reward is?"

"Sure, I guess." Max put the vehicle in gear and started off toward the ranch, as he had taken to thinking of the Phantom's hideaway.

"They haven't asked for anything yet. Nothing. Oh, I've given them enough to cover expenses, and a little extra. But they believe in the future. They know that if they are loyal to me and do good work they will be rewarded. It is the right way to do business."

If you're on your end of the transaction, Max thought but decided to keep it to himself.

Glancing in the rearview mirror, he saw two figures, a man and a woman (the Butcher and Lovinia Dulcet, perhaps), stepping from around the side of the dune in a hurry. This, too, he kept to himself as he smiled a little and drove on.

"What kind of wildlife do you see around here?" he asked, more to keep the Phantom from turning around and spotting the figures behind them than out of any real curiosity.

"Wildlife? Do I look like a writer for *National Geographic*? I'm the only wildlife you need to concern yourself with."

"Fair enough. Just trying to show an interest."

"Well don't."

Max responded with a curt nod, and miles of silence followed.

✳ ✳ ✳

"That noise," Lovinia turned away from the prison once more and ran back to the far side of the sand dune.

"Dammit!" the Butcher shouted. "Another couple of minutes and we'd have had them." He went after her.

"Shit." She stopped once the departing SUV was in view. "My bad. I'm the one who wanted to crawl back out."

The Butcher caught up and joined her in staring after the vehicle.

"You couldn't have known," he said. "We could have been under there all day. Who do you suppose it was?"

"The Phantom, probably."

"Maybe. A pretty short trip, though. Especially since he must not have actually gone all the way to the prison or he would have seen that we'd escaped. He'd be searching high and low for us."

"And if it *was* him, he brought a visitor this time."

"Huh?"

"You can't tell now anymore, but when they were still closer I could make out two figures in the vehicle."

"Jesus, what do we do now?"

"The only thing that's changed is that we have fresh tracks to follow. Let's go back and see if the others learned anything. Then we'll head back into the desert."

"Odd." The Butcher's voice was low as he walked away from her.

"What's that?" She was quickly at his side again.

"I'd have thought they would have seen us in the rearview mirror. Movement catches the eye in a big open space like this. I would have seen us if I was the driver. Why'd they keep going?"

"A riddle for another day, I guess."

"Yeah, they're piling up."

* * *

By the time the Butcher and Lovinia arrived back at *la Tarte*, everyone had freed themselves. They milled about in the circular courtyard as if strangers at a cocktail party. But one was missing.

"Where's Davenport?" Lovinia asked no one in particular.

"Flew the coop," Robin Varnesse replied. "Said something about tending to the Black Phantom on his own."

"Wants us to get to work dismantling the bastard's network," Abel Hazard said. "The Phantom was here, you know, and not alone. We heard voices close by. Did you see anyone?"

"Yes," Lovinia said. "We saw them drive off."

"So Davenport's gone, just like that?" the Butcher said. "He set off in the wrong direction if he headed east. The Phantom hightailed it that way." He jabbed a thumb over his shoulder to indicate the dune beyond the jail's entrance.

Twitch Markham added, "He thinks the Phantom actually did us a favor by bringing us all together in the Sahara. Says he's long suspected that LeGrand has a lot of his operation here, using South America as more of a red herring."

"I thought we were going to keep this kind of chatter to a minimum in the presence of spies." Miranda Gissing nodded in Dr. Intaglio's direction.

"Yeah, well what are we going to do, kill them?" Abel said.

Lovinia saw Mr. Bonnet shake a little at that.

"So they're *our* problem," Lovinia said flatly. "Convenient for Davenport. What's his game plan?"

"He didn't say much," said Robin. "Just that he was pretty sure we're near a place called Tindouf, and that it's the nearest urban center. It also has a large lake nearby. I don't know if he's going to try to fly out of there, try to track down some info about the Black Phantom, or just gather his strength for whatever comes next."

"Well, Godspeed to him," Lovinia said. "He'll be lucky to survive till sundown in these elements. Did he take any water with him?"

"Drank most of what was in the jug in his cell and said that would have to do," Robin said.

"Then that's what *we* do," the Butcher said. "Drink as much as we can and head in the direction LeGrand was traveling in. We'll only have the benefit of his tire tracks until the wind dusts them away."

"Maybe it gives us a head start on dismantling that network Davenport was talking about," said Abel.

"Yeah, or maybe it gets us all killed," said the Butcher. "Either way, I don't see a better option."

The Butcher would never lead the Nine, but he was uniquely respected among them. It amounted to the same thing at times. If those around you are unlikely to question you, Lovinia figured, your way stands. No one questioned the Butcher's assessment.

"There *is* no better option," Dr. Intaglio said.

All eyes turned to the turncoat psychiatrist, who had remained quiet until this outburst.

"Yeah?" Twitch said. "What do you know about it?"

"Twitch, my good man, I know that more than one of you would like to tear my eyes out right now, leave me as blind as Bonnet over there. Maybe more so, since I wouldn't have his powers of preternatural observation. But I can assure you that my time to enjoy the Black Phantom's confidence is over, which I should have thought was made abundantly clear by the fact that I shared in your predicament of being incarcerated in this godforsaken desert.

"We can stand around here gabbing and taking in the occasional whiff of each other's excrement buckets, or we can get a move on. There aren't many universal truths in this world, but I know of one: time is the enemy of success."

"So is treason," Abel added under his breath, but not so far under that it wasn't heard by everyone.

The Butcher stepped to Abel's side and placed a hand on his shoulder. "In time," Lovinia overheard him whisper, "there will be justice. But we're not going to assassinate our former colleagues in the desert like dogs, no matter how far they've strayed. Besides, they know a thing or two about the Phantom that we don't, yeah? That knowledge might prove useful."

Abel blinked and nodded, looking a little embarrassed to have had his thoughts called out so plainly. Lovinia had no idea if embarrassment was conjoined with fear and therefore absent in one without an amygdala, but the last thing her overheated brain needed was a brainteaser, so she let the question drift away.

"The doctor is right," said Miranda, making her way out

of *la Tarte* and into the vast Sahara Desert beyond. "Time's a wastin'. Besides, it gives me the creeps hanging around a make-shift jail that I just broke out of. Feels like we're tempting fate."

Lovinia hung back as the others filed out, half expecting that no one would bother to look after Mr. Bonnet. He didn't appear to require much looking after, though. Before she could express a word of encouragement, he was through the entrance-way and nearly caught up with the group outside.

Falling in stride with him she asked, "Okay, I can't resist. What can your hallucinations possibly be showing you out here where there's nothing to base them on?"

He smiled widely. "You want to know the truth? We're all a bunch of chickens that have just busted out of the coop, kind of like Davenport. But even stranger than that, I see us walking through a barren desert."

"You don't suppose ..."

"That my vision is returning? Doubtful. Just a trick of the mind, I'm sure."

Soon the eight of them were beyond the first dune and the Black Phantom's pen was out of view behind them. With SUV tracks as their only guide, they ventured into the unknown, not certain how long they'd be walking, but knowing that it was better to die in the sand than to rot in a cage.

CHAPTER 37

Davenport liked to think of himself as the Portable Nine's wanderer. Their nomad. They had all been to corners of the globe not thought about, let alone traveled to, by most westerners. But everyone in the gang besides Davenport had a home base, even if it changed every few years. Davenport only felt alive when he was on the move. It kept his mind sharp and allowed him to acquire knowledge that was invaluable to him in the work he did. So while Twitch, Miranda, Butch, and Lovinia had put down roots of a sort in the States, and while Intaglio, Bonnet, Hazard, and Varnesse had found their various paradises farther afield, Davenport had remained a citizen of the world.

The weeks he'd spent in the vicinity of Morocco with a beautiful French novelist were paying for themselves now as he lay in the shade of a date palm near the edge of the very lake he'd hoped to find here—not that those weeks, days, hours, and minutes had been a misery requiring compensation. The two of them had spent several days near the very spot where he now rested, reciting poetry to each other between bouts of passion. From her he had learned many lessons. One was that it was possible to appreciate the everyday existence that most people tolerated, endured, and even, in rare cases, enjoyed—without succumbing to its humble charms. It was a theme running through all six of her novels, she insisted, and most of her collected short stories and poems. It resonated with him at the time, but only now did he realize what an impact the notion had had on his occupation. During his struggles with right and wrong and his desire to be on the correct side of morality in the long run—

even if, in the short term, certain allowances had to be made— Cécile's precept had always been there, goading him on. It was *those* people he was doing all of this for. The working stiffs, the families, the traffic cops, the bureaucrats, the weak. What was he warring for if not for the preservation of their peace of mind and a certain measure of status quo in the world? He wouldn't have wished such an existence on himself for a king's ransom, but it gave him something to believe in, something to keep him from going mad with the suspicion that he wasn't on the side of justice at all, but just another shadow in the dark. Besides, the status quo had a place in the world, and every corporation and government, every institution, had limitations preventing them from crossing certain lines to maintain that status quo, even if the will was there. The Portable Nine had no such limitations; crossing the line was practically their creed.

He wouldn't be able to lounge around this sand-meets-water paradise much longer. His reasons for being in Africa were much different than they had been when he brought Cécile here as his lover, and his visit to this oasis had a similarly more pragmatic purpose to fulfill than his first encounter with it had. The waters had cleansed his body and slaked his thirst, and fallen dates had filled his belly (and his pockets). Soon it would be time to visit the nearby towns and villages to learn what he could of Pierre LeGrand's history in this part of the world, and what plans he had for the future.

Then, to an airport, because if he knew the Black Phantom at all, the enigmatic man had already slipped out of reach again, if not out of the country. Davenport wished his friends success, but he wouldn't have bet money on it.

CHAPTER 38

"Well I'll be damned." Twitch pointed across the flatlands at a low structure. "Maybe we haven't been chasing geese after all."

"We never were, you mite." The Butcher laughed at his own jab. No one else was in the mood.

Robin was the only one who hadn't stopped walking when Twitch made his observation. Now he did stop so he could turn and address them. "Am I the only one in this club who's learned not to celebrate prematurely? I see a building. It's probably our destination. Might not be, but let's say it is. Is our man hiding out there, or has he already moved on again? Say he's moved on. Has he left any food and water behind? Again, probably, but let's not get excited."

"Always looking for ways to make both sides of the ledger add up," Abel muttered.

"Shut up," Miranda said. It was all she had the energy for.

If exhaustion and thirst had an advantage, it was that they kept people mostly quiet. They covered the rest of the way to the small house in relative silence. As Lovinia rounded one corner she noticed that the SUV she and the Butcher had seen earlier was parked out front. *Shit*, she thought and rejoined the group.

"The SUV is here. Should we bum rush the place, scare him out?"

"Let's circle around, check all the windows," Miranda answered. "I'd rather not panic him into doing something rash."

"What, do you think he's a match for all of us?" The

Butcher laughed again, but not loudly enough to be heard from within the house.

"What if he's in the sedan chair, either hiding or ready to move?"

All eyes went to Bonnet.

"What the fuck's a sedan chair?" asked Abel.

"It must be what he sees instead of the SUV," Intaglio said.

Lovinia could tell that Mr. Bonnet was irritated at being spoken for, though he said nothing more.

"Bonnet's got a point," she said. "Why don't Butch and I head for the vehicle, while the rest of you circle around back and check for any signs of life indoors. And don't forget, we're looking for two, not one."

On the way to the SUV, the Butcher said, "Now *you're* calling me Butch, too? It's only ever been Davenport I've let call me that."

"Haven't we been through enough together yet? How do I earn the privilege?"

"I guess you have."

"Good. I'm glad to know you won't be taking my head off for it while I sleep."

He looked a little crestfallen by that remark. The sudden show of emotion silenced her cold. Then he lightened up again.

"You're safe for now. The bastard has my axe."

Lovinia opened the driver's-side door and stood on the running board to scan the interior of the vehicle. The Butcher opened the unlocked passenger side as well.

"All clear?" he asked.

"Except for a thick coating of Saharan silica."

The Butcher climbed in and sat facing forward without closing his door. He appeared to have something to say, so Lovinia did the same.

"The house is empty," he said in a low voice.

"How do you know?"

"The windows are shuttered. The others will need to crack them open to look inside. LeGrand never lets himself be closed in even that much, not since his time in the clink."

"You know a lot about him, don't you?"

"Some. We go back a piece. But I've heard a lot from Davenport, too. He's developed a spooky sense of the man."

"Can I ask you something?" She wrapped her hands around the steering wheel and studied her knuckles.

"Sure, I guess."

"You don't like some of the things you've done, do you?"

"Do you? Do any of us?"

"You're a little beyond, though. You know how we distance ourselves from you a lot of the time. We value you. We know why you do what you do, but we're all a little wary, too. You must know all of this."

"Yeah, I know."

"I've never really stopped to think about whether or not it bothers you, but I think it does a little."

The Butcher drew a deep breath and let it out in a thick sigh.

"I was thirteen when my father almost killed my mom. He was a worthless shitkicker drunk for as long as I can remember, but this night was different. I don't know if he mixed whiskey with cheap wine or had his ass chewed out especially hard that day at the lumberyard for being a hungover waste of oxygen. Hell, maybe he was trying some *new* kind of chemical out on himself. All I know is that he got angrier than I'd ever seen him."

"Anger like that is shocking to a kid," Lovinia said, wishing it hadn't sounded as lame as it did.

"He would have gutted her like a tiger shark," Butch went on, "left to his booze-addled will. But I'm not telling you this for sympathy, or so you'll think there's some justification for how I live my life. When I saw the way my father had Mama backed up against the wall with that paring knife, and how he kept her tight like a knot by pulling at the back of her hair with his free hand …

"Well, it wasn't the way people sometimes describe that

sort of thing. Nothing snapped. I didn't have any kind of break from reality. My memory of everything that followed is completely intact. I ran out the back screen door and picked up the axe my my father used to chop pinewood for burning. And you know what it was like more than anything?" He trained his steel-blue eyes on her. "It was like I'd been waiting for the sonofabitch to do something bad enough to set me free, because I'd been wanting to cut into him for a long time by then." He looked back toward the building.

"So you see, I don't blame him for what I've become. I was already more or less fully formed by the time that night rolled around. I was going to claim a first victim sooner or later. He made it sooner is all. And I don't suppose Mama's spent more than a day or two missing me since I walked out of her life that very night. I hope she's found a little gratitude at the bottom of her heart by now, and a little peace, but I don't like to think she's wasted any time pining for what could have been. Life don't work that way."

It was clear he was done talking about his troubled childhood, but there was a long pause before Lovinia said anything.

"I'm not sure I've ever been told a story where the teller didn't want to be patted on the back, forgiven, or encouraged in some way. I'm not sure how to respond. We all have our stories. None of them are very pretty, I guess. You don't get this job for wearing a suit and showing up on time."

"I just felt like unburdening myself, I guess. You're right that all of the Nine are outcasts, some more dangerous than others. None of us were meant for the straight and narrow. If fate hadn't drawn us together, Intaglio would have found some other way to be a fraud. Robin would be embezzling money. You'd probably still be doing porno."

"Directing by now, I think."

He chuckled at that.

"But did you ever wonder what I'd be doing?" he went on, looking at her again. "You think I'd be pulling petty crimes, breaking into people's homes at night and liberating their valuables?"

"No, I don't think that."

"Because I'd be out there doing what I do anyway, slaughtering people."

"I don't know." She met his gaze. "There's a weird morality to how you go about your business, the same as all of us."

In the pause that followed, they both looked ahead again. The rest of the Nine were coming around the side of the house now, realizing what the Butcher already knew, that the Black Phantom was gone, even though he'd left his SUV behind. Someone must have come to retrieve him—and his guest.

"Listen," Lovinia said, "don't go down the same road as Twitch. Once you start pulling at the thread of morality, the next thing you know you've unraveled your only sweater, and winter's on its way. You do what has to be done. We all do. As far as I'm concerned, you've never crossed a line that wasn't justified by the bigger picture."

"The ends always justify the means, eh? Maybe. I never worried about it when I was in the Army. I could never understand why some guys didn't like being asked if they killed anyone in Iraq or Somalia or wherever the fuck. I got a kick out of owning up to my record. I'd been given a license to kill and I figured that came with a license to talk about it, too."

"You don't owe anyone an explanation. We do mean, ugly work that no one else has the courage to do or the graciousness to thank us for. We keep the world on its axis while politicians and billionaires take the credit, even though it's usually their mistakes we're cleaning up in the first place."

"Better head inside and see if Monsieur LeGrand has left behind anything that might keep us alive for a while."

"Whatever you say, Butch. Promise me one thing?"

"What's that?"

"That you won't go ballistic if he hasn't."

He chuckled again as he stepped out of the SUV and headed for the entrance of the dwelling. Lovinia watched for a moment before stepping down from the vehicle herself, realizing there was a haunted quality even to his laughter.

CHAPTER 39

As the sun drew a curtain across the vast and noiseless desert, the Portable Nine—minus Davenport, Intaglio, and Bonnet—made themselves as comfortable as possible in the main room of the house. Candles burned on a large coffee table. Lanterns hung from nails in two of the walls. Those who weren't sprawled languorously on a pile of blankets on the floor had taken up seats on the humble sofa and chairs the room offered. These comforts wouldn't have meant much, of course, if Abel hadn't located a cellar door hiding under a weathered rug in the small kitchen. Crawling down the ladder stairs with a burning lump of tallow to see by, he soon discovered a well-organized and sufficiently stocked pantry lined with shelves of oranges, grains, salted meat, preserves, and other edibles. They had already located a cistern out back, so their food and water needs were sorted in the short term. Why not make the most of a less-than-ideal situation?

"All this party needs is some quality beer." Miranda had inadvertently sat across from Robin. His eyes were especially beautiful in this light. Sometimes she really hated life on the go, running on the wrong side of the law, naive as the law often was. It was hell on the sex life.

"No dice on that front, love," Abel said from the chair on which he sat with one leg flung rakishly over an armrest as he peeled an orange. "I searched high and low."

"You know something?" It was Twitch speaking from a nest of blankets on the floor. "This is the first time since I received Davenport's invitation that it's really felt anything like old times."

"Yeah," Miranda replied, "it's too bad about Intaglio and

Bonnet, though. I would have been tempted to ask them to leave if they hadn't volunteered to keep each other company outside."

"Fuck them," the Butcher said. "They only went outside when they learned I'd found my hatchet in the Phantom's bedroom." He patted the weapon, which lay across his lap. "Along with Davenport's King Cobra, by the way." Now he stood up and turned his back to the others so he could lift his shirt to reveal the handgun he'd tucked into the waist of his pants. "They can sleep with the other lizards for all I care." He sat back down.

"I have some news that might just keep us in our best spirits," Robin said with a thin smile. The floor was his immediately. "Inspired by Davenport's false reason for bringing us together in Seattle, I thumbed my way into the ledgers of Cloft Industries and quickly discovered a significant sum waiting to be plucked, ripe and plump. It had been set aside for that very purpose, just not with me in mind as the harvester.

"I won't bore you with the details. I know how you all get. First the glazed expressions, then the fluttering lids. Pretty soon there's snoring. Let's just say that I tracked some of the illicit activity that made this money available to one Elaine Rafferty, the bank president who handles some of Cloft Industries' more complicated affairs. I went to her, perfectly willing to split the profits down the middle, five million for her and the same for me. She found the amount laughable, considering the risk. And you know what? She was right. Her refusal to make a deal for an amount that was less than what she could legally walk away from the bank with any day of the week got me thinking. Maybe she and I could perpetrate the same scheme across multiple divisions within the bank and increase our take rather neatly."

"You're starting to bore," Twitch joked.

"Yes, yes. Okay. So it's five million each for now, and I got her to agree that for six times that in the long run she could justify flouting the law, and the will of Cloft Industries. In other words, my portable friends, we are not stuck out in this godforsaken desert without funds. Well, we are, temporarily. Until I can get to a bank, or at least an ATM. But the next phase of operations is financed, and the one after that, and the one after that. We'll have to see how the collaboration holds up, of course. So, not quite the sum from Davenport's ruse, but ..."

"Well, okay," Miranda said. "Nice work, Robin. It doesn't exactly get us out of this fuck hole, but it gives us a reason to try like hell. I swear to god if I'm injected with anything one more time ..."

"You know, you almost became part of my little plot with Elaine."

"How so?"

"I was prepared to ask you to play the role of my attorney, but it didn't become necessary. Not yet, anyway. But I hear you about being drugged, even though Lovinia and I missed out on the nerve-agent party. I wish the bastard had tried to stuff us into those cages without using chemicals."

"And I wish we had some beer." Abel swung his foot to the floor and pounded a fist onto the coffee table for effect. "Do you suppose the Black Phantom has gone teetotaler?"

"No," Lovinia said from the side of the couch opposite Robin Varnesse, "but I'll bet he enjoys forcing himself to go for long stretches without a drop. Part of some half-baked macho philosophy, no doubt."

"You know what bothers me the most, in some ways?" Twitch said. "The way he hauled us here like cattle. We wake up forty-thousand feet above the jungle, our hands and feet bound. Almost as soon as we land we're hit with the knockout drops again. Several days later we're in Marrakesh, getting doped once more and drifting off as we're prodded into the back of a truck bound for *la Tarte*."

"And he saved the worst for last," Miranda added. "Give me the steamy jungles of South America over *this* any day."

"Give me rainy Seattle," Robin said.

"I'd drink to that," Abel said, and they all shared in a murmur of laughter.

Even without alcohol to lubricate conversation and

play its odd tricks with time—simultaneously quickening and stretching the minutes and hours—the Portable Nine did their best to keep their spirits high, and Robin couldn't have been more pleased to be partly responsible for the relative jubilation. He contented himself to sit back, legs crossed, with that smile of his as the others reveled and chatted. Even with his suit caked with desert grit and torn through in places, he looked the part of the very devil to Miranda.

❊ ❊ ❊

The sun had been gone from the windows for hours by the time Twitch heard the faint rumble of an engine in the distance. Headlights grazed one wall, which prompted everyone to stand.

"What the hell do we have here?" The Butcher moved to the front window. Standing to one side, he peered into the darkness. "Seems to be coming our way, whoever it is. No surprise there."

"Friend or foe?" Abel asked. "That's the question."

"I'm surprised our little turncoats haven't come running back in yet." Twitch rubbed at his hair.

"I say we investigate." Abel moved for the door himself.

Twitch reached out and grabbed him by the shirtsleeve. "No, fuck that. I'm tired of this pins-and-needles bullshit."

He flung open the door and bolted into the unknown.

"Whoa," Abel said to the others, a little embarrassed by what had transpired. "I'd say the worm has turned."

"And a little child shall lead them." The Butcher was the only one to laugh at his joke. "Okay, okay. Let's give him a hand."

Headlights bobbed up and down, veered left to right, growing larger and brighter by the moment.

"You'd think if there's one place on earth where a road could be a straight line this would be it," Miranda commented. "Guess not."

No one paid any more attention to her remark, as they

all filed out of the house, than they had to the Butcher's joke. A hush fell over them, its source instantly identifiable as a shared observation. Miranda followed their collective gaze to a spot in the sand barely in range of the lantern Robin had brought from the house. There stood Twitch Markham, looking back at them, his arms out in a gesture of incredulous surrender.

"Where the fuck are the blind man and the shrink?" he asked.

"Sonofabitch," Miranda said. "The keys must have been in the SUV. How did we not hear them leave?"

"Must have rolled the fucking thing away from the house," Lovinia guessed, "waiting until they were out of earshot to start the engine."

"Would have been a pretty big job for the two of them," Robin said.

"They didn't need to push it all the way to the road," said the Butcher. "Just down this slope and behind the first dune, to muffle the sound of the engine."

"Goddammit." Lovinia sounded as though she couldn't believe they'd been double-crossed again, but that couldn't have been true. There was still hope for Mr. Bonnet. Miranda honestly believed that, but as long as Dr. Intaglio had a hold over him, neither of them would ever be above suspicion again.

"Look, this is disappointing." Miranda positioned herself between Twitch and the rest. "But it's down our priority list by at least one rung."

As if she'd conjured an ancient sand demon with her words, the oncoming mystery vehicle crested the nearest rise, washing the Portable Nine and the front of LeGrand's hideaway not only with light but with sound.

She saw that the Butcher's small axe hung at his side and adrenaline squeezed her guts tight. She hated watching him work. Not only was the brutality appalling, but it reminded her that she was really no different.

The vehicle appeared to be a sedan, which didn't strike Miranda as the most desert-friendly mode of transportation, but she also figured you took what you could get out here more often than not. It came to a stop twenty yards or so from where they stood. The driver cut the engine but left the lights burning. A car door opened but it was difficult to tell which side.

"You are friends of Davenport?" came a man's voice with a thick Algerian accent. A voice that could set the earth rumbling if turned up in volume.

Still, Miranda relaxed a little and could tell the others did as well.

"That's right," Twitch said.

"Good. He has secured travel for you. Helicopter to Marrakesh or Casablanca. From there, small plane if you want to go to Europe. Said you would know where to wait for his call there. If you'd rather exploit contacts here on Dark Continent, that can be arranged as well. Either way, I take you to Tindouf. Then make decisions."

"Jesus Christ," Abel whispered to Lovinia. "Dark Continent? Did we step into a Conrad novel?"

But Twitch was already walking to where the driver stood, and Miranda realized that she hadn't felt truly free until the car had arrived. Sure, they had freed themselves from the Phantom's *Tarte*, but they had remained cruelly imprisoned in his vast desert nonetheless. Even as they conversed and reminisced in the almost-cozy living room of LeGrand's shack, there had been a sense of unease about their immediate future. Not one of the Nine was unfamiliar with that feeling. It was with them constantly, but the further out they could push the worry the better. It was all they could hope for, really.

She heard Twitch ask the driver, "Did you pass a black SUV on your way out here?"

"No," came the reply, "but there is a fork in the road a few miles back. Driver of SUV may have taken the other branch."

"And where would that lead him?"

"Toward Morocco, same as us. But where in Morocco? This is impossible to say."

Soon the available number of the Portable Nine were piling into what turned out to be a jacked-up stretch limo, which allowed them to continue their banter and relative camaraderie. The only holdup was Abel running back inside to fill a burlap sack with fruit and canned goods, and make sure no fires were still burning. There was no good way to transport water from the house, but all were relieved to discover bottles of water in the limousine.

"Shit, Brahms," the Butcher said over his shoulder to the driver, who hadn't yet raised the glass between them, "this is what you'd have to call a reversal of fortune."

"The name is Walid," said the driver.

"Don't mind Butch," Lovinia chimed in from her seat opposite the Butcher. "He calls everyone Brahms."

Maybe it was because no one had ever heard the Butcher call another living soul Brahms before. Maybe it was because he had never been known to appreciate classical music. Or maybe it was that the opportunity for levity didn't come around all that often. More likely it was some combination of factors, but whatever the case, the limo filled with laughter as the driver raised the glass partition and drove away into the night.

* * *

The laughter died more quickly for Lovinia than it did for the others. As the uneven ride lulled them all into a quiet half-sleep, she slid her hands along her outer thighs and froze when she realized that her Twin Delights were no longer sheathed on either side of her skirt. The discovery left her concerned and embarrassed. Until she knew for certain who had her weapons, she wouldn't breathe a word to anyone. Everyone in the car was a suspect, as were the two runaways. And Davenport.

She'd taken them back from Abel, hadn't she? Yes, of course. She must have. But she watched him a bit more closely now, would be watching them all a bit more closely from now on.

CHAPTER 40

Dr. Intaglio drove in silent darkness for many miles, seeing the world as though all had been obliterated but what he was allowed by the beams of the SUV's headlights. Where Dr. Intaglio saw headlights, he had been told, Mr. Bonnet watched clusters of yellow–green fireflies in the middle distance, as if from the shore of a lake from his childhood in northern Sweden.

It was Bonnet who at length broke the silence.

"Round and round we go, you and I. Did you really think we could accomplish so much more with the Phantom than we could as the Portable Nine?"

Intaglio said nothing, so Bonnet continued.

"You said I could come with you or remain with the others, as I wished."

The doctor grunted.

"But we both know that wasn't true. I could hear it in your voice. Once you saw that the keys to this thing were under the visor, you meant to drag me along if I resisted, even if it meant alerting the house. What is it about me that you put so high a value on? Surely I slow you down more than anything."

"I guess I had my quiet time." There was irritation in Dr. Intaglio's voice. "Now there's to be talking the rest of the way, is that it? So be it. There's courage in you, Bonnet. There, I said it. It's the same reason you've been one of the Nine all this time. You may lack the sense of sight, but the struggle has made you strong. We've always been able to rely on you for duties requiring extreme subterfuge. You can gain the sympathy of strangers much more quickly than any of us, and the trust. I still rely on you for those qualities."

"Well maybe you should try treating me like it."

"I don't know if I'll ever grow accustomed to the new you. What is it that's made you so much more ..."

"Outspoken? I suppose being pushed off the ship changes one's priorities. I don't know, you're the head-shrinker. You and I were settling into our lives as collaborators with the Black Phantom. At least I was. It had grown somewhat comfortable. Then Davenport had to send that goddamn note, and suddenly the world was full of options. For the first time in who knows how long, I felt like I might have a say in my own fate, as opposed to being dragged around like a dog on a lead."

"But now you've chosen me for a second time."

"Yeah, well, like I said, it wasn't much of a choice this time. It seemed like the most peaceable course."

"And so here we are."

"Here we are. The question is, Where are we going?"

There was a pause before Intaglio gave an answer.

"If we can make our way to Algiers, I can get us on a boat to Malta." His voice was lighter than it had been, almost enthusiastic.

"Malta? What the hell is there for us in Malta?"

"Secret histories."

"Ah, you mean Davenport."

"It's a shot in the dark, I'll admit, but it's a starting point. More is known there of his history than anywhere else on earth. But Malta is a place of closely guarded secrets. We'll require the help of a man named Chesterton if we want answers, and he doesn't come cheap."

"And your plan, once you have these answers about the reserved Davenport?"

"You talked about options opening up for you when he called the Portable Nine together again. Well that's what I'm after: options."

"In other words, you have no plan. You just want to lug me all the way to Malta in the hopes that a man named Chesterton still lives there and can tell us about Davenport's past. Then, armed with options, the world will be our oyster. Is that the long and short of it?"

"Our sardine, actually." Intaglio could hear the smile in his own voice.

"Excuse me?"

"Chances are we'll have to stow away on a sardine boat to get to Malta without leaving a trail. Same for the return trip."

"Your pitch could use some work, but I have to say I don't have a better idea. Can we agree that all of this may lead to some kind of arrangement with Davenport, as opposed to making him an out-and-out adversary?"

"Bonnet, you may have outgrown your britches, but it only leaves you naked and vulnerable. We will play this exactly as I say, and you will do exactly as you're told. Are we clear on that?"

Bonnet didn't say a word, only stared ahead at the fireflies above the lake. Did the insects now swarm in two fitful whorls, their color tinted several shades toward red?

Dr. Intaglio smiled at the thought as he drove on.

CHAPTER 41

"Welcome to Tindouf," Walid said into a microphone that transmitted to speakers in the rear of the limousine.

The city wasn't what any of them would have called beautiful under ordinary circumstances. Where flat tenements didn't litter the landscape before them, aging high-rises appeared to teeter like sand-blasted threats to anyone who might dare to walk in their shadows. All of this could be made out by the dim pink of sun that had been pretending to rise for the past forty minutes. The unique beauty of that desert pink was part of the reason a kind of hushed awe had fallen over the Portable Nine, Abel suspected. Also, impoverished as it obviously was, Tindouf was a fairy-tale kingdom compared to *la Tarte*.

There was a touch of melancholy in Abel Hazard's appreciation of the scene, however. He had never told anyone that he sometime had regrets about his decision to have his amygdala removed, partly because the reason was difficult to put into words. What many people didn't realize, or bother to contemplate, was that fear and wonder were intimately connected. A poet might have made a career out of pondering such a thing, but for Abel the understanding was second nature. He wasn't without the capacity to appreciate beauty, or to enjoy depth of feeling, but such moments came without the immediacy they used to have for him. There was no sense of worry that they would be gone before he could take from them their intended lessons. That diminished them somehow. It diminished life, if he wanted to be completely honest with himself.

Of course, he was drawing on memories from back when he still believed in God, another casualty of a life lived without fear. Where there was no dread, or any strong attachment to the sublime, there was little use for God, and no concern for the possibility of the Devil. He got the feeling Twitch Markham would give a year's salary to spend a day feeling the way Abel did. He wasn't sure he wouldn't do the same to spend a day as Twitch, even with all of his anxieties.

And so it was that Abel rode into Tindouf with the closest friends he'd ever known, for better or worse.

"Soon we'll be at the hotel where your friend has secured rooms for you," Walid said into the microphone.

"Is he there?" Miranda turned her head toward the glass partition behind her. No answer. "Dammit," she said. "Must not be a microphone back here. I don't trust this guy."

"We won't have to trust him much longer," said Lovinia. "He's just a ride to the hotel."

"Yeah, a ride who knows what we all look like, and about our predicament."

"Davenport trusted him," Robin said.

Miranda slammed the end of a fist against the glass partition, and the car swerved a little. After a few seconds, the partition whined down partway.

"You'll find two buttons on either armrest. One is to engage me, the other is to disconnect. I prefer that you use those."

"Is Davenport waiting for us at the hotel?" Miranda demanded.

"No, he is not."

"Where is he, then?"

"He is a long way from here by now. Took a helicopter to Marrakesh, same as you will. From there he had many options. Flights are cheap and frequent."

"How do you and Davenport know each other?"

"We don't. Just as I don't know you. You get a good day's sleep, and this afternoon I drive you to heliport. Arrangements still need to be finalized. So if there's nothing else ..."

She leaned back, and up went the glass.

"Smug bastard."

"Do you suppose we'll have any say in where the airplane out of Marrakesh takes us later today?" asked Twitch.

"Not likely," said the Butcher. "My guess is Montpellier."

"France?" Twitch said. "God, I'd like to walk on some American soil again."

"You will, my boy. You will. But France is our safe spot. A good place to regroup. It has to be what Davenport had in mind. Even if not, I think it's where we should go."

"Should be beautiful this time of year," Twitch said, all sarcasm.

"It's not winter yet," the Butcher said with a smile.

"Too close for comfort," was the nervous man's response.

Miranda stared at the side of Walid's face, probably wondering if he had some way of listening in on them, whether the switches in back were engaged or not. If so, he had just gotten an earful.

"You know," she said, "it can't be rocket science, getting a ride from the hotel to the airport. Maybe Walid of Tindouf will run out of usefulness by the time he's dropped us off at the hotel. Maybe he'll meet with an accident."

If she was testing the limo's communication system, it proved either that Walid was an impeccable actor, or he had been telling the truth about not being able to hear them unless they wanted him to. Whatever the case, Miranda's suggestion was met with silence all around.

She let out a breath of laughter and said, "I'm just kidding. I'm sure Walid's a perfect mensch."

* * *

Miranda lay on her side, doing her best to mimic the breathing patterns of someone asleep. When she heard the same deep breathing from Lovinia, who occupied the other twin bed in the room, she assumed the others would be asleep in their rooms, too. Best not to involve anyone else in her plan. Some things were best dealt with as discreetly as possible.

Exiting the room without being detected was the hard part because the thinly carpeted floor had more squeaks to it than a sack of rats. But she made it across the floor and through the cheap wooden door to the hallway without waking her roommate. The door made its own irritating complaints as she swung it closed, but it was a relief to be out of the room.

The corridor had its share of loose boards, too, but nothing like her room. The light that drifted down from fixtures in the ceiling seemed vaporous and too yellow, as though it were a poison meant to provide a drastic cure for somnambulism. And did the hallway actually elongate as it struggled to reach the lobby? Surely not.

To call it a lobby was a laughable exaggeration, she was reminded when at last she turned out of the dark hallway and into the more brightly lit area, where a pretty young woman smiled at her from behind a check-in counter.

"You don't have a cigarette, do you?" Miranda asked.

"Sure." The girl drew a crumpled packet from a blazer pocket.

Miranda noticed as she leaned in to take the cigarette that the clerk had on a loose-fitting skirt and sandals below the up-market navy blue blazer. Poverty was a bitch.

Still, she needed the cigarette, even if it meant taking a little food from the clerk's mouth. "Thanks." She passed through the lobby to the small parking lot out front.

The air conditioning in the hotel was a joke, but it was better than nothing, she realized as a wall of desert heat enfolded her. A breeze bowed a row of palm trees across the street and carried a spicy, unidentifiable scent, but it brought no comfort. Nor did the hazy view of squat, unevenly situated buildings that dotted the small city.

And here we have proof that people are capable of living just about anywhere.

She figured she'd find Walid somewhere nearby. Drivers, in her experience, were a lot like dogs: reliable and predictable, except when they weren't. He stood several yards ahead of the limo, leaning away from her with his hands wide apart on a low brick retaining wall that had been painted white a thousand years ago. A photographer might have taken a shot of him from behind like this and photoshopped in a vast sea for him to be peering across, instead of the derelict sprawl he actually took in. Poverty wasn't a subset here, it appeared. It was simply the way of things.

"I don't suppose you have a light?" she asked.

He spun around, startled.

"You," he replied. "Yeah, I have light." But he made her come to him.

She bent to meet his flame and inhaled deeply, holding the smoke in her lungs for a moment. "Mmm, that's good. I don't smoke often, but I love it."

"You should be asleep. You'll need rest for the journey ahead."

"Couldn't get the Sandman's attention. And then I got to thinking about that mustache of yours."

"My mustache?" His eyes narrowed.

"It's hot. You know, sexy."

"Are you … coming on to me?"

"You're not going to tell me it hasn't happened before."

Bulls-eye. His eyes widened and his shoulders relaxed. He'd let his guard down, if just a little.

"No, I wouldn't say that." He smiled and ran an index finger along the underside of his mustache.

"Look, I generally like a little more romance than this myself, but time is kind of short, and I feel that you and I have a connection."

"What are you suggesting?"

"Okay, to the point. I like that. Well, I sweet-talked the gal behind the desk to secure me a separate room, away from the others, and without a roommate. Said I wanted it to be a little remote."

He swallowed hard but said nothing, so she continued.

"I'll tell you what, I'm going to turn around and walk back into the hotel. If you follow, we'll head up to the seventh floor. Otherwise I'll turn down the hall and climb back into my lonely bed and try to catch a few hours of sleep.

"Why don't you come in through the side entrance, though. No need to test the check-in girl's tolerance."

He eyed her up and down but remained mute. He would follow. She was almost sure of it. But to be absolutely certain, she added a little swagger to her gait as she crossed back toward the main doors.

By the time she reached the elevators, he was walking in through an entrance to her left. The elevator was in an alcove that kept them out of sight from the hallway, and there was a wall between them and the front desk. She pressed the up button and waited.

After a series of grinding sounds that called to mind cables being strained beyond their grade, the elevator arrived, signaled only by the lighted button going dim and the doors banging open. There was no bell.

Stepping inside was an act of courage, but it was the only way. He joined her immediately, much more relaxed and confident now.

"Seven, you said?"

"Mm-hmm." She smiled up at him and caressed his necktie.

He reached for the button and Miranda tensed, knowing that her timing would have to be impeccable. His finger connected with the button, and at the first shudder of the doors coming together, she darted through. Her caressing of the tie had turned into a fierce grip. She held firm as the doors slammed shut between them. Here's where the plan became a little flimsy. She expected to have to hold onto the necktie until the elevator stalled. Beyond that, details dissolved, but she did her best thinking on her feet. Even if all she accomplished was trapping him in the elevator, that was probably enough, especially in a lifeless town like Tindouf. Somehow she didn't think the Otis repairman would be showing up wearing a freshly ironed uniform and swinging a toolkit any time soon. In fact, Walid, the poor bastard, might die from thirst in there.

But that's not how it played out. Thinking it would require more force than it did, she yanked on the necktie to hold it in place as long as possible while the elevator chauffeured Walid upward. What she ended up doing was pulling the man, hard, into the doors, triggering them to open halfway, stalling him between floors. There he lay on his stomach, dazed, level with her line of sight.

Shit, she thought. Now there was nothing to prevent him from jumping down to the floor and exacting his revenge. Yet she held onto the tie. He reached toward her, and her hold on the tie caused her to inadvertently pull him closer to her. His head and chest were hanging over the edge of the elevator when the grind of cables moving through pulleys started up again and Walid was thrust quickly upward. He bobbed along with the car several times as it jerked to a stop at the ceiling. The impact must have cut him nearly in half. His face went red and blood trickled out of his mouth.

Better blood than word of the Portable Nine's future plans, she thought, satisfied with the results of her prank. No one else may have noticed in the limo ride to Tindouf, but the hired driver had flinched when she brought up the idea of doing him in. Her conviction on the point wasn't one hundred percent, but nothing ever was. He probably flinched. Might have. Could have. Whatever. There was no cause for that sort of thing if he hadn't been listening in, and no use risking a more generous assumption.

She dropped her cigarette butt to the carpeted floor and ground it out with her heel before returning to her room for whatever restless sleep she might be able to conjure. That's when she realized that her entire plan for doing in Walid had been based on the assumption that the old building's elevator doors would not be equipped with proximity guards or sensors. That the assumption had been correct did not prevent her heart from banging against her chest wall now.

CHAPTER 42

Davenport watched the Black Phantom move among the sharp rocks and rain-slicked trees. A black cape flowed behind him; at times it was all that could be seen of him. Phantom indeed.

The hike—now up a steep embankment, now down a treacherous drop-off clotted with ground cover—would have been a challenge under the best of circumstances. Trying to keep up with the nimble Phantom through such terrain was daunting. Davenport would have guessed himself to be the man's equal in terms of fitness and agility. He was not.

He followed the Phantom down into a thicket of amber-tinted brush and crooked trees that looked to be adapted specifically to pierce the flesh with their spindly boughs. His adversary pushed his way through with no little effort. But was that a clearing Davenport detected on the other side of the thickest foliage? Maybe not much of one, but sunlight seemed to be finding its way into a region beyond the trees. He hoped it was the Phantom's destination, not only because he was exhausted, but because for the first time since this chase began, he had lost sight of the man as he burrowed into the dense copse.

About to press through the last row of trees, Davenport had to check himself. He retreated a couple of steps to avoid being noticed. The Black Phantom had indeed reached his destination, and it was more than a clearing. Here the density of trees ended, giving way to a flatter, emptier expanse. The Phantom stood at one end of the plateau they both occupied. Davenport thought the Phantom was staring at a rock face at first, but no, there was a man-made structure there. This was the object of the Phantom's intent gaze.

The time had come for Davenport to announce himself, but before he could break free of the clutching flora, another figure emerged from the far side of the structure. A familiar figure, boasting a many-colored sport coat and a tan porkpie hat.

Wishing he hadn't been forced to leave his Colt King Cobra behind when he was imprisoned in the desert, Davenport adjusted his black leather fedora and stepped into the clearing.

"Well, shits and giggles," he said in a booming voice. "Isn't this a happy little reunion!"

The woozy beads that passed for eyes in Max Brindle's head rolled in Davenport's direction. The Black Phantom merely lowered his head, keeping his back to Davenport.

"I would have thought my luck had run out by now, but dammit if this isn't a gift from the gods. What's the term? A twofer! God damn."

Those eyes of Brindle's flared to life, and he came at Davenport with a darting finger.

"I've had it with your cocky shit. You know that? And I wouldn't be so sure you know what the gods have in store."

"Do I really have to countenance a lecture on hubris from the little hypocrite here?" Davenport asked the Phantom, who still refused to turn from what appeared to be some sort of cell or enclosure. Then, turning to Brindle, he said, "I'd put that finger away if I were you, and think long and hard about taking another step in this direction." He wasn't sure he bought Brindle's indignation, but he could play along as well as the next man.

"You had your chance with me, and you fucked it up," Max went on, "just like you've fucked everything else up in your pathetic life. I came out on top of this one, and you can't stand that. I'm so far beneath you. Isn't that it? But who do you have to blame but yourself? You could have ended this back in Florence, but you didn't have the sac for it."

"Careful, Max." It was said in guttural tones, the Black Phantom the speaker, though he still didn't turn to face the two men.

The command had been issued to the wrong party, however, for it was no longer in Max Brindle's power to influence fate. He had had his say, and now the outcome was set in motion.

Realizing that Max's act was likely for the Phantom's benefit, not his, Davenport nonetheless lunged, simultaneously grasping the smaller man by his colorful lapels and forcing him backward as if pushing a tackling dummy in American football practice.

"I'll put some sense in you yet, Brindle." He slammed him against the enclosure the Phantom was so preoccupied with.

Something went wild in Brindle's eyes, but not in a threatening way. It spooked Davenport. He stepped back, expecting Max to stumble forward or slide to the ground. He did neither, which further unnerved Davenport. The eyes had gone from wild to terrified to accepting, and Davenport couldn't figure it. It shouldn't have been a truly damaging slam against the curved wall of the rock-and-concrete bunker. But something was wrong.

"Say something, you little prick!" Davenport shouted.

Curiosity perhaps got the better of the Black Phantom, but only to the extent that he swiveled his head in Brindle's direction.

Brindle's eyes fluttered and his head bobbed a couple of times, as if he were in an important meeting and trying without success to fight back sleep. Eventually his head hung slack and all movement ceased, until the body fell slowly forward. Protruding from the wall of the structure was a six-inch bolt or length of rebar, now glistening scarlet, and dripping crimson.

Davenport's head spun. He'd been given a second chance in Florence, an opportunity to change the way he conducted business, if not get out altogether. Now this.

"You stupid sonofabitch," the Phantom said.

Davenport couldn't take his eyes off Brindle's limp body. Realizing the man's thigh lay partly on his shoe, he recoiled with a shudder. That's when he noticed that the door of the enclosure before the Phantom was ajar. It was a tall, arched affair made of iron, now russet in color. Something about the way the door hung open, no more than a foot or so, triggered awareness in Davenport. This must have been the cell where Pierre LeGrand's father—Jacques—would have breathed his last lungful of Caribbean air if not for the fateful eruption of *La Grande Soufrière*, which left him badly burned but free as a bird. Davenport knew it was in this vicinity, but he had expected something more grandiose. The rest of the prison had apparently been razed.

What a grim pilgrimage he had interrupted here. He almost regretted getting on LeGrand's tail so soon after his escape from *la Tarte*. Again fate seemed to be working against him. If he had let a little more dust settle before jumping on a plane out of Marrakesh, Brindle would be alive and the Black Phantom would have had his chance to make whatever peace he intended to make here. But then Davenport thought of his aunt, and his blood pumped a little faster, a little hotter.

"Where does this put us?" Davenport asked.

The Phantom exhaled sharply through his nose. "You follow me all this way. You kill my business partner. And now, like a timid mouse, you ask what's next? Dear God, such an insult!"

"What was the plan here, LeGrand? I think I know what this place is, but what were you and Brindle hoping to accomplish?"

The Phantom swirled his cape as he turned to face Davenport at last. He took a step toward him.

"The truth?"

It wasn't rhetorical the way he asked it. He expected an answer, as though it was a decision with some weight. Davenport nodded.

"Only one of us was going to leave this island. He thought it was going to be him. You'll find a peashooter in the pocket of his sport coat."

"But you were never going to let that happen."

"No," LeGrand said with a grin.

A sudden implication occurred to Davenport then. If LeGrand had been prepared to defend himself against an armed Max Brindle, surely he was now counting on doing the same against Davenport. He let his eyes rove the area, trying to avoid detection in the process. There must be some clue or weapon here.

The door. At the open edge was a bracket, welded in place and running perpendicular to the door frame itself. It stuck out about three inches and had a one-inch-diameter hole in the center. The bracket was designed to meet its partner when the door was closed so that some kind of locking mechanism could be slid into place. Another bracket with a hole in the center stuck out from the jamb on the hinged edge of the door, which was old but must not have been the original. This cell had been repaired somewhere along the line, if crudely.

Then he saw the locking mechanism leaning beside the door. The Phantom took a sideways step to block Davenport's view again, followed by a slow backward-shuffling stride. He was going for the damn thing, which was a long metal rod, the perfect diameter to shoot through the eyes of the brackets of the cell. Or to knock a man senseless.

Or both. Not necessarily in that order. Suddenly the stakes felt very high.

"Look," Davenport said, masking his nervousness as best he could. "We have some shit to work out, you and I, but can we agree to set aside our differences long enough for me to tend to Brindle here?"

"You mean a Christian burial?" The Phantom threw back his head and howled with deep-throated laughter.

It was likely to be the best chance Davenport would have to act, and he took it. Leading with his shoulder, he rammed into LeGrand's broad chest, slamming him backward into the door's bracket. The door didn't budge and the Phantom's hand shot to his back, unabashed agony distorting his features.

Davenport used the momentum from the assault to drop and roll to his left, pulling at Brindle's sport coat as he hit the ground. It gave him enough purchase to stop his roll, and his hand slid into one of the dead man's pockets in search of the gun LeGrand had referred to. Empty. He threw a glance at the Black Phantom, who was still in pain but recovering. Davenport had to prop up Brindle's bulk to get at the other pocket. It was worth it. He withdrew his hand, along with a 9mm Glock.

"You're well and truly fucked now!" he shouted at the Phantom.

"What are you going to do, shoot me?" LeGrand moved away from the entrance, his breathing heavy. There was no blood on the bracket. "Is the Mad Marksman of Malta going to blow my fucking head off?"

"For what you did to my aunt I should do worse than that. You fucking *scumbag!*"

"What's it going to be, then?"

"That rod." Davenport inclined his head toward it. "Toss it over here, very gently."

"What rod?" LeGrand craned his neck to follow Davenport's gaze. "Oh, that. What do you want it for?"

"I want it away from you. Now send it this way."

LeGrand took the rod in one hand and held it like a staff for a moment before heaving it into the air. It arced toward Davenport and fell across Brindle's corpse. The Phantom's face seemed to say, "Satisfied?"

"Okay, good," Davenport said. "Now, I don't want to shoot you in the ankle. I really don't. But if you don't squeeze yourself through that opening and into the cell, that's exactly what I'll do. I even know how to make sure you don't bleed to death from the wound."

"You don't want to do this."

"Oh, but I do."

"Then mark this down, Davenport. On this day you are declaring war. There are people expecting my presence soon. When I do not appear, they will know to seek out a document, though they do not know what it contains."

"And what, may I ask, does this document contain?"

"Everything I know about the so-called Portable Nine, yourself included, of course."

"That can't amount to much."

"You don't believe that."

"Step into the fucking cell."

"You will regret this day a million times over, and as of today I have no greater enemy on Earth than a stinking rat known as Davenport."

He spit angrily on the ground and turned to do as he had been told. It required some effort to press himself through the opening between the door and the frame, but he got it done without having to remove his hooded cape. Now the question was, Would Davenport be able shut the massive door behind the Phantom?

"All the way to the back of the cell," Davenport instructed, unable to see the Phantom in the darkness of the enclosure. "Find something you can use to tap on the wall. I want to hear you."

Soon there came the steady rhythmic pulse of a stone clacking against the rear wall. There was a slight echo to it.

"Good. Keep it up."

Davenport began to push against the door, still holding onto the gun. It seemed hopeless at first. The damn door wouldn't budge. But looking down he could see that the door had scraped and flattened a fan of earth where it had been opened. Where it had stopped, a rounded clod of grassy soil blocked it. Maybe a slight grade meant the door could be closed more easily than opened. He went at it again, grunting with effort until sweat popped on his brow.

"It's a heavy bastard," the Phantom said from within, the echo of his voice sending a chill through Davenport's extremities, despite the damp heat. The tapping had stopped.

"Keep knocking," Davenport replied through gritted teeth.

The tapping of stone on stone resumed and Davenport redoubled his efforts. This time the door moved. Not much.

Maybe a couple of inches, but it was progress. Putting all of his weight into the job, he jerked the door free of a stone or root and it shot forward, barely touching the ground. It hit the jamb and bounced back.

"I see that there's a barred vent built into the top portion of the door," he said. "I'll be at work burying the dead if you have any parting words of derision for me. Am I right in assuming you've already outfitted the space with foodstuffs and water for Brindle's sake? This was your plan for him, wasn't it? Or something like it?"

The tapping slowed, and anger seemed to billow out of the cell in waves. Davenport reached into his pocket.

"Oh, I almost forgot. I have something for you." He tossed a Polaroid into the space. "You have a flashlight in there?"

"What is it?"

"That's your father. And that busted-open pod next to him? That's the Brazil nut fruit that fell on him and brought a swift and embarrassing end to such a merry life. I think you'll recognize the photograph."

He lifted the rod from Max's body, pressed the door all the way shut, and slid the rod through all three brackets: a neat fit. The Black Phantom was caged, and he howled like the devil to prove it.

"Sam Gutterson would approve of this, by the way. I wanted to tear you limb from limb, but he said I should keep you alive if possible. Send my regards to the goon who killed him, by the way. If you ever get the chance. Anyway, my friends will also be pleased to have a say in your ultimate fate. So for those reasons, you live another day."

Without waiting for a response he moved on to the business of digging a grave. It was going to be sweaty, tiresome work in the merciless sun and cloying humidity, but it had to be done. He'd been playing with moral fire for too long.

Then it would be time to catch a boat back to the mainland, and leave the Black Phantom, formerly of Caracas and points south, to howl in solitude until help came. Because help would come eventually. Help always came for the undeserving. But the man who might walk out of that cell in a week's time, or a month's, would be a changed man—and he would remember who had changed him.

ABOUT THE AUTHOR

Pete Mesling

In addition to writing fiction and poetry, Pete Mesling composes guitar music and laments the current moratorium on road trips and afternoons spent at coffeehouses. He lives with his wife and daughter in the Pacific Northwest.

BOOKS BY THIS AUTHOR

None So Deaf

Out of print.

Jagged Edges & Moving Parts

In these collected tales of terror, you will visit worlds familiar and foreign, witness frights credible and extraordinary ... encounter villains human and otherworldly. It may not be the magnitude of the darkness explored here that is of greatest interest, however, but the fact that unexpected moments of humanity, courage, and thoughtfulness are allowed to gain a foothold from time to time, often against seemingly impossible odds.

Jagged Edges & Moving Parts may be an exploration of the darkest corners of our shared existence, but it is also rooted in a belief that if people can be as ruthless as monsters, they can also be every bit as astonishing.

COMING SOON FROM
PETE MESLING!

The Wages of Crime:
a collection

The Maker-Man of Merryville:
a fantasy novel for young readers

AND ...

The Portable Eight:
a sequel to *The Portable Nine*

Made in the USA
Middletown, DE
09 February 2021